A BOOKISH ROMA

ALLISON JONES

Distribution by Bublish, Inc.

ISBN: 978-1-64704-262-2 (Paperback)
ISBN: 978-1-64704-261-5 (eBook)

*I want to thank everyone who scrunched
their noses at me when I told them I was a writer.
This book is a giant middle-finger to you; but
thank you for buying my book.*

Ten Years Earlier

The doctors say it won't be long now, but my mother is stubborn. Her will to live far exceeds any medical expectations. She glides between reality and another dimension. And sometimes, I am not sure which is which. Margaret Snyder is a formidable opponent for death.

She comes from old money, where image is everything. On the outside, she always seemed kind, loving, and very generous. Behind closed doors, the truth was a completely different story. She hid her unhappiness in a bottle, disappearing both emotionally and physically for days at a time. As a child, I thought it was me. That if I were different, she would love me. But now I realize there was nothing I could have done to fill the void in her soul.

Abandonment.

Emotional and physical neglect.

Distrust.

The foundation for every relationship I have ever had. Except for Owen. Owen has always helped me feel less broken, less unlovable, and less unwanted.

"Addie! Addie, where are you?" The bellowing echoes through the halls of my childhood home. It is my mother, of course, who is yelling at the top of her lungs even though I only left the living room for a moment. We transformed her once opulent living room into a veritable hospital ward to accommodate her impending transition from life to death. Of course, this transition has been going on for a year, and I am simply trying to keep my shit together.

If I'm honest, the only reason I'm even living here is because of Owen, my twenty-year-old brother. Born with Down syndrome, he is one of my greatest teachers. He is a complete smart-ass and loves to challenge me, but I adore him. He fills the emptiness. When my mother became ill, she made me his guardian. Truthfully, I was already raising him anyway. Neither of my parents could deal with an "imperfect" child that wasn't "normal." Cue the eye roll and middle finger salute.

My father left not too long after Owen was born. My mother did her best to ignore her son, but she made sure all of her "social friends" saw her as the doting maternal figure. No matter what illusion she managed to craft, she couldn't take away my memories of her passed out in the middle of the afternoon while Owen screamed in his crib. Or the times when she would disappear with no explanation. There were times when a maid would drop in, but even that wasn't consistent.

Alcohol was the only thing worthy of my mother's undivided attention. It has been just Owen and me all along.

I suppose most people would be resentful if they had been placed in this position. If their mother's inability to cope had robbed them of a typical childhood. Truthfully, I have walked through the anger, hate, and resentment. Sometimes residue seeps in when I least expect it, but my life is better with Owen in it. He inspires me and motivates me to be the best person I can be. Maybe it is because he sees our mother with love and compassion. He accepts her for who she is and doesn't try to change her. He doesn't have unrealistic expectations. He simply loves her.

I exhale before I enter the room, and when I walk in, my eyes meet hers. She looks small, vulnerable, lying in the hospital bed cloaked in blankets that, unfortunately for me, don't warm her cold nature. Her youthful beauty has been ravaged by aging and, more importantly, her life choices. A stranger would see her and think "fragile." She appears to be so sweet with her ready smile and fake warmth. But her bitterness bites like a rabid dog. I have lost count of the revolving door of caregivers who have come and gone. She despises strangers inhabiting her home. If they are overweight, they are sent packing. Yes, thank you very much; she is prejudiced against those with a little extra junk in the trunk. She fears that they will fall on her and kill her. I'm not even joking. *Would that be a bad thing?* I wonder. I know those thoughts are awful: but when you spend twenty-four hours a day in an emotional hostage situation, evil thoughts tend to rise to the forefront.

"Mom, what is it?" I ask, hoping she isn't gearing up for one of her rants about my weight or lack of a spouse. Apparently, being thirty and single is taboo in her eyes. And the body image issue? Well, it has always been a sore spot. When I was a child, I was enrolled in anything that would keep me moving in an effort to keep the fat at bay. I didn't inherit my mother's slender frame; instead, I got the soft, curvy appearance of those on my father's side. I'm not and never have been obese, but when I look in the mirror, I always see someone who doesn't quite measure up.

Let me clarify: I am not a troll. Not that I have anything against trolls. I am sure someone thinks they're attractive. But me? Well, let's just say that I am vertically challenged, coming in at a solid five feet even. My short blond hair is spikey and unruly; it's the only edgy thing about me. One guy I went out with said that my "blow job" lips were my best asset. Those were the first words out of his mouth when I met him (along with, "So when are you giving me a blow job?"). That date ended before our drinks were served. So, yeah, apparently, my plump lips rival the filler-laden pouts of celebrities and porn stars.

"Addie, I'm so sorry. I thought I was doing the right thing. I'm so sorry." She keeps repeating the apology over and over.

"What are you sorry for, Mom?" There could be a multitude of things. My mind is racing. This is completely unlike her.

She grabs my hand and looks at me. Her stare is vacant. Death beckons. Her last breath leaves her parted lips, and I am left without the answer to her deathbed apology.

Addie

Present Day

I look around my modest Brooklyn apartment and exhale. It isn't extravagant, but it is all me. A slew of well-placed bookcases hosts my collection of literary classics. I won't lie—when I say literary classics, I am referring to the romantic-themed kind. Still, I would describe myself as a voracious reader. I love the escape books provide, and since I haven't seen any action since the Clinton administration, it's nice to see *someone* is getting some, even if they are fictional.

Picture windows frame the living room where I have a prime view of the street below. Cozy, oversized chairs provide a place for me to read or write. I love the energy of our Brooklyn neighborhood. It's so full of life. It became a soft place to land after my mother died.

A month after my mother's passing, I was let go from my duties as a freelance columnist for a local newspaper. I should have known something was up when my editor approached the conversation as a sympathetic counselor would.

"Addie, how are you doing?" my editor, Joyce, asked me as we sat in her office, her brow furrowed.

"I'm doing okay. Adjusting to our new normal." I twisted my hands in my lap, a lame effort to ease my anxiety. To be completely honest, the only grief I felt was for the mother I deserved but didn't get.

"Good. It will take some time. The reason I called you into the office is that we are making some changes, and I thought it was only right to tell you in person since we've worked together for so long. Unfortunately, we aren't using a freelancer anymore for your home section. As you know, print is suffering, and we feel that an in-house person would save us money. I'm sorry that we have to let you go. If you need a recommendation letter, I'm happy to supply that. You have been an asset to the paper, and we are sad to lose you." She didn't make eye contact with me, and an awkward silence fell over the room. There goes ten years down the drain.

"Oh. Wow. Umm, well, okay. Thank you for the opportunity. I've enjoyed the last ten years working here." I seriously sounded like a robot. In my mind, I was going out in a blaze of glory with my middle finger raised in the air. Instead, I stood, shook her hand, and left her office in a daze.

I wallowed, consoling myself with ice cream and wine as I sat around in my favorite pair of pajamas. Darkness became my friend. And not just in terms of my mood. I literally didn't turn on any lights. By the seventh day, my apartment was littered with empty food containers, and an ineffable stench permeated the air. After some investigation, I found the source of the smell. It was me. Showering hadn't even been on my radar.

In actuality, the monotony of writing about home design week after week was getting tedious. I had grown to hate it, but it gave me purpose. It gave me an identity. After being let go, I was plagued with thoughts that I wasn't good enough and wondered where to go from there.

I inherited a considerable amount of money from my mother, which provided a generous cushion. On the eighth day of my reclusiveness, I realized that this could be the moment to step out of my comfort zone. You know how we all talk about taking a goal to task, and then we add, "Someday I'll do it"? That day was my someday. Well, In fairness, I postponed that someday to the next day; I still had some more ice cream and wine to consume, but not together, of course. That would ruin them both.

But after that, instead of waiting for the light at the end of the tunnel, I lit that bitch up myself. In my head, I am a badass. However, in reality, I am fearful of change. Fearful of not being accepted. So instead, I take care of everyone else to simply avoid the possibility. That's me: the caretaker. After days of mourning the loss of a job that, quite frankly, was lacking inspiration, my attitude began to shift. Instead of looking at the loss of my job as a bad thing, I decided to see it as an opportunity. Incredibly healthy of me, don't you think?

Writing a book has always been in my peripheral vision. The idea of creating a fictional novel about a forty-something woman navigating life seemed to speak to me. As a single woman, society deems me a spinster or a lesbian. I hold nothing against either, but I simply do not belong in either of those groups. Still, according to society, I should be hoarding cats by this point. And for the record, I do not have even one cat, but I do have Owen, who is as moody as any four-legged feline.

People are immediately drawn to Owen—to his infectious grin and laughter. We have the same blond hair, but his is coarse and thick while mine tends to be thinner, hence the reason I keep it in a short pixie cut. His low muscle tone could be a detriment, but he never lets it stop him. His exuberance for life is inspiring, and when he says, "I love my life," it makes all the "big" stuff that I worry about seem so unimportant. He is open to any possibility.

He adjusted well after Mom died, but the reality is that it has always been just the two of us anyway, so we quickly settled into a rhythm. He is employed at a neighborhood grocery store that happens to be down the street.

"What are you doing today?" he inquires, breaking me from my memories.

"Writing," I respond.

"Again?" He rolls his eyes.

"Yes, again," I state, my voice dripping with annoyance.

"Maybe Mr. Schmitt will hire you at the store. You could work with me, and I would be your boss." He grins and giggles.

This is our conversation every day. He doesn't understand that I'm really writing a book and have been for quite some time; that writing is my job even if, at this moment, it isn't lucrative; and that someday, someone and maybe several of their friends will want to read it. I watch him walk to his job.

For the first few months, I walked him to work every day, which elicited innumerable complaints. "Addie, I am thirty. I am a man. I can walk alone." Whatever. So instead, I watch from the stoop of our apartment building, asking him to text me when he gets there. His text always reads, "I'm here. Get a life."

He's right, you know. I *will* get a life after I complete this book. The finish line is on the horizon.

I was ten when Owen was born; he was a late "oops" baby. Since my parents opted out of raising him, I became his caregiver, advocate, mother, and sister; and he—well—he became my everything. When he was younger, I walked him to school every day, his chubby hand connecting with mine. His smile was infectious. Once we would reach our destination, he would turn to me, open his arms, and give me the best hug I have ever encountered. There was never a better way to start my day.

My life is so much better with Owen in it—even when he gives me the finger (which happens regularly). His developmental delay has never been a hindrance. It doesn't define him, and if anyone feels sorry for him, they are missing the bigger picture. He is thriving, appreciative of the present moment. While the rest of the world stresses about mundane issues, Owen lives his life with ease. He is a contributing member of the community, and most of all, he is loved. He is a walking example of living life in the moment. I want to be like him when I grow up (but without the attitude).

I shuffle over to my laptop, settle into my writing chair, pray for some creative mojo, and delve into the project at hand. My book, *Finding the Light,* centers around Sherry, a forty-something woman on a quest to find herself, even with the layers of baggage that bind her. Along the way, she opens her heart to love while uncovering secrets that have plagued her family for generations. Sounds nice, right? There are some characteristics that we share, but I shape her into being a lot of things I don't see in myself. She is poised and beautiful but still struggles with finding her way in the world. That latter part is what we share. I want to fit. I want to find a place where I belong. I want the happy ending.

Lost in thought, I barely hear my cell phone ringing. The name on the screen makes me grimace. It's my cousin-in-law, Dorothy. Dorothy is married to my cousin, Matthew, a passive, unmotivated individual who uses me as his personal ATM. Dorothy, on the other hand, has a penchant for not asking and simply taking items that don't belong to her—like jewelry. Yes, Dorothy is a shoplifter and has been caught on numerous occasions. She seems to skate through the court system and is never accountable for her actions. Oh, and she might also be a hoarder. However, she maintains a façade of success with her designer duds and perfectly coiffed blond hair. I suspect that the money I "loan" them goes toward Dorothy, always looking like a million bucks instead of toward their bills. Color me surprised. Her willowy figure and manicured fingernails complete the illusion. She is a real piece of work.

Why do I continue to participate, you ask? I'm not sure. Maybe it's because, besides Owen, this is the only family I have left. It's toxic and dysfunctional, I know, but I crave acceptance and love. My hope that people will change and start to care about me consumes me. Logically,

I know it's not going to happen, and yet I continue to play the game, thinking that one day, people will treat me the way I deserve. I am sure a psychiatrist would have a field day with my issues.

Anyway, like a dumb-ass, I answer the phone. It is simply the next stage in the cycle of insanity.

"Hey, Dorothy." My voice is emotionless.

"Addie, I'm just calling to check in with you. Are you doing alright? I miss you." She sounds loving. Her tone is so overly saturated in sweetness that I might actually get a cavity. But it's a lie, just like everything else about her—cue my exaggerated eye-roll. There was a time when I thought we might have a nice familial connection, but what I have learned is that under Dorothy's compassion, an ulterior motive is always at the root. She's the type of person who presents herself as someone she's not. People gravitate to her. She spins lies like cotton candy—and they believe her. It took me a long time to figure out that she wasn't a safe person, so I disconnected, except for the "loaning" part. Somehow, it keeps them from inserting themselves into our lives. It gives me a slight reprieve—family in name only, but family, nonetheless. This process is exhausting, and so are my mixed feelings about them.

"We're doing well. How are you all?" I ask, but I don't care. I am currently having an inner argument with myself for even answering the damn phone.

"You are so sweet to ask. We're struggling. Matthew lost his job, and it's really hard for us." Whenever she is trying hard to put on her "sweet" personality, she tends to use her fake Southern accent. I sigh.

What a surprise. Matthew loses jobs like water through a sieve. I wonder if the ink has ever dried on any of his applications before he's been let go. I don't take the bait. I know she wants money. The suggestion is there.

"Gosh, that's too bad. I'm sure he'll find something else." I say it with such conviction that I almost believe my own bullshit.

"Of course. I know you're right. It's just so hard living in a place where I don't know if we can even make our rent. It is so scary. But we can't move to another place with lower rent. Those places are sketchy and riddled with crime. No matter how badly off we are, we simply can't put our lives at risk. And even so, if we…"

At this point, I am no longer listening, and I'm itching to end this conversation. But with Dorothy, it's difficult. She talks endlessly, and I often wonder how she accomplishes it when she rarely takes a breath. It is a talent. She is completely self-absorbed and irritating.

I listen to her chatter, and when I feel a pause coming, I jump in with a resounding, "Dorothy, I have to go. Someone is at the door." Okay, label me a liar, but I prefer to call it self-preservation. Don't tell me you've never done the same thing. Anyway, she reluctantly releases me from the current hostage situation and promises or threatens—depends on your outlook—to be in touch soon. I can't wait.

On the bright side, I didn't take their financial crisis bait.

Baby steps.

Dorothy

That bitch. *Ugh.* I didn't even get a chance to ask for money before she disconnected the call. Honestly, we deserve that money. Her ungrateful mother should have left something for Matthew. After all, he is her only nephew. Margaret Snyder always thought that she was better than everyone else. She had her nose stuck up in the air, always looking down at me as if I was trash. Sure, I grew up in a trailer park, but at least I had the ambition to get the hell out of there. And Matthew was my ticket. I mean, I was attracted to him and even fell in love with him, but it was what he could do for me that was the hook.

I remember when I first met him back in high school. Matthew was a football player. Guys wanted to be him, and the girls just wanted to be with him. Tall and muscular, he oozed sex appeal. He was the most popular boy in school—a true bad boy. A bad boy with money, or so I thought. You see, his parents weren't in the picture, so he lived with Addie. Their mansion boasted a pool and décor that made my mouth water. So I zeroed in on my mark. Since I was the head cheerleader, the process was easy. I mean, come on—who else would he even date? I am a total catch. We were the "it" couple all through high school. College wasn't in the picture for either of us. Matthew flitted between jobs, and I didn't think much about it, since his family was loaded. He got a monthly allowance that made my minimum-wage job at a local boutique seem like chump change.

Before I knew it, we were engaged and planning a small wedding. But I wanted an extravagant wedding. You know, something that would make a statement to all of those haters who didn't think that I would amount to anything. It would have been like flipping off everyone who had dismissed me. However, cheapskate Margaret Snyder wouldn't bend to my will, and I was stuck with an unmemorable ceremony and an even more mundane reception. I muddled through it while keeping my eye on the prize.

Tapping my fire-engine red, acrylic fingernails together, I decided that I need to be more persuasive in my loan presentation with Addie. "Borrowing" items from stores isn't as lucrative as it used to be since my arrests, and the pawnshops are onto my game. I need another means, and if Addie doesn't cough up some cash, I will have to put my plan in motion. But first, I will put Matthew on task since family reigns supreme in Addie's eyes. She has always had a soft spot for Matthew. Of course, their relationship changed once I came into the picture. I hate Addie. I hate everything about her. She is such a goody-goody. Naïve. Oh, and don't get me started on that her disabled brother. Owen gives me the creeps.

The front door of our modest apartment opens, and in walks the man of the hour. I smooth my blond bob and stick out my ample chest. He loves me in short designer skirts and stilettos, which happen to be my standard form of dress. Matthew is still as attractive as he was in high school, but his lack of social status clouds the appeal. I put on a fake smile, walk over to him, and rub my hand down his chest.

"How was your day, baby?" I don't care, but he has gotten a new job that I am hoping he keeps longer than the last one.

"It was fine until my boss criticized the way I was loading the boxes into the truck, so I quit. I mean, why'd he have to be so picky? He should have been grateful that I was loading them at all."

I try to keep my reaction in check. Nothing good ever comes from me pointing out the obvious: he is the problem. Now, if we had a ton of money, this would not be an issue, but obviously, if I'm shoplifting and playing nice with Addie in hopes of a "loan," that isn't the case. My patience is wearing thin. So I do what I do best. I manipulate.

"Oh honey, that's too bad. Their loss, right? Well, don't worry about it. Why don't you just pay a visit to Addie? You haven't seen her in a while, and I bet she would help us out until you find something else. That's was family does, right? We help each other." The words almost choke me.

"Thanks for your support, babe. You get me. You understand that these places refuse to see my worth. Yeah, I'll go visit Addie. She owes us since she's got her hands on what should have been *my* inheritance. That bitch of an aunt didn't leave us shit. I mean, I took care of her, too."

"It just isn't right that you were left out, so I bet Addie will be happy to give us a helping hand in our time of need." I coo.

"I'll go and see her tomorrow."

Matthew is such easy prey. I just hope Addie is as easily manipulated as my gullible spouse. Momma needs a new Prada bag.

Addie

Owen became my priority after our mother crossed over to the afterlife. Okay, he has always been my priority, but now, I am his sole guardian. Legally. Honestly, I'm not sure where my mother ended up, but hopefully, the restraining order God had in place has been lifted. She was the most ungodly woman on the planet. I guess that makes me a bad daughter, and I'm sure there is a place reserved in hell for me, too. I hope it's in the front row.

Most mornings, I revel in the quiet sanctuary of my apartment, but there are days when I take a field trip to the Coffee Shop on the Corner. No, that isn't my nickname for it. It is literally a coffee shop that resides on a corner, and that is the clever name the owners, Mike and Sal, decided on when they opened this gem in our neighborhood. Mike is fit, burly, and extremely good-looking, while his partner in life and business, Sal, is physically slight in appearance and rocks his intellectual vibe. His classic uniform consists of khakis and crisp Oxford button-downs, while Mike goes for jeans and tight-fitting T-shirts.

The first time I met them was at the grocery store where Owen works, where we bonded over our mutual adoration of liquor-infused sorbet. If you haven't tried this delicious concoction, you must do so.

But not right now, because I'm in the middle of my story and I need you sober. Anyway, they told me about their quaint coffee shop, and I will admit, I was a little giddy.

So, it has been a ritual of mine for the last few months to settle into one of their cozy chairs and create some magic. When I arrive, there is always a piping hot cup of java waiting to jolt my brain into the creative process along with one of their homemade chocolate croissants, served warm. The coffee shop is a slice of heaven with its mocha walls that host colorful art created by Sal, along with black-and-white photographs of various European cities that he and Mike have visited. There are several intimate seating areas that invite customers to sit and relax. Mouthwatering pastries, muffins, and scones peep out from glass display cases.

I visit the cafe when I feel stuck or lack the inspiration to put some life into these characters. Sometimes, I think my characters judge my ability as a writer, and most of the time, I'm right there with them. Writer's block is no joke. For me, it means that my characters have gone radio silent. Maybe they're pissed about the directions that their stories are going. But there is something about this coffee shop that turns my garbage into magic.

The aromas of coffee and warm baked goods caress my senses as I open the door. Mike strolls over and envelops me in a comforting hug. Another bonus of coming in here is the abundance of love and kindness these two have for me.

"Addie! So happy to see you. How are you?" he asks me.

"I'm good. Just hoping your coffee and croissant will inspire me to finish up this book. I'm close, Mike." I exhale. While I don't have the experience of delivering a baby, this book feels very much like giving birth. It's years of work and emotions that have bled onto the pages. My pride and joy. My labor of love. Once it leaves my hands, I am powerless over the outcome and that scares the living shit out of me.

My stomach knots at the thought, but it subsides once I touch my chocolate croissant.

Diligence pays off as I plow through chapter after chapter, revising, editing, and developing my characters. On this gloomy Monday afternoon, I exhale in triumph. It's done! I'm grinning like a fool despite efforts to maintain my composure. I lean back in my chair and close my eyes. While intense relief overwhelms me, it is peppered with anxiety at the idea of releasing it to the world. Now it's just a matter of sending it to my close friend, Nina Wentworth.

Nina is a literary agent who just happens to own The Wentworth Agency. We met at a writing workshop six months ago. I pitched my story idea, and she was very interested. We just clicked. Odd, since we're total opposites. She is poised, gorgeous, and fashionable with sleek, long black hair that accentuates her olive skin and slender figure. She probably wouldn't be caught dead wearing yoga pants or a T-shirt. She probably doesn't even own any. I imagine she sleeps in her Chanel suits. Kidding. Well… maybe. Still, she is kind, sweet, genuine, and encouraging. Honestly, she is the first person in a long time who has believed in me.

Matthew

Approaching Addie's apartment, my anxiety quickly dissipates as I rationalize the reasons why I'm entitled to my aunt's money. Honestly, I should've known my aunt wouldn't leave me anything, but my monthly allowance was the least she could've left. Without that, I had to start working…for other people. I mean, I wasn't meant to be told what to do. I was meant to be a leader.

A sexy woman is leaving Addie's apartment building. I take the steps two at a time to catch the door before it shuts. I wink at her as she holds the door for me, and she blushes. I've still got it. My power over women is how I managed to score Dorothy. All charm, all the time. I hustle up the four floors to Addie's apartment, grateful I didn't have to press her buzzer. Sometimes I think that Addie ignores me when I come over. The element of surprise is on my side today.

I knock and wait. She never asks who it is, which is another bonus. The door swings open, and there stands my cousin, who, by the way, doesn't look the least bit shocked to see me.

"Matthew, to what do I owe the pleasure?" Her face is a blank slate, not betraying the slightest emotion.

If I didn't know better, I would think she was annoyed with me.

"Addie, can I come in? We haven't seen each other in a while, so I thought I would come by and check on you." I smile at her warmly, throwing my charm her way.

Sure enough, she opens the door and gestures for me to enter. I enter and head for the couch, where I make myself comfortable. Addie follows suit, and we settle in awkward silence.

"So, what have you been up to? Are you still 'writing'?" I do air quotes because "writing" is just a lame excuse not to work. Okay. I know what you're thinking. You think that I shouldn't judge because I don't want to work, and she doesn't need to. But it's not that I don't want to work—it's that I don't want to work for *someone else*. If I had the money—the inheritance money I'm owed—I could start my own business. What kind of business you ask? I want to start a consulting company. Sounds a little vague, right? Well, I didn't say I knew what I wanted to consult on; I just know that I want to be the boss.

She smirks at me. "As a matter of fact, I just finished my book and sent it off to a literary agent."

Whatever. Sending it off to some lame agent in the hope that someone will buy it is pathetic. It isn't like she needs the money -what a loser.

"Oh, well, that's great. Let me know how that goes," I say acting as if I am interested.

"How's your job going? Are you still a customer service rep with that medical device place, or did you already quit?" She scrunches her nose at me.

"Oh, I moved on to a company where I was loading trucks, but that didn't work out. They didn't see my potential."

"Well, that's unfortunate. So, let's cut the shit. Why are you here? Need a handout? Following up since your wife wasn't successful yesterday?"

She can be a bitch when she feels like it. She reminds me of her mother.

"We could use a little help. With me between jobs, things are tough." I try to look sincere, but it's hard. That money is *owed* to me, after all.

"Since I'm in a good mood, I feel generous. This is the last time, Matthew. You all need to get your shit together."

She goes over to her bag to retrieve her checkbook, and I hope she's making out the check for at least the same amount she always gives us. She hands it to me. Yup, same amount. I take the check.

"Always a pleasure, Addie. Thank you so much." I turn away from her and leave with a smile on my face, not bothering with goodbyes. Dorothy will be pleased.

Addie

Sucker. I have sucker written on my face. Honestly, I wasn't surprised when Matthew showed up. Since I interrupted Dorothy in her quest to ask for monetary assistance, I figured she would manipulate her spouse into doing her dirty work. I know I should stop the cycle. Sometimes, it is just easier to give in, as it will give me a reprieve for a few months. And at least I plucked up the courage to tell him it was the last time. He won't listen, but I did try.

I am baffled as to why my mother didn't leave anything to Matthew. She wasn't a fan—I do know that, but he lived with us for several years since his parents weren't in the picture.

"Addie, Matthew has hit his peak," she would say once in a while. These were the moments when she wasn't criticizing me.

"What do you mean?" I would ask.

"He's popular. He's the football star. He has it easy. He has too much. After high school, he won't amount to anything. He's weak and lazy, and all he's learned is that he doesn't have to try. That's going to hurt him in the long run."

I look back on those conversations and wonder if she was psychic because she was weirdly on target. Maybe that's why she didn't leave him anything. I guess I will never know. Just another mystery left behind by my dearly departed mother.

Addie

It's been three months since I sent my book to Nina. Waiting is hard. Sure, she is encouraging and keeps me posted. We made a pact that we would not insert our business relationship into our friendship. Besides, she knows how annoying I would be if that boundary hadn't been set. I pass the time by escaping with my book boyfriends and their adventures. When I was in college, my intellectual classmates would discuss their latest literary exploits. They would drone on about the impact authors like Sylvia Plath and Ernest Gaines were making on their lives. While they rambled on, I was quietly pining for the romance novel left under my pillow. I don't apologize for my lack of literary savvy, but I don't advertise it either. I would nod in agreement and insert things like, "Their words are so profound." I like to think that they thought I was more of a quiet intellectual.

My trip to love town is interrupted by the loud blast of "Baby Got Back." Owen has been playing with my phone again. *Sigh.* I see that it's Nina, and my heart starts to pound. My inner dialogue is at war. If I answer it and it is bad news, then what am I going to do? But if it is good news, I will miss out if I don't answer the phone. Maybe she wants to meet for a drink. Jesus. My inner bitch screams, "Answer the fucking phone!" So I do what she says. She's scary.

"Hey! What's up? How's your day?" I try to sound calm, cool, and collected. Instead, I sound like a wound-up talking doll.

"Addie, you don't sound like yourself. Are you okay?" she asks. Her voice is laced with concern.

"Um, I'm fine. In true transparency, this waiting is killing me. I know we set a boundary about work and our friendship, but three months is a long time for me to be patient and not ask about my book," I answer honestly.

"Are you sitting down?" she inquires. Her voice is neutral.

"Yes." I grip the phone tightly.

"Big Sky Publishing wants to buy your book." Nina's voice goes up an octave.

"What?" I only heard the word *book*. I might have blacked out a little. Nina slows her speech.

"Big. Sky. Publishing. They want to buy your book."

I gasp. Holy. Shit. Balls. Then I scream, "Fuck yeah!" I am classy like that. She laughs.

"I'm so proud of you! I knew you could do it." I feel her smile through the phone.

"Nina, this is a celebration of you, too. You're the one who pushed me to finish," I replied emphatically.

"Oh, sweetie. I know you had it in you all along," Nina says.

"Okay. So what's next?" I inquire.

"Ashley Eberhardt from Big Sky will be calling you. We'll meet with her and go over the contract. Then the fun begins."

"Fun?" I ask.

"Yes, Addie, the fun. Well, first, there's the editing and all that boring stuff, but then the good stuff. Book launch, signings, interviews—you know, the fun things that go with becoming a published author." She says it like we're going shopping. Which, for the record,

I despise. Okay, now I am internally freaking out. I am an extroverted introvert. I like people, but I don't. I know it sounds odd. I have a very tiny circle of people that I communicate with, and frankly, being alone is quite appealing. Maybe I didn't think this writing a book thing through. Damn. My stomach clenches. My hands get clammy, and my breathing hitches.

"Addie, I can practically hear you thinking through the phone. Stop. This is going to be fine. You'll see. Allow yourself to enjoy this. I will be with you the whole way, both professionally and as your friend." She has the most amazing way of grounding me.

"Alright. I will calm my inner thoughts." I laugh. Honestly, my thoughts are like squirrels at a rave.

"Oh, and for the meeting, wear something other than your typical attire." She has now switched to "professional" Nina.

"What's wrong with my attire?" I ask, even though I know the answer.

"Addie, business attire should not scream I-just-rolled-out-of-bed-and-don't-give-a-shit."

"Ugh, okay," I say with less enthusiasm.

"If you need me to come over and help you pick out something, I can," Nina quips, but I know she's serious.

"No, I can dress myself," I state. She laughs.

Bitch.

We say goodbye and end the call, and I am left to process this life-changing development.

Addie

Later in the day, my phone rings again. It's a number I don't recognize, but I answer it in case it's the publishing house.

"This is Addie." I try not to sound annoyed just in case it isn't a telemarketer.

"Addie! Hello! This is Ashley Eberhardt from Big Sky Publishing. I'm sure Nina already told you that I finished reading your manuscript. I have to say, it's magic! We're interested in signing you, so I'd love to meet you and go over the details. When are you available?"

Instead of answering, I find myself at a loss for words, paralyzed by my inner dialogue; those bitches don't know when to shut up.

Bitch, what is your problem? Answer her!

Stop overthinking.

If you answer her like you've got your shit together, you can finish off that ice cream that you've been eyeing since breakfast.

"Addie, are you there?" she asks.

"Oh, I'm so sorry. Yes, I would be happy to meet with you. I mean, I am completely open. Nothing happening here. You know how it is, the glamorous life of a freelance writer." I start giggling as I ramble. I'm pretty sure that this Ashley woman might already be having second thoughts about signing me. My face contorts in a silent reaction to my ridiculousness.

"Please, Addie. Don't worry. You aren't the first writer to react that way. How about tomorrow at nine? I will have my assistant send you the details. But be prepared because I think this is the beginning of an amazing journey."

I accidentally squeal a little—with joy, not like Miss Piggy or anything—thank her, and hang up the phone. Owen walks in from work. I run over and hug him, practically squeezing the life out of him. He gives me his usual blank look.

"Addie. Stop! I can't breathe." By this time, I am giggling like a drunk clown.

"Owen, a publishing company just called, and they want to buy my book. Do you know what this means?"

"They did? Addie, you are the best writer. I like the stories you tell me. I knew you could do it." He smiles at me. "Does this mean we're eating Mexican tonight?"

"Yes! We're celebrating!"

"Good, I'm hungry." He turns and heads toward his room.

He leaves me with a big grin because while I may have just sold my first book, he lives for the simplicity of chips and salsa.

Addie

I enter the upscale, plush New York City office and find it laden with sophisticated furniture clad in linen. Infused lavender permeates the air. I suppose the ambiance should relax me, but there is that unceasing, nagging voice in the back of my head, trying to remind me that I am unworthy. As I inhale the sweet scent, a level of satisfaction bubbles up, and I'm all smiles as I approach the reception desk and make small talk with Ashley's assistant, Sally.

Sally escorts me to Ashley's office, a mix of classic decor sprinkled with modern elements. Contemporary art decorates the walls along with photographs of the authors whose books Big Sky has published. I go a little fangirl as some of them have created my book boyfriends. I can't believe I'm in their company. Nina is standing near the windows soaking up the spectacular view of the bustling city. She turns to greet me with a slight smile. I know I'm going to get a lecture because I might have ghosted her yesterday.

"You didn't call me back. I left you a couple of messages." She raises her eyebrows at me. Sometimes she can be scary.

"I know. Look, I'm sorry. I was pretty sure you were calling about my ability to dress myself. And for the record, I *can* dress myself. Look, Mom, no yoga pants." I laugh.

Nina doesn't laugh. Instead, she puts her hands on my shoulders, which is more like the Eiffel Tower looking down on the Seine River—huge height deficiency on my part—and lovingly says, "I know that you're nervous. I know that it makes you incredibly uncomfortable to have the focus placed on you. But you are an incredible human being, and this book is part of your journey." She backs up before continuing. "As we progress in this process, you might want to consider a publicist. I have someone in mind. Oh, and you, my beautiful friend, are getting a stylist." She grins.

I stare at her like she has two heads. My breathing stutters. Could this be a dream? I always hoped that my book would find a way to reach the masses, but then that would be it. I would go back to my simple, boring life. And a stylist? Please. I think I did a great job with my attire today. I selected a pair of black slacks, along with a white cotton blouse. How could that be wrong? Sure, I just realized that there's peanut butter on my pants, and I am wearing my cat socks, which, by the way, are a hot commodity since I saw them on *The Ellen DeGeneres Show*. As if Nina can read my mind, she grins and rolls her eyes.

When I first lay eyes on Ashley, I am overwhelmed by her stunning beauty and instantly feel self-conscious. I lack self-esteem. Feeling "less than" is my default setting. Ashley blankets herself in designer labels, sports perfectly coiffed hair, and oozes sex appeal (with curves that rival Marilyn Monroe's).

"Addie, it is such a pleasure to finally meet you. I can't tell you how much I enjoyed reading your manuscript. Now the real work begins. I just want to prepare you. Your life is about to change. Are you ready for this?" She waits for my response, but I feel that she doesn't want my honest answer.

Addie

It's been nine long months since my initial meeting with Nina and Ashley. It has been a process of editing and strategizing that has required me to embrace this new adventure. I have passed the time by starting a new writing project, keeping regular date nights with my book boyfriends, as well as martini drinking with Nina. This keeps my squirrely thoughts at bay. Mostly.

I stroll down the busy Brooklyn sidewalk to my four-story walk-up apartment building. It is easy to be energized by the vibe of the neighborhood. The eclectic group of people that reside here and the stories that accompany them weave a rich tapestry of culture and personality. The mix of young and old occupants sprinkled with individuals from various ethnicities is the foundation of this community.

The climb to my apartment on the fourth floor is the only thing I would change, but I count it as exercise, so that's a bonus. As I enter my humble abode, I catch a glimpse of myself in the full-length mirror in my bedroom. Why I would even purchase this reflective spawn of Satan is a mystery, but I allow myself to look. My pixie hair sticks out in all directions, and my face is devoid of makeup. I am wearing my standard yoga pants and an oversized T-shirt that reads, "Writer's block happens when your imaginary friends stop talking to you."

The status of my body has always been a source of my lack of confidence. I accept the reality that a size two is not in my future. After all, the height fairy skipped over me and left me vertically challenged. The damn fairy couldn't even spare another inch or two. I'm curvy and slightly overweight because, duh, I adore food and despise exercise. Since being forty-something is an introduction to aging, my boobs have started to embrace gravity and hang lower than they used to.

My moment of critiquing my body is interrupted by the sound of my intercom. I buzz them up. Now, don't gasp. Nobody buzzes me unless they know me. Plus, New York is not as scary as people make it out to be.

When I hear a knock on the door, I stroll over and open it to what appears to be a mirage. There in front of me stands a man—not just any man, but a man who literally takes my breath away. He is at least six feet tall with a muscular build. Light dances in his brown hair with flecks of silver, and his eyes—well, I'm completely lost in them with their piercing green hue. His chiseled face is a work of art, and ladies, his suit is fitted, accentuating his fine assets. If he were a fire, he would easily be of the four-alarm variety. Am I panting?

Silver fox, I think. The problem is that what I am thinking slips through my lips. It happens to me when I'm nervous. I lose all filters. Probably one of the reasons I haven't dated in a very long time. I will explain that issue later, but let's get back to the hottie in my doorway.

"Excuse me?" says the tall drink of water.

I decide that my best course of action is to pretend that I don't hear him.

"Oh, um, I think you have the wrong apartment. This is 4B. Stella lives around the corner."

Stella is a stacked blond who "entertains" regularly. It wouldn't be the first time her "friends" got the apartments mixed up.

"Who is Stella? Never mind, are you Addie Snyder?" When I nod, he continues, "I'm Jameson Ford, your new publicist." He stares at me. It is disconcerting.

I stand there, stunned. I assumed Nina would hire some adorable twenty-something girl who would be perky and happy. Jameson is a far cry from perky or happy. He looks pained. I realize that I might have forgotten about a meeting that Nina said she had set up with my new publicist. I need to start writing shit down. Plus, she never shared that she hired a hot-as-hell man. I am going to kill Nina. Too bad. I kind of like her.

Jameson

I take one look at the quirky woman standing in front of me and feel an instant twinge of regret about taking this job. After all, I am highly sought-after in the publicity world, so I really don't need to take on yet another client, but Nina and I go way back. I did this as a favor to her. Addie isn't what I expected. She is wearing clothing that hides her figure; her hair is short and unmanaged. Her nervous energy is palpable as she wrings her hands while her eyes gravitate to the floor.

I subtly peek behind her at her apartment. As a former Navy SEAL, I thrive on structure and discipline. I don't have room for disorganization in my life, nor am I remotely flexible in that area—and it's nothing I'd ever want to change. From the looks of Addie's place, I feel smothered. The place is cozy but packed with knickknacks, photographs, and books. Good God, the books. It looks like a library has vomited in her apartment.

"Are you done passing judgment?" She eyes me suspiciously.

How did she know? Is she a mind reader?

"I'm admiring your place," I say.

She snorts and lets out a laugh. I like her laugh, and that smile, well, it lights up the room. Shit, what the hell is happening here?

"Well, I thought Nina was going to send a woman," Addie says. "No offense. I'm not sexist or anything, but…well, okay, I'll now shut up. I tend to ramble when I'm uncomfortable."

"Good to know. I assure you, Ms. Snyder, I am the best in the industry, and Nina wants you to have the best." Sure, I sound egotistical, but in this industry, you *must* have a lot of ego to get to the head of the pack.

"Please call me Addie. I don't know what the big deal is. I mean, I wrote one book." She waves her hand dismissively.

I study her. She doesn't have any idea what this process entails.

"Addie, we need to start the promotion process now, before release, and then once your book is released, we'll need to make the media rounds. This means interviews like *Good Morning America* and *The Today Show,* along with using social media. Not only do you need my help, but things are going to change. My rules. And you might want to stop letting just anyone into this building without first identifying who they are."

Her eyes narrow, and she blows out her breath harshly. "Listen, I don't take instruction well. I am forty-something…and I have been on my own for a long time. We can work *together,* but I make the rules." She thinks she's intimidating. How adorable.

"Are you done?"

She remains silent, appearing satisfied that she's getting her point across.

"Look, we can work together, but you need to let me help you navigate this. It can be intimidating at best." I scrutinize her attire. "On a more important note, Nina has scheduled a stylist for you."

"Yes, Nina told me about the stylist. Apparently, I can no longer dress myself." She sighs. "I just thought that the book would be released, and I could simply sink back into my regular life." I can tell she's starting to panic. It happens. Writers tend to hide behind their words. Words become a comfort—an outlet, a place of retreat. This client will probably require a lot of handholding. Christ, now I'm thinking about holding her hand.

"Then maybe you shouldn't have written something that would change the landscape for the average middle-aged woman. I'll be in touch." I smirk, opening the door to leave.

"Wait, you read my book?" Her expression softens.

"Of course. I have to be able to promote it, and to do so, I have to know the material."

"What did you think? I mean, did you like it?" Her eyes search my face.

"I think Sherry is a strong, formidable woman. I particularly liked how funny and relatable she was despite her insecurities." I am not bullshitting. I enjoyed it and know that I can promote it successfully. *If* I have Addie's cooperation, and that means *my* rules, like it or not.

"Wow. Thank you so much." She whispers the words, and a slight smile tugs at her lips.

"Of course, the romance was unrealistic, but it's exactly what your target readers want, so it works." I need to be honest. Romantic love is not real. It simply doesn't exist.

"So you have never been in love?" she inquires, furrowing her brow.

"Lust, yes. Love, never. It is a setup for hurt, and I, for one, don't believe in it."

"Good to know. Well, it was delightful meeting you, and it should be interesting working with you." She smirks. Her tone is laced with sarcasm.

"Here's my card. If you have any questions, call me." Ignoring her last remark, I hand her my card. Our fingers touch, sending sparks through my body. I walk away as fast as I can.

Addie

Holy shit! What is happening? The silver fox, a.k.a. Jameson, is pushy. A big, hard, muscular know-it-all. When our fingers touched while he was handing me his business card, I felt my lady parts wake up from their long winter's nap. My hoo-ha is Rip Van Winkle. His presence made me tingly. Jesus. Anyway, I could hardly focus. He's ridiculously handsome and a great big asshole. I am torn between hate and lust. I mean, he's demanding, judgmental, and he literally doesn't believe in love. Who thinks that way? I didn't have a great example of love growing up, but I know it exists. I know there is a possibility of me finding it. Even if I simply find it by creating it for my characters.

All I heard was him spouting nonsense about our next steps, including the words "tour," "appearances," and "stylist," which are up there with bad words like "diet," "chocolate shortage," and "no wine." My mind is reeling. I am going to murder Nina. Grateful he's gone, I pull out my cell phone to text the bitch.

Me: *Thanks for the warning. This publicist is bossy, annoying, and a complete asshole.*
Nina: *Oh, good. You met him.*

Me: *You are dead to me.*
Nina: *Going through a tunnel. Losing you. Talk soon. (Heart emoji, heart emoji)*

Even though I love her, I hate her.

Me: *That only works if we're having a voice call.*

Radio silence

Me: *(Middle finger emoji)*
Nina: *(Laughing emoji)*

I need to find a new friend.

Jameson

I am affected. Just so we're clear, I don't get affected. If being a Navy SEAL taught me anything, it prepared me for the unexpected. Meeting Addie threw me a curveball, but I'll manage. This is a job—a much safer job than my previous one. The PTSD has eased. With the help of my psychiatrist, I've gained some valuable skills to cope when it rears its ugly head, and for the most part, I am able to function without isolating. The only physical reminder of my mission gone wrong is a scar on my chest, where they removed some shrapnel. I was one of the lucky ones. I came home.

But I also became a statistic when I got here. The readjustment, after all of the horrors I went through at war, was harder than recovering from my physical injuries. I don't miss the nightmares, the inability to leave my apartment, and my need to numb with alcohol. I was left with no choice other than to seek outside help. It was either that or become a recluse—and I almost chose that unsavory option. But through the "encouragement"—aka the insistence—of my best friend, Harrison McCall, I did the "right thing." Now I have tools to help me deal, like exercise and mindful breathing, and I'm participating in life again. Still, working on the emotional connection portion of the program, though.

The publicist gig was something that fell into my lap. After getting home and realizing that my career as a SEAL was over, I isolated myself and pushed everyone around me away. But Harrison would not back down. He refused to accept that this was how the rest of my life would be.

Harrison and I met while going to Yale. We're an unlikely pair— him being a blue blood and me being a product of the projects. While Harrison never wanted for anything, my mother scraped to make ends meet. When I wasn't working multiple after-school jobs, I was studying. Fortunately, my hard work paid off and joining the Navy allowed me to attend this very prestigious university. I fulfilled my mother's dream of going to college. My goal was to create a life that would make it so my mother would never have to work again and get her out of her dismal apartment in an area high in crime. She deserved only the best; her life was a series of disappointments and heartaches. My dad left shortly after I was born, so it had always been the two of us. Yet even when things were tough, she never wavered in her positive attitude. She made everything better.

While I was overseas, she passed away from an aneurysm. The guilt of not being here for her still haunts me. She died alone, and her death was the same day that I was injured in an ambush while on a mission. By the time I was sent home, she had already been buried. Harrison took care of everything. He is my brother in every sense of the word.

The last conversation I had with her was about two weeks before her death. It was the last time she said her famous quote to me—the one she'd told me so many times before to lift my spirits: "If you want to make your mark on the world, be true to yourself. Don't follow the pack. Lead them." When I got home, I had that tattooed on my chest as a reminder that she is always with me.

Six months after my mother's death, Harrison came over to my apartment and did what he did every day—he opened the shades to let in the light and set down some food on the counter. He was never invited, but that was not an obstacle. He sat down and looked at the sullen, sunken face of his college friend who had once shown so much ambition and promise.

"Man, this has got to stop. You have spent six fucking months feeling sorry for yourself, and it's time to move on. You have a full life ahead of you. Your mother would never have wanted this for you."

"Don't you dare bring my mother into this. You have no idea what it's like to watch your comrades, your friends, die in front of you, and not be able to help them. I failed them along with my mother. I couldn't help anyone. What makes you think I can help myself now?"

"Do you think they would want you to sit and waste your life? Your only failure is not living. What would your mother think of you now, after she worked so hard to get you what you needed to build a good life for yourself? Celebrate being here. You got a second chance. Not many people can say that." He sounded exasperated.

"Wait, where are the cameras? Are we filming a fucking Lifetime movie? Take your inspirational crap somewhere else."

"Fine, but before I go, I have an offer. I've been thinking about this for a while. Join my company. You did some publicity work before you joined the SEALs, and you were good. I need help. We are drowning in business. Please consider it. You owe me, and I know you could make a good career out of this."

I did owe him. He was the only one who had stuck by me after my mother died, took care of me while I recovered from my injuries, and despite what an asshole I had become, kept being my friend.

When I first came home, I was inundated with friends trying to help. They would bring me whole meals and try to draw me out of my miserable existence. One by one, the visits diminished. I had successfully pushed everyone away, with the exception of Harrison. That fucker is stubborn.

"I'll think about it," I said. And I meant that. Maybe he was right. Maybe it was time to move forward and start living again.

"Wait, did you just say you would consider it?" He grinned.

"Don't get all excited. I haven't said yes."

"Yet. But you will."

And after that come-to-Jesus talk, I agreed that the only way to honor those who lost their lives was to move forward with mine. Working gives me purpose. But personal relationships, aside from my friendship with Harrison, are not on my radar. Sure, I engage in mutually satisfying physical encounters, but I make sure they know the score. I don't get attached. It helps me avoid the pain of loving someone. I can't allow myself to feel. It hurts too damn much.

Addie

"You could have prepared me," I say while having lunch with Nina the next day at a swanky restaurant in Midtown Manhattan. As usual, I'm dressed for comfort versus style, while Nina is dressed for Fashion Week. And by the way, it is not Fashion Week. Our friendship remains a mystery.

"Prepared you? What fun would that have been?" Nina smirks while I roll my eyes.

"I was expecting a woman, and you sent me a brooding man who looks at me like he can't believe he got the booby prize."

"Jameson is very good at his job, and you need the best. Plus, he isn't bad to look at, is he? You can thank me later." She continues to gloat.

My lady parts clap in agreement. Traitorous bitches.

"Okay, so he is attractive in an annoying bully kind of way. I told him that I was in charge, so I think we established how this is going to work." I give her a satisfied smile.

Nina laughs. She laughs so hard, she snorts. Nina never snorts. Her laugh is refined and classy. Being such an immense source of hilarity for my friend is beyond irritating.

"First of all, he needs to take the lead. You haven't navigated this process. Addie, this is big. When people figure out who you are, you will not get a moment's peace. Your book is going to be huge. I can literally feel the success you're going to have. You're giving humor and lightness to menopausal women. You're giving them hope that their lives haven't ended simply because a man left them or their bodies have changed the rules." Nina does an excellent job of switching from friend to literary agent without hesitation.

I allow that to sink in for a moment as I munch on my last French fry while my friend eats her kale salad. Maybe I should start eating kale. Wait, I hate kale. Then a thought slams into my mind. People are going to see me. Like, physically see me, and that brings up a new level of anxiety. My face drains of color.

"Maybe this was all a mistake. I kind of wish I hadn't written this book," I whisper.

"Too late for that, my friend. Let's bask in your moment. I will be with you every step of the way, and so will Jameson." A smile spreads across her face, and I sigh. I guess this will be an interesting adventure.

Addie

I walk into the reception area at the salon of the stylist that Nina had arranged to meet me. Unfortunately, yoga pants and food-stained T-shirts don't scream "success." A small bit of panic bubbles up, and it makes me search the abyss of my purse for something sweet. Some people carry a flask or a stash of Xanax. I carry chocolate. A sigh of relief escapes my lips as I unearth a lone wrapped piece, and my fingers go on autopilot to unwrap it. As I close my eyes, enjoying the heavenly treat that feels like a party in my mouth, a familiar masculine voice interrupts my bliss. I might have moaned a little bit—for the chocolate, not the man.

"Sorry to interrupt your intimate moment, but George is ready for you." Jameson's eyes seared into my skin. He isn't big on greetings like, "Hello! How are you?" Nope, he's like a robot. Devoid of any emotion. This is going to be painful.

"Crap, I didn't know you would be here," I blurt.

"Obviously." He glares at me. Color me fifty shades of annoyed. I gather my purse, reluctantly following Jameson. "Nina thought it best that I meet you here. You know, to make sure that you show up."

"Whatever." I turn my attention to the person who will be dressing me.

George Benson is gorgeous and completely flamboyant. His tall, slender stature is draped in a stylish Armani suit. His styled, slicked-back, jet-black hair highlights his high cheekbones and almond-shaped brown eyes. George is hot.

"Addie, George. George, Addie," Jameson says in what's supposed to be an introduction but is so dull that I almost fall asleep.

George greets me with an exuberant hug and then proceeds to do a complete up-and-down of my attire. He looks deeply concerned. Then he does a once-over of Jameson, and a smile tugs at his lips. He looks deeply interested.

"I don't suppose you hit for the other team," he says to Jameson, flashing his megawatt smile and batting his eyelashes.

"No." With that, Jameson goes to sit down. George laughs.

"Addie, I am so excited to meet you! Nina tells me that you have many appearances and events lined up, so you'll need some clothes that make a statement. Plus, we have a makeup and hair team, so you won't have to do anything. Just sit back and enjoy this incredible ride." He's grinning at me. I might puke out of anxiety.

"We are going to burn this outfit and anything else resembling it. Now, go into the other room and strip down to your panties. I need to see what I'm working with, girl, and I can't get an inkling until I get you out of those clothes."

I stare at him, overwhelmed with mortification. He wants me to undress? Like, in front of him? I strive not to see *myself* without clothes, let alone allowing someone else to see me without their protection.

"Sweetie, I'm gay. You in your panties is not a big deal." He waves his hand, dismissing my insecurities.

I move toward the door feeling Jameson's eyes boring into my back. I close myself into the spacious dressing room and strip. The insult of having a full-length mirror adds to my reluctance, but I close my eyes and do as George instructed. As I am disrobing, I am assaulted by memories of my mother. Every day, her passive-aggressive words would singe my self-esteem.

"Addie, why can't you just go on a diet? Then you would get boys to notice you."

"When we are at the club, I need for you to order a salad so that the ladies think you're least trying. It is so embarrassing to have a daughter who is overweight."

My ugly trip down memory lane is interrupted as George knocks on the door, enters the room, and evaluates the situation. I hold my breath.

"Addie, you are gorgeous. Look at you with your curves. Honestly, if I style another anorexic model, I think I might scream. Is it mean that I eat cheeseburgers in front of them?" He giggles. "But girl, what panties are you wearing? My grandmother wouldn't be caught dead in those. Of course, she has a grandson as a stylist, so she has no choice in anything she wears."

I burst out laughing, and for the first time in a while, I relax. "George, nobody even sees my panties, so that doesn't matter."

"Umm, girlfriend, when you are getting your sex on, do you want your man looking at your panties wondering if you raided your grandmother's underwear drawer?"

"Well, that isn't an issue at this point." I look down at the floor. My vulnerability is overflowing.

"Honey, having the right undergarments will make you feel sexy. Confident. And when that lucky man unwraps you like the present you are, it will set the tone for the experience." He wiggles his eyebrows at me.

I smile. Jameson's face pops into my head. I am in so much trouble.

George takes my measurements and brings in a few items for me to try on. Unlike most women, I hate shopping and have cultivated a knack for buying online to avoid the unforgiving mirrors and lighting that taunt me. Plus, it isn't like need to be fitted, since I only buy yoga pants and T-shirts.

"We are introducing colors into your world, Miss Thing. No more drab for you. Your body was meant to be on display. And heels. You must wear heels to give you some height and elongate the body. We are going to have so much fun!" Unfortunately, his excitement is not contagious.

Fun is not the word that I would use to describe this situation. Maybe the opposite of fun. Like visiting the dentist. And heels? That is a recipe for disaster. The last time I wore heels was when I attended Matthew's wedding, and I fell. Not just a subtle fall, either. No, when I humiliate myself, I commit to it fully. I fell face-first into the wedding cake. It's on video and everything. Dorothy made sure to post it on any and every social media site. When confronted, she told me that since there's so much sadness in the world, laughter is the best medicine. So apparently, my humiliation gave others some healing comic relief. You're welcome.

After George finishes measuring, tugging, and violating a lot of personal space, I get back into my clothes and leave the dressing room. George wraps me in a warm hug.

"I'll bring the clothes to you tomorrow. You are fabulous, Addie. You and I are going to be great friends." His genuine smile brightens his face.

I feel a little overwhelmed. It doesn't help that silver fox has been staring at me while George and I talk, his gaze dark and intense. A stare that kind of scares the shit out of me. I exhale, sigh, and whisper, "Okay, well, see you later." I walk out the door only to find that my new, brooding appendage is following right behind me.

Jameson

With any new client, I do a background check. An important piece of my job is to stay ahead of any complications that might threaten to arise. I want to make sure there won't be any surprises, and with my extensive connections in law enforcement, it is never an issue to expedite a deeper investigation.

There are a few unexpected blips on Addie. Her mother is deceased; her father seems to have disappeared not long after her brother was born, and she has a loser cousin who goes from job to job, has filed for bankruptcy, and married a woman with sticky fingers. This is not the best scenario when working with a public figure. When a family member starts making bank, roaches start crawling out of the woodwork, so I have to make sure those individuals don't ruin my client's reputation.

I'm relieved to see that other than those few issues; she is clean. No arrests, tickets—not even an overdue library book (but after seeing her book-laden apartment, she probably doesn't need to borrow government-owned books). She pays all of her bills on time, and she keeps only a few close friends. It seems straightforward, but I know to always expect the unexpected. And some of the unexpected is already happening. I find myself surprisingly overwhelmed by an unusual sense of responsibility for Addie. I've never felt this way about anyone except for my mother. And that petrifies me. It is unsettling and beyond confusing.

My mother was the best example of someone happy despite her circumstances. She was never bitter about being a single mom, and she was the epitome of unconditional love. Even when I was deployed, she looked at me with tears in her eyes and said, "Go make the world a better place. You were meant to make a difference." She always made me feel valued. No one has been able to infiltrate my walls since she died. No one has measured up.

After we leave George's place, Addie walks a few feet ahead as if she's trying to lose me.

"Addie, the car is right here," I shout over the crowd of people navigating the sidewalk.

"Car? I take the subway. I don't have a car." She gives me that "you're a dumb-ass" look.

Then she spots the sleek black town car and her eyes widen.

"Nina wants you to be shuttled around by car for these kinds of appointments, and for events, too. This will be our mode of transportation."

I can see by the expression on her face that she is trying to process this change among a host of others. I catch up to her and put my hand on the small of her back to ease her toward the car. She shudders at my touch, or quite possibly she is chilled, but I feel electricity. Could she feel the same strange connection as I do? She hops in the front seat. The driver looks at her like she's an alien, and I smirk as I slide into the back.

"Back seat, Addie," I say.

"Oh, well, of course." She avoids my eyes. She smiles at the driver, eases herself out of the car, and slides in next to me. She smells good, like vanilla. I can't help but notice she's fidgety, her hands clasping and unclasping in her lap. My ego would like to think that I make her a little nervous.

"We need to go over next week's schedule. First up, *Good Morning America* is scheduled for Tuesday. The car will be at your apartment at seven a.m. You'll be on during the eight a.m. segment. George will meet us at *GMA* to dress you, and they'll do your hair and makeup. Right after that is *The View*."

"Do I really need all of this help? Clothes? Makeup? Hair? It seems like overkill. I'm not a celebrity."

I look at her with a cool stare.

"Okay, maybe I need a little help. Oh God! This is really happening. I mean, I wrote a book. This is too much too fast!" She covers her face with her hands and proceeds to hyperventilate.

"Breathe. Just breathe," I whisper with a gentleness that startles me a little. My sense of protecting her is heightened. I want to soothe her. Assure her. But most of all, I want to ease this anxiety that tells me she doesn't think she is deserving or worthy of this opportunity.

Addie slowly regains a normal breathing pattern.

"Thanks. I don't think I'm prepared for this whirlwind. I mean, I wrote a book. Just a book."

"Addie, you keep repeating that you wrote a book. But it's a book that will make an impact. Be proud. Enjoy the moment. Celebrate it. Stop looking at this as if it were a bad thing."

"You're right, of course. It's just my experience that with something good, there is always something bad to follow. I'm waiting for the other shoe to drop, the shit to hit the fan, the floor beneath me to drop, the—"

I interrupt her. "I get the idea, Addie. It's perfectly normal to feel anxious, but you have a team of people who will have your back every step of the way." I itch to touch her, but I need to remain neutral. No emotional attachment. This is only a job.

Addie

I feel uncomfortable the moment the words leave my mouth. I don't want to appear vulnerable. My whole life has been a series of unfortunate occurrences. Giving Jameson a glimpse of my insecurities, well, it was not a part of my plan. I like to keep those things closely guarded. Besides, his body language tells me that he's currently experiencing extreme discomfort, or perhaps he just always appears constipated. Maybe I'm not so bad off after all. Now, if I could get my lady parts to agree that this isn't anything more than a business transaction. But no, the proximity of his hot body has them singing the "Hallelujah" chorus. Bitches.

"Sorry for my little meltdown. I just can't seem to process all of this, and I am a little freaked out, to say the least," I whisper.

"No worries. This isn't the first time that I've had a client panic," he states, completely monotone.

Right. Client. *Geez, Addie, remember you're simply a paycheck to him.*

The car slows at the curb in front of my apartment, and the driver opens the door for me. I glance at Jameson and give a slight smile before turning to leave. I feel his hand grab my wrist and jump at the firmness of his grip.

"Not so fast. I thought I could give you a few pointers that will make you feel more comfortable during the interviews you'll be giving." He is still holding on to my wrist. I look down, and he instantly releases it. I miss the touch.

He clears his throat. "First, the producer will run over the questions they'll be asking, so you will have that information in advance. The best advice I can give you is to focus on the interviewer. Pretend it's a conversation with a good friend. Doing that will relax you."

"That makes sense except that there are cameras, lights, and millions of people watching me." My voice raises an octave.

"I think you will surprise yourself, Addie. Your book is relatable, and so are you."

Before I can even respond, his warmth dissipates, and the colder, more stoic Jameson emerges. "And remember, push the book as much as you can during the interview. You want to sell it, not just have a chat. It's all about promotion. The more you promote, the more sales you will make. I'll be back at seven a.m. on Tuesday to pick you up. George will meet us there with your outfit, and then you'll go to hair and makeup. Don't be late."

I nod that I understand even though my mind is reeling. I get out of the car and look back, but he's looking at his phone, dismissing me.

I walk into my apartment, and the buzzer immediately assaults me. Adhering to Jameson's concerns, I ask for identification. It's my cousin, Matthew. Again. I imagine that this isn't a social call but more of a monetary request disguised as a social call.

I open the door and gesture for him to enter. It astounds me that Matthew is still as good-looking as he was in high school. He is of medium height, has black hair, and his arms are lined with tattoos (which are mostly covered by the leather jacket that he wears). It never fails to amaze me that at one time, we were close—but something shifted. When we were younger, he was like another brother. When Owen was born, things changed. Maybe he was uncomfortable with his disability, or quite possibly, he was discovering the world of the female persuasion. Possibly both, but there had been a growing distance between us for years. Once he met Dorothy, our relationship evaporated. He draws people in with his charismatic, engaging personality. He's one of those people who could sell ice to an Eskimo. Too bad he doesn't use those skills to keep a job.

"Hey, Matthew." I try to sound chipper.

"Hey, yourself. You didn't even tell your only cousin about your new book. I had to hear about it from Dorothy, who saw it on Twitter. That hurt my feelings." He pouts. I soften as I feel the old Matthew emerging. Sweet. Caring.

"Well, it's kind of new to me, too. Plus, it's a tad overwhelming. I haven't had a lot of time to adjust." It's the truth. I feel like I'm living someone else's life.

"Really? A windfall of money is overwhelming? You wrote a stupid book. Big fucking deal." Nice. Yep, ladies and gentlemen, the real Matthew is back. The cold, spiteful man who feels that the world owes him. I tense up instantly.

"There hasn't been a windfall of money. We are just starting to promote it, so…" I stop mid-sentence, knowing that an explanation will simply fall on deaf ears. "What brings you here, Matthew? You aren't here to talk about my book." I sigh.

"Oh Addie, you've always been so sensitive. Look, I just need a little loan until I find another job. After all, we *are* family, and family helps each other." He is looking at me expectantly. Normally, I would roll over and comply with his request. Didn't I *just* give him a handout a few months ago? Maybe it's the fact that I'm emotionally spent—that I am currently trying to navigate this newfound status. I'm a little tired of taking care of everyone else, especially people who are perfectly capable of taking care of themselves. Maybe I'm tired of being told what to do, what to wear—well, the list is lengthy. There's no room for this fresh hell. All of the emotional baggage of constantly enabling my cousin bubbles up and spews out. My brain is screaming, "There she blows!"

"Let me get this right. I slave for a decade creating a book that I hoped someone would be generous enough to publish, and you, who goes through jobs like women go through chocolate, want a piece of the action? I've 'loaned' money before that has never been repaid. Several months ago, I wrote you a big, fat check that should have kept you afloat for a while. I am tired of you and your wife idly expecting me to bail you out while Dorothy goes and 'buys' a new Michael Kors purse." I do air quotes on 'buy' because let's be honest, convicted or not, she is a shoplifter.

"Matthew, while I'm on a roll, I will tell you that your freeloading days have officially ended. There will be no more handouts. You and your shoplifting hoarder of a wife need to get jobs." I exhale. Wow, that feels fucking amazing. The guilt I thought I would feel simply isn't there.

"You know she was never convicted, right? It was all a big misunderstanding." He's looking at me like he's still trying to convince himself- cue my exaggerated eye roll.

"Is that the only message you got from what I just said?" I am so done at this point.

"Are you kidding me right now? It isn't my fault that I can't find or keep a job. It isn't my fault that your selfish mother refused to leave me any money. You. Owe. Me." His face darkens. His finger points at me. To be completely honest, I am a little intimidated and very surprised, but I won't let him steer me away from honoring my truth.

"My mother owed you nothing. I don't owe you anything. Stop blaming everyone for your own shit. When did you become so entitled and bitter? There was a time when we were close. I don't even know who you are anymore." I shake my head. Tears threaten to fall, but I resist the urge to show any vulnerability.

He smirks. "Whatever, Addie. You have always thought you were better than everyone else. I guess family means nothing to you."

"Family does mean something to me. I thought that giving you money all of this time would make us closer, but the reality is that it seems to have done the opposite. You don't care about Owen or me—you simply want to use me as your own personal ATM. I'm done, done trying to make us have a relationship that doesn't even exist, and done being used. But most of all, done being the pushover I've been for years. Grow up, Matthew. You and your wife need to find someone else to manipulate."

"It's cute that you're standing up for yourself. Little Addie, who couldn't even get a date. Whose only friend is her retarded brother. But even with this book, you are still the pathetic, fat loser you always were. Watch your back because your high and mighty days are numbered."

"Are you threatening me?"

"I would never threaten family. Have a good day, Addie." He turns and walks out the door.

Could this day get any stranger?

Addie

I can hardly sleep. The thought of being on television for the whole world to judge me elicits tremendous anxiety. At seven a.m., I am staring out of the window, willing Jameson not to show up. But when I see the town car pull up in front of my apartment, I go numb. My stomach churns. I hesitate to leave my sanctuary. I might hyperventilate. What if I make a fool of myself on national television? What if I can't remember anything about my book? Suddenly, my legs are walking to the door without my permission. The next thing I know, I'm standing on the sidewalk in a trance, frozen, staring at the black car idling at the curb. My stomach rolls…oh God, I might throw up right here in full view of everybody. I see the back window of the car open.

"You have to get into the car for us to get to the set," Jameson deadpans.

His voice jolts me out of my stupor, and I swallow down my nausea. *Deep breaths. Don't show weakness,* I tell myself. *I can do this. I brought chocolate with me.*

I narrow my eyes, covering my fear by giving him my best glare. On a good day, I'm not overly intimidating, so I sigh and assume the seat next to the brooding publicist. Jameson smells good. I just want to sniff him vertically and horizontally.

"Are you sniffing me?"

I realize I'm leaning toward him while making a sniffing sound. *Oops.* My lady parts comment, "Good job," and I tell them to hush. I said that last word out loud, too. He gives me a strange look.

"Don't be silly. It's the coffee I'm smelling. Did you bring one for me? Isn't that part of your job?" I stare at him expectantly.

He smirks and hands me the cup of liquid gold. I might have moaned, and he raises his eyebrow.

As we pull up to the back door of the studio, my breath catches. My nerves are at a rave.

"Addie, if you hold your breath, you will pass out." God, he is so annoying.

"Thanks for the reminder, Captain Obvious. I will keep that in mind for future reference." I mock salute him.

He smiles at me, or maybe I am so far gone that I'm simply hallucinating, but I swear there is a slight tug of his lips, and teeth are exposed—a rare phenomenon.

As we enter the building, I see that George is waiting impatiently.

"Girl, what did I tell you about this sorry excuse for clothing? You can look cute and stylish while being comfortable. Never mind. First things first, and we need you, Addie Snyder, to put the FAB in FABULOUS. Fortunately, you have me to help you get there."

Seriously, it is the butt crack of dawn. Why is he so perky? I nod in agreement since he's right. I am a hot mess who needs any help she can get.

There are so much touching and various invasions of personal space. First, George buttons and zips and pulls at my clothes, then the makeup girl is all over my face *and* neck, next the hairstylist gets close, and then a slew of miscellaneous assistants proceed to feel me up. I haven't had this much action in, well, let's just say my lady parts have cobwebs, and if Christopher Columbus were alive, he would think he found a whole new world. I might be a virgin by default.

By the time everyone is done, George looks at me and says, "Addie, you look amazing. I mean, I am amazing, but it helps to have something wonderful to work with, and you are beautiful." He says it so matter-of-factly that at that moment, I have no choice but to believe him.

He positions me in front of the mirror, and I gasp. I am wearing stylish, fitted black pants with an elegant pink silk blouse that accentuates my assets. The "girls" look like they're waving "hello" instead of dragging along the waistband of my pants. George chose low-heeled pumps since he knows I'm fearful of falling in heels, and my pixie cut is styled in a way that frames my face.

I stare. George grins, and Jameson appears to be having a stroke.

Jameson

I am not sure what it is about this woman. She's not my type. I'm usually drawn to glamorous, refined women who are easily disposable. I don't want the emotional tendencies that lead to the R-word: relationship. The word makes me break out in a cold sweat. But Addie, she is another R-word: refreshing. I like how she greets everyone with kindness and a smile. I enjoy how astonished she is when she catches a glimpse of herself after George styles her—and I can't help but stare at her transformation. And it is amusing how she searches her large purse in hopes of finding a piece of chocolate, and when she does, pops it in her mouth like a Xanax. Lucky piece of chocolate.

What the hell is happening to me?

The interview goes without a hitch. She is incredibly relatable, and her nervousness barely shows. My phone buzzes nonstop as we head over to the set of *The View*.

"You did fantastically. After *The View*, we'll meet Nina for lunch to go over the book tour, and then we'll head back to Rockefeller Center to meet with the producers of *The Tonight Show*. Same deal as *GMA*. They will go over questions with you, and then you're done for the day." I am still looking at my phone, not wanting to make eye contact.

Silence.

"Addie, did you hear me? Are you okay? Look, I know this is all very overwhelming—"

"Do you? Do you know this whole situation is making me want to scream? I am trying very hard to be excited. To celebrate this moment when my dreams have come true. But I'm seriously wondering if I'm cut out for this. That interview was terrifying. I am a behind-the-scenes person. This," she gestures to her new look, "is not me."

I am used to the diva meltdowns. The outrageous demands of celebrities and what happens when they don't receive their requests. But this—this is a totally different beast. I have never had anyone who didn't want to be the center of attention.

"Addie, I can't imagine the kind of pressure you're feeling, but this is part of the package. You are under contractual obligation to fulfill these appearances until after the book tour." I say it with firm conviction, but I regret the words the moment they spill out of my mouth. This probably isn't what she needed to hear.

"I should have known you wouldn't have a human response. You know, to be sympathetic to my feelings, my fears. I guess you aren't paid to be a support system." She turns and looks out the window.

For the first time in a while, I am speechless. I can placate the most difficult individual, but the authenticity of this woman is gutting me. How do I handle this?

"I am paid to keep you on schedule. I'm a publicist, not a therapist." Once the words leave my lips, I can hear the hurt in her gasp. From what I saw in my background check of Addie, the people in her life are users and always have been. The only ally she seems to have is Nina, and maybe one day, I can be that as well. I need to do a better job of not being an asshole.

Addie

That night, I stumble into my humble abode, depleted. There is something about this apartment that honors the real me—a writer who wants to write. I strip out of my fancy new clothes and cloak myself in my pajamas. Too keyed up to sleep, I open my laptop and start to write.

The door buzzer startles me awake, and when I immediately fall back asleep, my phone starts ringing. And the door buzzer goes off again, on steroids. I feel the indentation of the keyboard on my face from the night spent on my laptop. Owen beats me to the buzzer. Somehow, it's eight a.m., and I need to be on a local morning show at nine. Shit.

"Who is it?" My brother loves to act like he is the guardian of our domain.

"It's Jameson. I'm Addie's publicist," his sexy voice announces.

"What's the password?" he asks.

"Um...e-excuse me?" Jameson stutters.

"The password. You have to say it before I let you in."

I intercept the buzzer and let Jameson up.

"Hey! He didn't know the password. You told me not to just let anyone up." Okay, have I shared that Owen can be a little inflexible?

"Yes, Owen, I did, but this is the guy who's helping me with all of this book crap. He's the one getting me spots on television, so you can share the password with him once he gets up here."

"That's dumb." He flips me off.

My phone continues to buzz. The caller ID reveals it's Dorothy. I hesitate to answer but realize that it's either now or later that I will have to speak to her. She's persistent when she doesn't get her way.

"Dorothy, I can't talk right now. I am running late and—"

"Listen, I need to talk to you. I had a vision, and I can't shake the feeling that something bad is on the horizon." Did I share that Dorothy believes she is psychic? Yep. Lucky me. I'm just grateful that she isn't a mind reader.

"Well, I am going to have to call you back. I'm already running late." Click. I breathe deeply and exhale in order to deal with the next issue at hand: the visitor at the door. Jameson.

He glares at me. I glare at him.

He pauses and then says, "You look like hell." As he eyes me, I feel judged.

"Always doling out flattery. Let me grab my stuff, and we can leave. Oh, and Owen, this is Jameson. Jameson, my brother, Owen."

"Hey, Owen! Great to meet you." He smiles. Wow, his lips do move away from the permanent scowl he's always wearing.

"You didn't know the password." His eyes narrow at Jameson.

"Well, maybe you can tell me what it is. I'm so glad someone honors the safety code. Your sister needs help in that area." He eyes me.

"I know, right? She's the worst. She won't listen to me. I'll think about giving you the code. Later." And with that, my brother strolls away.

Jameson smirks at me. "Your brother is funny. At least he's mindful of being safe. By the way, you have a keyboard imprint on your face."

"Well, I was busy writing last night and fell asleep doing it. I was inspired!" I gloat, proud of my diligence.

Jameson takes a quick glance at the screen. He snorts. That's when I realize the product of my inspiration is page after page of absolute gibberish.

Jameson

The emails regarding Addie have been overwhelmingly positive. I can't keep up with all of the demands as I sort through the many requests for her presence. I am also continually pestered by the conversation we had the day before. You know, the one where I referred to her as a job. I was such a gigantic asshole. Being a NAVY Seal taught me not to feel, not to get attached, and I used to think that was a good thing. I can't help but continue to carry it through my everyday interactions. Always in control. Never ruffled...until now. Addie is complex, but the added factor of her brother and the love she feels for him draws me to her even more.

Harrison strolls into my office and leans heavily on my desk. The lights of the bustling NYC skyline twinkle from the expansive windows.

"Let's get out of here. I could use a drink."

"Man, you have no idea." I sigh.

"Is Addie difficult?" He looks concerned.

"Difficult? Annoying, frustrating, and sarcastic describe her best. I mean, I have been on missions that were less complex than her. She needs to come with an instruction book. Oh, and she eats chocolate from the bottom of her purse. Who does that?"

The corner of Harrison's mouth tugs. "You like her."

"She's a client. It's just hard when she's so resistant to being in the public eye. It's foreign to me—most of our clients beg for it." I am in defense mode.

"Uh, huh." He chuckles, slowly nodding his head.

"Can we go drink now and talk about something else? What's going on with you?"

"Just keeping people happy. Living the dream and hoping to get some action tonight, so come on. Maybe you need to get laid, too."

Christ, I can't remember the last time I got laid, and oddly enough, I have no desire to scratch that itch.

We arrive at a hip bar in the West Village. Honestly, is there any bar in New York City that isn't hip? The corners of the bar feature leather sofas that give the place a cozy, intimate vibe. It's crowded with high-end clientele, all dressed in designer clothes. We settle into a corner spot, and women start eyeing us immediately. An attractive blond at the bar winks at me. I contemplate my next move, but I feel nothing. Normally, I would buy her a drink, make idle conversation, and head back to her place. Nothing has felt normal since I met Addie, and I can't understand what it is about this woman that has me so off-balance. Our waitress returns with our drinks—whiskey neat for me, craft beer for Harrison. The amber liquid trickles down my throat, an instant relief. I close my eyes to enjoy the flavor.

"You're awfully quiet. Any of these women catch your eye?" He wiggles his eyebrows.

"Nope. Not in the mood tonight. Just looking to relax and catch up with my friend." Honestly, I would prefer drinking alone and possibly into oblivion, but I did that for far too long. Isolating. Drinking to forget. Quenching my guilt. Guilt over being the only survivor and not being there for my mother. But the alcohol-induced haze was a temporary fix. It only exasperated my PTSD issues.

"Tell me about Addie. Nina raves about her." I am intrigued. Harrison and Nina have a tenuous relationship. The air is thick with sexual tension when they're together. The sparks are palpable but generally overshadowed by Nina's coldness toward him.

"Addie is different. She doesn't want the attention. She's resistant to me being in charge. Her sass is annoying, and I can't begin to tell you how frustrating it is." I take a long drink, letting the alcohol take effect. He smirks at me and raises his eyebrow. "What?" I bark.

"Nothing. I mean, you certainly seem a little edgy. I just wonder if maybe this woman is inching her way into being more than a client. You have always been closed off, but more so after your mother died. It's okay to feel again." He sounds like Dr. Phil.

To feel again. The idea seems so foreign. After everything I have been through, the thought of allowing myself to become attached to someone scares the hell out of me. Loss and sadness are already my constant companions. Maybe I am too broken to be fixed. All I know is that in order to survive, I must keep a wall up. It keeps me protected, always has. I don't think I could survive another loss.

"Addie isn't my type," I say this as if I'm trying to convince myself.

"Jameson, your type are the ones that don't require anything of you. The faceless women that serve a purpose, and then you discard them. I don't believe you've ever had a girlfriend." He's challenging me.

"Of course, I have. Plenty," I counter.

"I'm talking long term. Commitment." The "C" word is as bad as the "R" word. This conversation is making me squirm. It's uncomfortable, and it's making me think about Addie. I finish my whiskey and raise the glass to the waitress, indicating I need another. Harrison observes me, nodding as if he is all-knowing. Asshole.

I turn the tables. "What about you? When did you have a relationship that lasted longer than a week? Tell me what the deal is with Nina. You all seem to have some sort of history. And she seems like she can barely tolerate your existence." The waitress returns. I grab the glass from her. Taking a long drink, I stare at him, challenging him back. Two can play this game.

"Touché. I just haven't seen you undone by a woman before, so it makes me curious. And there is nothing with Nina. She just doesn't like me." He shrugs. "Let's talk about sports. I feel like I'm starting to grow a vagina as we delve into our relationship issues and feelings." He snickers, and I laugh.

"Cheers to that!" We clink our glasses and talk about ESPN.

Dorothy

Everything is abuzz with the new sensation: Addie Snyder. That bitch. I am so sick of everyone asking about her. Everyone is so enamored. I'm not about to let my cousin-in-law reap all the success. After all, I'm due *something* from her and my spineless husband. After Matthew came back empty-handed from his visit with Addie, it was time to flip the switch on being nice and pretending that I'm interested in her life and her retarded brother. I am going to get a piece of Addie's success or die trying. Fortunately, my plan is already in motion.

"I know that look. What are you up to?" Matthew inquires.

"Oh, nothing. Just reading about Addie and how she's taking the world by storm. I'm super happy for her. Wouldn't this be a great time to find your uncle? A reunion for Owen, Addie, and their father would be a wonderful story."

"Why would that make her happy? My uncle abandoned them. He cut off all contact and fell off the face of the earth. Wait a minute. Are you trying to stir up something that would tarnish her success?"

"Matthew, I can't believe you would think that. I just feel like maybe there could be some resolution; uniting a family that was torn apart. You know, love heals and I just want to help facilitate the process. Wouldn't this be a nice time for Addie's family to come back together?"

If anything, I am an excellent actress and I hope that my dear spouse believes my intentions. We have been together for a while. I steal things in order to pay the bills. I get arrested, am immediately released, and then Addie gives us money to continue this ingenious cycle. We have the ideal marriage. I don't think this is a good time for her to finally find a backbone.

"Why are you staring at me? Can't I be happy for your cousin? She's our family. I want to see her get what she deserves." I grin.

Let the games begin.

Addie

Nina warned me about reading the stories and comments people write about me. Even if there are positive ones, there are always those individuals, because they lack purpose or perhaps a soul, who will do their best to murder your character. Well, like a petulant child, I didn't listen.

First, I found a sweet article about my book from someone who received an advanced reader copy. Then there were a few about my television appearances. George will be pleased—they loved how I looked. Then I saw it—a picture of my long-lost father. It's recent; age has changed his hair to salt-and-pepper. He was always an attractive man, and he's still tall and slender and impeccably dressed. I would have recognized him anywhere. Except there's a vacant look in his eye. Cold. Unfeeling.

The headline is misleading: *"Bestselling author, Addie Snyder, keeps disabled brother from knowing father."* I will give them credit. It is a solid piece of fiction.

There's a recent photo of Owen on his way to work and another of us at dinner. It's creepy. Invasive. And I am pissed. How in the hell did this happen? Okay, I know what you're going to say. That I am now in the public eye, and this is fair game. Yes, of course, you're right. Don't get cocky though. I don't admit that easily. But as uncomfortable as this is for me, Owen didn't sign up for this. The circus has come to town, and someone is the ringmaster. I just want to know who. Not many people know the story. For fuck's sake, I don't even know all of it. One day, I had a family. Imperfect. Dysfunctional, but we were together. Then, *poof,* my father disappeared, never to be heard from again.

The odd part is that my mother never seemed alarmed by that turn of events. She seemed relieved. They never fought. Honestly, they barely interacted; but as a child, I thought that was typical. Shit, she didn't interact with anyone unless they served a purpose—her children fell short in that area.

As I continue to pop chocolate to mitigate the anxiety that's bubbling, I think about my next step. So I text Nina.

Me: *Okay, you are going to be mad, but I just looked myself up on the internet.*

Nina: *Were you ignoring me when I told you not to do that?*

Me: *No, it was opposite day, so I did, you know, the opposite.*

Nina: *How old are you?*

Me: *Depends on the day.*

Nina: *I am coming over and confiscating all electronics with internet capability.*

Me: *That seems a little extreme. Can we pause this argument for now and address the elephant that is now on* Page Six?

Nina: *Okay. I am mentally filing this away. What happened?*

Me: *There is a story about my father with recent photos of him, along with several of Owen.*

Nina: *Well, shit. Okay. Take a breath. Are you eating chocolate? If not, then start. Do you want me to come over? Have you called Jameson?*

Me: *Breathing. Many chocolates popped. No, you don't have to come over, and I haven't called Jameson.*

Nina: *You need to call him. Meanwhile, let's meet for drinks tomorrow night. Give yourself a breather.*

Me: *If you eat bar food, I will come.*

I laugh because, at this moment, I can practically feel Nina shuddering at the thought.

Nina: *Ugh. Alright. See you tomorrow night at seven at our usual haunt.*

Me: *Can't wait. The wings are calling you.*

Nina: *I'll eat extra kale at lunch to prepare.*

I dial Jameson's number and hope he has a large shovel to clean up the shit that is hitting the fan.

Jameson

Women are always attracted to me, but tonight the field holds no appeal. They lack in most everything, and the fact that I have no physical reaction is alarming. I nurse my drink, watching Harrison effortlessly work the room. After a while, I wave goodbye and head out into the chill of the night. I could have taken a cab or gotten on the subway, but I walk instead in the hope that it will help clear my mind and allow me to process the discomfort I'm experiencing.

I have money. I even have a few friends, but ever since I met Addie, the emptiness has become palpable. I don't want a relationship with a woman. It's too much effort. Plus, being involved means the possibility of loss. Abandonment. Heartache. I had a front-row seat to my parents' disaster of a marriage. The anger I had for my philandering father percolated through the years as I watched my mother live in a land of denial while Dad slept his way through various cities as he traveled. When he was murdered, I didn't shed a tear. The walls I built shielded me from feeling. I might be considered a womanizer, but the women I go to bed with know the score. No strings. Purely physical and never emotional. If they get clingy, I cut them loose. It might make me a bastard, but at least I'm an honest one. Commitment isn't on my agenda; I just need to keep reminding myself of that fact where Addie is concerned.

In mid-thought, my phone rings, and speak of the devil, it's Addie. I could ignore it, but seeing as it's eleven at night, I figure there must be an issue.

"This is Jameson," I answer, knowing that by acting as if I don't know who's calling, I'll irritate the shit out of her.

"Really? That's how you're going to answer the phone? Seriously, your phone tells you it's me, right? Do you know how to read?" she spews.

The annoyance in her voice is music to my ears, and I smile. "Oh, hey, Addie. Sorry, I haven't gotten a chance to add you to my contacts yet. What do you need?" It's a lie, but I enjoy taunting her.

"What do I need? You haven't seen the story trolling the entire internet. Everyone knows now. I thought writing a book would be a source of celebration. I worked so hard to complete this story, and now its success is bringing me misery. I didn't want anyone to know." I hear soft sobs coming through the phone. Now I feel like crap.

"Okay. Relax. How bad could it be? There is no bad publicity. It keeps your name relevant." I'm trying to sound upbeat but can barely believe my own bullshit.

"That's it? Well, mister publicity guru, the media has gotten wind of my long-lost father. On top of that, Owen's pictures are splattered everywhere. I don't want to be in the public eye, but I don't have a choice. My brother does." She sounds exasperated.

I am at a loss. The emotion seeping through the phone is something I'm unprepared for, and apparently, I need to find her father before he comes crawling out from whatever crevice he's hiding in and nip this in the bud.

"Calm down. I have a friend who is a PI. Maybe he can get a location on your dad. Do you want to find him?" I ask.

There is silence.

"The man who left us is not my father. He abandoned the family because Owen wasn't what he considered normal. My mother was an emotionless shell who drank herself into oblivion, disappearing for days at a time. I essentially raised my brother, so no, I don't want to find him, but I do want to save my brother from any pain. He never knew our father, but I did, and frankly, Owen didn't miss anything. I mean, there were moments that were special—moments when I thought that he loved me; but they were few and far between."

The silence lingers, and then she quietly adds, "I don't want him to get hurt. I know that I have to be exposed to the media, but he didn't sign up for this."

"Let me get my friend on this, and I will deal with the media. Owen is lucky to have you, Addie." I mean it. She loves him fiercely, and it just makes her even more perilous to my heart.

"No, I am the lucky one, Jameson. Before he was born, I was invisible to my parents. My mother was too busy perfecting her image while my father was always distracted. But Owen came into this world and gave me hope. He saw ME. He saved me and gave value to my life. He needed me, and in turn, I need him. He loves me unconditionally, and in my family, that is like winning the lottery. He is truly the only person on this Earth who accepts me for me and vice versa. We are a team, and I don't want to let him down."

"You aren't letting him down, Addie. I promise you that I will help you protect him. The kind of love you have for him is rare and pure."

"Jameson, that was probably the kindest thing you've ever said to me. Thank you for helping me with this. I feel better talking to you." I can hear her smile through the phone. For a brief moment, I feel my shield cracking, but then I remember the pain of feeling and I shut down.

"Don't get used to it. I'll be in touch. Good night, Addie." My voice is gruff.

"I won't. I'm sure it was hard for you to say. Good night, Jameson." Her voice drips with sadness.

And with that, she hangs up. She continues to surprise me, while I continue my streak as a grade-A asshole.

Addie

I look at my phone as if it were an alien. The conversation with Jameson was unsettling. The fact that he was seemingly supportive and wants to prevent any harm to Owen should have made me feel better. Instead, I am confused. I didn't peg him as someone who would be moved by another person's circumstances. The whole situation is baffling.

I reluctantly go into my bedroom, throw the clothes that litter the bed onto the floor, and lie down. With no energy to spare, I fall asleep immediately. I wake up to sunlight—and the chilling sensation that someone is watching me- my skin prickles. I scream and arm myself with my very dangerous pillow. Adrenaline pumps through my veins as I pummel the unwelcome guest repeatedly. At some point, I recognize a voice that could only belong to Jameson. Shit.

"What the fuck, Addie?" he shouts as he fends off my feathery assault weapon.

"Um, well, you know, I thought you were an intruder. And by the way, how the hell did you get into my apartment?"

"Well, when you didn't answer the phone or the intercom after several attempts, I called Owen, and he let me in. He finally gave me the password. Also, he likes doughnuts, so that helped. Anyway, it's after nine, and we're late for our meeting. I thought something happened to you." His voice is laced with worry.

"Oh, that is so sweet! That, you know, you were distressed over my well-being. Okay, well, I'm ready to go. Sorry about the misunderstanding. Wait. How did you get Owen's number?" I pause, looking at him for the answer.

"Nina, of course, was kind enough to give me his number. So, let's reevaluate *this* situation. First of all, you are not ready to go. I saw you in that outfit yesterday, so there needs to be a shower in your immediate future. Also, you're my client, so I'm always concerned about your well-being."

"Right. Client. Got it. Okay, so I'll jump in the shower, and then we can get going. Sorry about the pillow bashing, not answering my phone, and the litany of other charges that I am guilty of doing. I'll try to be your star client from now on." My clipped tone drips sarcasm with a hint of hurt, and I mock salute him.

I gather my things and slam the bathroom door in his face. The maturity level today is at level zero.

Jameson

The ride to Nina's office is overcrowded with layered silence. As we ride the elevator to Nina's office, I break the tension by asking about Nina's relationship with Owen.

"We do brunch together most Sundays. He thinks Nina is his girlfriend." A grin spreads across her face that melts a bit of my frozen heart.

As the doors to the elevator open, her phone rings.

"Sorry, I have to get this. It's Owen. He doesn't usually call while he's working."

I nod, but I am reluctant to move from her side. After a brief, hushed exchange, she ends the call, and a smile tugs at her lips; tears are pooling in her eyes.

"Owen just saw his picture in the paper. He isn't upset. He says that customers want his autograph. Gosh, I had hoped to keep him private—not because I'm ashamed of him, but because I know how cruel the outside world can be to someone different. I'm so glad he's taking this well." She avoids my eyes. At a loss for words—seemingly my constant state of being in her presence, I simply nudge her toward Nina's door.

As we spend the next hour hashing out the book tour, I find myself lost in thought. I'm so captivated by this woman. It isn't about her looks, although she's gorgeous even with her peanut butter stains and her lack of fashion sense. It is her inner beauty that radiates. It's what translates in her book, which is why the entire world is just as awestruck as I am.

"Hello…Jameson. Are you even listening?" Nina's voice interrupts my thoughts.

"Yes, of course, I am." Jesus, I need to get my shit together.

Nina smirks and rolls her eyes.

"Alright then, we're all set. You'll leave on Monday and head to LA. All the arrangements have been made. Get excited, Addie! This is going to be amazing." Nina was probably a cheerleader in high school.

Addie utters a weak "yay" with an added raise-the-roof hand gesture.

"Now that we have the tour settled," I say, "let's chat about your father. His resurfacing might be disconcerting, but we can control the narrative. Do a few interviews so that your side can be noted." I'm treading lightly because I'm not sure how she'll take the idea.

"Fuck. No. I will not be commenting on my loser father and the mess he left behind. It's no one's business." Her face is flushed with anger, a reaction that doesn't surprise me in the least.

I hold up my hands in surrender and say, "Okay. For now, we'll do it your way; but if things escalate, we need to stay ahead of it. The story will be shared by other parties, so it's important that your side is on the record."

She nods in agreement, but I know there will be a fight about it later.

Addie

The week was hectic between the multitude of appearances and the hassle of trying to pack for LA. Of course, George made several visits to my apartment to help me get my shit together: you know, scoffing at my choice of luggage, judging my collection of vintage T-shirts and yoga pants. Speaking of luggage, he's probably jealous. Hello Kitty is adorable, and I have never lost my luggage on that ridiculous carousel. While other people are panicking trying to find theirs, mine screams, "Here I am, Addie!" He snickers at me when I slyly try to insert some of my comfort clothes into the mix. While I think that my actions aren't being observed, he's quickly unpacking them and throwing them on the floor.

Owen is all smiles because he gets to stay with our friend and neighbor, Emily. Emily is my stand-in when I'm gone for longer than a few hours. She's great with him, and I'm grateful to have someone who I trust to help me out when I need it.

"Owen, are you going to be okay with me being gone for five days? I mean, this is the longest we've been apart."

"I am a man now, so you don't need to baby me. Bye." He goes back to looking at the current YouTube video that he's obsessed with and ignores my existence. Typical.

"Aren't you going to miss me?" I sound like I'm begging.

"I will miss you, Addie. You will be okay without me." He gives me a tight hug and lingers. I take him in. This sweet human whom I love so much is the foundation for the good in my life. We let each other go, grinning at one another. I leave, dragging my suitcase behind me, and it makes a clunking sound down four flights of steps. As I step out of the front door, I am mystified by what I find in front of me. Jameson is leaning on a sexy sports car, looking very smug. It's quite a sight. My ovaries cheer. Bitches.

"Wait, where's the town car?" I eye the tiny, black BMW sports car suspiciously.

"Before I answer your question, please tell me: what kind of fucking luggage is that?" He's laughing. First of all, why does he have to be so hot while he laughs? Second, why is everyone so invested in my choice of luggage?

"Jealous? While you're trying to find your average black bag that matches everyone else's, I will be waiting on you with my delightfully cheerful suitcase. Now that that's settled explain this current car situation?" I tap my foot impatiently.

"I thought I would drive us to the airport. However, since you brought that creepy kitty luggage along, I am currently rethinking my decision." He keeps laughing. Asshole.

Annoyed, I stand there and glare at his hotness. Why must this man be attractive 24/7? Does he ever have an ugly moment? Jesus, why must he be so damn perfect? He interrupts my thoughts with his irritatingly deep, sexy voice.

"Are you thinking again? Come on, Addie. We need to hustle so that we can get to the airport."

"Be gentle with my kitty. She's sensitive." At that moment, I realize the innuendo. Wishing the ground would swallow me whole, I escape by getting into the car while he bellows in laughter. My mortification is complete.

The leather smell blends with the manly, spicy aroma radiating off of Jameson as he gets in the car. I suddenly realize that I am making sniffing sounds again.

"Allergies," I whisper.

He nods with a slight smirk. "Tell me about Owen and how you got to be his guardian." He starts driving.

"Well, my father left us shortly after Owen was born. I was ten, and honestly, I had never met anyone with Down syndrome. He's magic. The moment he looked at me, I was smitten. That was it. I was hooked by his natural ability to love without walls. He touches everyone he meets and doesn't allow his disability to limit him. Anyway, when my mother's health started to decline, she named me his guardian. It was all I ever wanted, really, and it wasn't a big change. I have been his advocate and mother-figure for years. It has always been Owen and me against the world."

There's a pause, and I'm not sure whether Jameson is processing what I said or if he wasn't listening in the first place. "I have my PI trying to locate your dad," he blurts out. Real smooth, hotshot. I open up to him, and this is what I get back. I sigh, my mind switching gears to a much less pleasant subject. Even though we had talked about involving another party to search for him, I'm still nervous about taking action. I'm fearful about what they might uncover.

"I could live my whole life never seeing him again," I say. "I don't need anyone in my life who doesn't accept Owen. There is enough of that in society. Who needs family like that? But with that being said, I guess I have to admit that you were right the other day. We need to keep ahead of him, just in case. I mean, I have no what kind of person he is today, and I want to keep Owen safe."

The day my father left was the catalyst for my trust issues with men. He came to me with tears in eyes and said, "Addie, sweetheart, I need to leave. Know that this has nothing to do with you, but I simply can't be with your mother anymore. Give me some time to get settled, and I will come back for you." I wrapped my arms around the man who had, when he had bothered with me at all, provided the buffer between myself and my prickly mother. He was the only person that I felt cared for me. I fell to my knees as I watched the taillights of his car disappear into the night. That was the last time I saw him. He never came back to get me.

Jameson jolts me out of my thoughts.

"I understand. With all of the press about your book, this could get ugly. Do you have any other family that helps you with Owen?

"I have a cousin, Matthew. But he doesn't help me with anything. He is all about himself and his shoplifting wife, Dorothy."

"They sound like a lovely pair."

"They are a delight." I sarcastically retort. "Matthew can't even care for himself. It makes it easier that he doesn't have any dealings with Owen. He doesn't need people who aren't consistently there for him. He needs stability, and after his upbringing, I want to be the person who provides that for him."

Jameson is silent, and I let the silence linger. Maybe he's figuring out some way to help keep Owen safe.

Addie

I try to act cool, but I'm flying first class, so I'm a little bit like a toddler at a toy store. I might have squealed. The flight attendant hands me a glass of champagne while eye-fucking Jameson. Typical. It has happened all morning. At the ticket counter. At security. He even got pulled aside by a female TSA agent who gave him a good pat down, then called over one of her colleagues, who proceeded to pat him down as well. Their hands lingering on his very tight, taut ass. Lucky bitches.

I chug my bubbly beverage. So much for looking confident and sophisticated. Jameson's eyes leave the book in his hand to study me. I'm sure he's counting the hours until these five days are behind us. Anyway, I am not going to allow his steely personality to rob me of my excitement. I keep thinking of the next trip I'll take with Owen and how he would be in heaven sitting in these seats.

"Enjoying yourself?"

"Yes!" I giggle and then promptly dig in my purse for some chocolate.

"What would happen if there was no chocolate at the bottom of your purse?" he asks, and I gasp.

"I would panic. Anxiety would overcome me. I might pass out," I say with a deadpan expression on my face.

"Really?" His face reflects honest surprise.

"No, I just wanted to see your reaction. It's kind of an oral fixation. I need to have something in my mouth. It calms me." Once the words leave my lips, I silently berate myself. The innuendo hangs there like an annoying gnat. There is nothing I can say to take it back, so I make it worse by saying, "Plus, chocolate is better than sex." And there, ladies and gentlemen, is the reason that I haven't dated in eons. I have no filter and easily get flustered. My lady parts sigh in disbelief and ask me to return my woman card.

He gives me a sideways glance and resumes his reading. This is going to be a long flight to LA, because now I'm thinking about sex, I'm sweating, and I keep popping chocolate like they're Xanax. And by the way, Nina suggested that I get some Xanax for my anxiety over the launch and tour. She isn't a pill pusher, but she does understand that I am an extroverted introvert. It's a thing. Look it up. The gist is that I like people in small doses, but sometimes people ruin it for me. Do you understand? People in large groups is a big fat NO. Unfortunately for me, I am going to experience masses of the human race. It sounds hideous. At that thought, I drift off to sleep. See? The thought of people makes me lose consciousness.

I am jostled from my slumber by Jameson. It's then that I realize I had fallen asleep on his shoulder, my hair sticking up in all directions, and I have left a thin residue of slobber on his shirt. Awesome.

"Enjoy your nap?" His eyes dance with amusement.

"Yeah, um, sorry I fell asleep on you." I quickly extricate myself from his shoulder while wiping the drool from my mouth.

"It's fine. There will be a car waiting for us once we get our luggage, and then we'll head over to the hotel. You'll have a few hours before we head to the party. George has scheduled hair and makeup for two hours before we have to leave."

As we make our way to the luggage carousel, a giggle slips from my lips as I navigate to the front to retrieve my Hello Kitty bag. Yes, I get looks of confusion, judgment, and probably a host of other aspersions, but I stand by smugly with my bag while they sadly continue to wait. I move to the side, waiting on Jameson. Thirty minutes later, we stand at the lost baggage counter, where he fills out a report. I can't help but be very amused. Luggage lost on a direct flight—a direct flight, people! Seriously. Understandably, he is a tad out of sorts. Being the smart cookie that I am, I zip my lips. It's a struggle because I had some good material to share. For example, "How do you like my kitty now?" or "My kitty never lets me down"… and then I realize that those sound sexual, so I'd better keep them to myself.

We make our way to the limo that is waiting for us, and as I am about to express my sincerest condolences, he glares at me and says, "Don't say a word." Well, that only makes me want to do it more.

"All I was going to say was that I could get you a set of Hello Kitty luggage. My treat." I grin at him.

He rolls his eyes while gritting his teeth.

Addie

L.A. is blanketed in plastic. Not the recycled, saving-the-Earth kind, but the kind where women's faces lack emotion, and their body parts don't jiggle in any of the right places. A façade of perfection: perfect skin, perfect hair, perfect clothes. I bet none of them would ever be caught dead in a T-shirt and yoga pants- their loss.

Anyway, the hotel room is gorgeous. I try to imitate Julia Roberts' scene in *Pretty Woman* when she throws herself on the bed and giggles. She did it better. Still, everything is so plush, elegant, and sophisticated. Floor-to-ceiling windows provide an amazing view of the bustling city and a bird's-eye view of the "Hollywood" sign. The linens on the bed, well, let's just say that they aren't Target brand. Oh, and the large Jacuzzi tub taking up residence in the bathroom might be my new favorite spot. I can't believe this is my life. I shiver, a ball of excitement peppered with anxiety. The party is in a few hours, so I decide that I'll take the time to check in with Owen, and then I'll have a date with that tub before the team of people arrives to help me get ready. I can't wait to go to the party with the poster child for grumpiness.

I dial Owen's number, and he answers, "Hey, sis."

"Hey, buddy! How was work?" I miss him already.

"Good. I got to stock the shelves today. Then Emily let me have pizza for dinner. She doesn't count how many pieces I eat." He giggles. Nice dig, bro.

I am constantly trying to get Owen to be conscious of his caloric intake since individuals with Down syndrome tend to struggle with their weight. He usually balks at me, rolls his eyes, and then comments that maybe I should stop eating chocolate. We end at a stalemate.

"Well, it sounds like you're having fun. After I get done with this book tour stuff, you and I are going to take a vacation. We can go anywhere you want." My wheels are turning at the thought of all of the uncharted territories we could explore together. Owen is a huge history buff, so the possibilities are endless.

"Really? I want to go to California. There are hot chicks there." Jesus. Take. The. Wheel.

"Let's not refer to women as 'hot'. How about saying that California has pretty girls?"

"Okay. They have pretty hot girls there." He laughs. I sigh and realize that this is just another battle that I am not going to win.

"So, think about all of the places you want to visit, and we'll plan a trip. Just the two of us."

"Can Jameson come?"

Well, that is a surprising development.

"Um, he's probably busy, buddy."

"I like him. He's fun, and he thinks I'm hilarious; plus, he can be my wingman." Wingman? Really? *Ugh.*

"We can talk about this later. I need to get ready. Behave."

"Addie, I am a man. I know what to do." His tone is laden with annoyance.

"Love you, Owen." God, I miss him.

"Love you too, Addie."

We disconnect. Before I even step away from my phone, it rings. Dorothy. Fuck my life. I answer it because she'll just continue to bug the shit out of me. I might as well get her out of the way.

"Hey, Dorothy!" I try to sound excited, but my tone ends up flat anyway.

"Addie, thank God I got a hold of you. I saw that your father resurfaced. Are you okay?" The concern I hear is fake, but I'll go along with it. I'm surprised it took her this long to call. She thrives on other people's drama.

"It's fine, Dorothy, really. I'm too busy with the book launch and tour even to think about it," I lie.

"You are so strong, Addie. You know, I had a premonition that he would come back into your life." Fun fact, Dorothy likes to dabble in honing her psychic ability. I use the term "ability" loosely.

"Oh, wow, that's fascinating. Well, I'd better run. I have to meet my publicist for the book launch, and I need to get ready." I can't wait to get off the phone.

"Of course! Enjoy the evening! Send me a selfie of you in your dress! I bet you're going to be gorgeous. Remember, Matthew, and I are here if you want to talk. I understand better than anyone." This whole conversation is giving me the creeps. And another fun fact, I don't do selfies. At all. I always end up looking constipated because I'm concentrating so hard on looking natural.

"I'll keep that in mind, Dorothy. Thank you." I end the call and exhale. She does understand—her father left her family at a young age—but I learned a long time ago that she isn't trustworthy. I shake off the feeling of dread and label it as nervous energy, knowing that any time I talk to Dorothy, there's always a sense of distrust that lingers. She isn't a safe person, and I know that I need to be wary of her agenda. Because she always has one. But I can't be concerned with her right now. My focus needs to be on the book launch and tour. For now, I have a date with a large tub that will be overflowing with bubbles.

Jameson

I wait in the lobby for Addie to come down. We're due at the party in less than thirty minutes, and with L.A. traffic, I know we're going to be late. Addie is always late. It's infuriating.

Right when I'm about to text her, I see her approaching. The simple black dress hugs her curves, its off-the-shoulder neckline giving a peek of her alabaster shoulders. Her short hair is slicked back, giving it an edgy, artsy look. She is stunning.

"You're late." I can't help but berate her. It's the only way I can keep my distance (and I love how flustered and annoyed it makes her). She's infiltrating my thoughts and breaking down my walls. I can't allow it. She shrugs and proceeds out through the doors to the waiting car.

"You look nice. Did your luggage ever find its way to you?" she asks as we get into the car. She tries to hide her smile, but I know that she is thoroughly amused by my situation.

"No, my luggage is set to arrive tomorrow. It had a lovely time in Boston. I had my assistant call and arrange for a suit."

"Well, I'm glad that you have someone so efficient. When is your birthday?"

"December twenty-fifth. Why?" Her line of questioning intrigues me, much like everything else about her.

"Oh, a Christmas baby! How does that work, anyway? Combination presents or separate? I mean, it would be ideal to get double the goods, right?"

"My mother was a single parent working two jobs to make ends meet. I hardly got any presents, let alone doubling the goods. You never answered my question. Why are you asking about my birthday?"

Her brows furrow, and I can see the pity in her eyes. It isn't as though I am embarrassed about my upbringing. My mom did the best she could. Sometimes she went hungry so that I could eat. Sometimes I would hear her softly crying when she thought I was asleep. It's just, I wanted so badly to repay my mother for her sacrifices, and by the time I could, it was too late.

"Your mother sounds like a special person. Do you get to see her often?"

"My mother died. Now answer the question. Why are you interested?"

"Oh, I'm sorry about your mother." Her eyes fill with sadness.

"Thank you. She was a wonderful person. Now back to your question." I desperately try to change the subject because talking about my mother stirs up both guilt and grief. I prefer to contain it by avoiding it at all costs.

"I asked because I want to know when I should send you some new luggage. Obviously, not like mine, since you've been so vocal about your distaste for it, but it does need to be unique. I was thinking of something colorful. Bold. You know, something that jumps out at you when it makes the rounds on the carousel." She snickers.

"Addie, can we stop talking about my luggage? Honestly, I have never had an issue before today. Someone more superstitious than I might think that losing it was linked to you. Maybe you're bad luck," I tease.

"No, this isn't on me. It's on your dull luggage that blends in with every other boring bag." She grins, and then her face pales as we pull up to the front of the Beverly Hills Plaza Hotel.

On the way here, I watched her fidget as we got closer and closer to the event. She has a pattern of smoothing her dress, then wringing her hands. I want to touch her, hold her hand. Assure her that this will all be fine. But instead, I look out the window to escape the feelings that are overwhelming my thoughts.

"Oh, my God! I can't even believe that this is the place for my launch party!" she says, her eyes lighting up as we pull up in front of the building. "Oh, my God! I think I'm going to puke. No, I think I'll just stay in the car. There will be too many people in there. What if I make a fool of myself? What if I trip in these godforsaken heels?" She looks at me for answers.

"Addie, you're going to go in there and blow them away. This is your moment. Nina and I will be with you the whole time." Now *I* sound like a goddamn cheerleader.

"Okay. I can do this. I worked hard to get here. I deserve this." She exhales, digs into her clutch, and pops a piece of chocolate into her mouth. "Let's do this!"

I feel like I'm watching her have an Oprah *aha* moment. What? I watch Oprah. She is the queen of living your best life, right?

As the driver opens the door, I slide out and then turn around and offer Addie my hand. She hesitates. Our eyes meet, and she puts her hand in mine. A sizzle travels up my arm, and the air crackles around us. I reluctantly release it and put my hand on the small of her back to ease her forward.

The flashes from the cameras are blinding. Everyone wants to know who Addie Snyder is and what makes her special. They don't know the half of it, but they will.

The moment we enter the ballroom, Nina approaches looking ever so calm, cool, and very collected. She is the epitome of grace and elegance.

"Addie, you look gorgeous!" She leans in, embracing Addie warmly.

"Nina, I am going to puke."

I grab two glasses of the circulating champagne and hand them to the ladies.

"You know, a little Xanax would help in this situation. I assume you have the equivalent of a candy store in your clutch." Nina smirks.

Addie scoffs. "A very small candy store, but this delightful bubbly is quite helpful." I realize that she is chugging it. Nina looks at me.

"Jameson, please make sure that her liquid courage doesn't get out of hand."

I nod in agreement.

"You're going to be fine," Nina soothes. "Remember, this is all for you and Owen. Everything you've worked for, all of the sacrifices you've made have all cultivated this moment."

"Now, I'm going to cry." Her eyes pool with tears. Nina cups her face.

"Now, let's curb the puking-slash-crying impulse. You are going to ruin your makeup. Let's circulate and meet some of these people."

We navigate our way around the room, stopping while Nina and I alternate introducing her to various individuals. I feel edgy. On alert. Reminiscent to when I was on a mission, oddly enough. There is something off about the vibe of the room. I don't spot anything immediately obvious as I casually glance around, but I know this uneasy feeling in my bones. I stay close to Addie. Nothing bad will happen on my watch.

Addie

I am not a paranoid person, but something isn't right. I try to shake the feeling—the intensity of being watched. I look around the room at the number of people in attendance. There is something so overwhelming yet humbling about being the focus. Maybe my paranoia stems from being the center of attention. After all, I certainly have never been one that people notice. I'm always the one hidden in the shadows.

You're not good enough.

You aren't pretty enough.

You will never amount to anything.

My mother's voice echoes in my head. I need to silence her and enjoy the moment. I refuse to allow a voice from the past to ruin this for me.

"Addie, I would like you to meet Cecilia Winthrop. She is vice president of Winthrop Entertainment and a big fan of your book." Nina beams, and I keep wondering why no one here is larger than a size four. Cecilia is stunning and statuesque with her slender figure and ivory skin. Her chic blond bob frames her face and her mermaid-cut dress molds to her figure. Her breasts are so perky; it's as though they're greeting me with a salute. I almost giggle, but I compose myself by stuffing a crab puff in my mouth. I am such a smooth operator. I hold up a finger to indicate that I will be with them momentarily. Meanwhile, my taste buds are having their own celebration with the delightful hors d'oeuvres. I must get a plate of those.

"Cecilia, it is a pleasure meeting you. Thank you so much for coming and celebrating my book." I don't give a toothy grin because I think I might have crab stuck in my teeth. As people pass by and tap me on the shoulder to get my attention, I give them awkward closed-mouth smiles and nod.

"Addie, such a pleasure. I loved your book and was chatting with Nina about the possibility of bringing it to the big screen." She smiles warmly at me.

Seriously?! Mind blown. Book to the big screen. That sounds crazy. Where is the guy with the crab puffs when you need them?

"Wow, Cecilia. That's amazing and so surprising." I am grinning like a clown, not even concerned about the crab I think is in my teeth. All of this is surreal, but I still can't shake the feeling that something isn't right. Paranoia envelops me.

It helps that Jameson is always by my side. More like glued to my hip. When I go to the restroom, he waits outside. When I want another drink, he goes with me. It is odd but weirdly comforting at the same time. Plus, for the love of God, he smells amazing, and that suit—well, it's molded to his muscular frame, accentuating the best ass I've ever seen. I think I'm sweating. Is it hot in here?

"Addie, I know that this is a lot to absorb, but trust me, this will be the next step in bringing your story to a larger audience. We can talk more later. Enjoy the evening. You deserve it." She raises her glass to me as she moves on to mingle with others.

A man approaches me. He gives me a slight smile.

"Good evening, Ms. Snyder. I'm Senator Wendell Brooks. I just wanted to come by and tell you how much I enjoyed your book." He looks a bit uncomfortable.

"Oh, thank you so much, Senator. I appreciate you taking the time to read it." While I am talking, I think about how odd it is that a politician would sit down and read a book like mine. I mean, isn't he busy crushing the dreams of the people he serves? I feel like I knew him at some point as if we met previously. But before I can ask, the hairs on my neck bristle.

Out of the corner of my eye, I notice a man. I turn to look at him, and the familiarity of his features takes my breath away. It can't be him. Jameson must notice how my body tenses because he moves closer. Normally, I would be all over that, but this isn't about my lady parts. This is about confronting my past.

"Hello, princess. It looks like you've done well for yourself." The man in front of me is my father, Richard Snyder, or Dick, as he despises being called. I don't honor him with the title of "dad." He is merely a sperm donor. He is the man who left because Owen wasn't "normal." He is the man who walked out the door, leaving his family to pick up the pieces. The rage within me is percolating. I need to escape but I am frozen. Just like in the picture I saw online, he's still handsome with his salt-and-pepper hair. His presence is commanding. Some might find him intimidating, but I don't. The smile he gives me doesn't reach his vacant eyes. "What? No hug for your father?"

Jameson moves closer. Our shoulders touch as he quickly fills the space. His body seems like a protective shield beside me. Jameson's warm breath tickles my ear as he leans in. "I can get security if you don't want him here." I shake my head, indicating that I need this moment, although it is comforting to know he has my back... and it is a shame I can't enjoy his closeness. Timing, friends.

"Why are you here?" I ask, but I don't want to know the answer. After the story was dumped on social media, I knew it was only a matter of time. Sweet. Baby. Jesus.

"Is that any way to greet me? You look well. I was sorry to hear about your mother." At this point, I start to wonder if I have been transported to an alternate universe.

"You don't get to express your sympathy. That right was surrendered when you walked out and never looked back."

"Oh, Addie. Always so dramatic. The reality is that you don't know the whole story. You have, of course, only heard your mother's side; but there is so much more to it." He smirks.

"What are you saying?" My head is spinning.

"I'm just saying that there's more to the story. You have allowed your mother to create this fictitious life, and you've believed what she chose to tell you." He utters the words as if he is ordering a meal at a restaurant.

"I didn't allow anything. I was a child. When you left, Owen only had me; Mother wasn't exactly maternal. So excuse me for not buying into the victim role you seem to relish playing." My body shakes with fury.

"Look, I'm just asking for some time to sit down with you. Meet Owen. After all, I don't know how defective he is with his disability. Plus, I want to share in your success. Isn't that what a family is supposed to do? Share." He smirks. Again. Can this man not even fake a smile?

"Defective? Owen is not defective. If anything, you are the one who is faulty. And are you insinuating that this little act is going to benefit you financially?" My anger wavers as confusion overtakes it.

"Well, that sounds so ugly, don't you think? I prefer to think of it as an investment. I'll be in touch."

As he saunters off, I am left stammering, speechless at my big party during my big moment. This feels like a scene that I would conjure up in my mind—a fictitious dramatic scene for a book. Arms envelop me, and I hear people talking, but I can't understand what they're saying. Then everything goes black.

Jameson

I watch the scene unfold between Addie and her father. It is surreal. My intel told me he was in town, but I wasn't given any information suggesting that he would be making his move toward Addie tonight. I feel like I failed her. I should have been informed.

As her asshole of a father departs, chatter and whispering spread around us like wildfire. Stares linger on Addie, despite my moving to block them, facing her to make it look like we're simply talking about what just happened. In reality, I think she might collapse. Cameras flash as the media circles their prey, ignoring my attempt to protect her. This is the last thing she needs. Her anxiety about being in such a social situation was almost too much for her to bear. Her need to be invisible is still strong, despite her sudden fame. This might break her. I feel like a total failure, but I can't think about that right now. The most important thing on my agenda is getting her out of here.

Addie's face is pale. Her breathing is rapid. She is definitely either going to pass out or hyperventilate. I block out everything around me and focus solely on her. I gently direct her to an isolated area near the staff exit leading to an alley where our car will be waiting. The moment that her father made an appearance, I texted our driver; I had a feeling the situation would not end well. Just as we make it out the door, her eyes close, and I scoop her up and head for the car. Getting her back to the hotel is my only priority.

A voice breaks through the chaos as the door starts to close behind us. "Ladies and gentlemen, I apologize for the distraction from Addie's launch party. Please continue to enjoy the celebration. There is plenty of food and drink. Cheers!" Thank God for Nina. As the slow-close door latches behind us, I hear it open again, and then I hear the echoing sound of stiletto heels quickly scuttling up the alley behind us.

"Jameson, you want to tell me what the hell that was?" Nina asks as she catches up with me at the car. She opens the door, and I carefully put Addie inside. For the record, she is pissed. She knows that I have people in place to deter problems like this for my clients. In her eyes, I have failed to do my job. She isn't wrong.

"Nina, can we talk about this later? My priority right now is getting Addie back to her room."

Her face softens as she looks at her friend. "Of course. But the three of us need to sit down tomorrow and figure out how to get that asshole to back off. Tell her that I'll call and check on Owen for her. I don't want her to worry."

"I'll tell her. Good night, Nina."

Jameson

In the car, Addie slowly comes around. Disoriented and confused, she looks up at me and smiles. Then as quickly as it appeared, a shadow blankets her face instead.

"Please tell me that my father didn't just show up and turn my book launch into an episode of *Jerry Springer*." I love a good family drama—if it isn't mine. Addie is my client, so it might as well be my own drama. It's a nightmare for both of us.

"Unfortunately, he did. We're going to meet with Nina tomorrow and strategize about damage control. How are you feeling?" My eyebrows furrow as I study her face while the car is stopped at a traffic light.

"Feeling? Well, confused. Pissed. A little embarrassed. Overall, I think I'm simply in shock. I haven't seen him in over 30 years. When he left, he said he would come back for me." Her eyes glisten, and then she gasps. "Owen. I need to call and check on him."

"Nina is doing that for you. She didn't want you to worry."

"Okay. Good. That makes me feel better." She exhales. "I don't remember anything after my father's veiled threat. Was I graceful when

I passed out? I didn't moon anyone, did I?" If she weren't so genuinely concerned about it, I would laugh.

"No one saw, Addie. I guided you to an employee exit away from the crowd before you passed out. You were very graceful." For the record, I liked holding her very much. And I don't like that I liked it.

"Oh, goody." Her voice drips with sarcasm. Then she softens her tone. "By the way, thank you for being there. You know, to catch me. Literally. I just don't want to be one of those videos that go viral with my granny panties exposed for all to see." She grimaces. "Um, not that I'm wearing granny panties. I just need to shut up now." She closes her eyes.

Okay, now I am seeing her in her underwear. Granny panties or not, it's sexy. I need to nip this shit in the bud.

The car stops, arriving at the hotel. "First, let's get you settled in your room. Hungry? You didn't get a chance to eat before the ordeal went down." Look at me being all diplomatic. Caring, even. I didn't tell her that Owen would have security so subtle that he won't notice.

"I would kill for a burger." Did she just moan?

"Okay, we'll order room service and try to salvage this night. It should have been a celebration, Addie. I'm so sorry." My voice wavers slightly. Hopefully, she doesn't pick up on the emotion.

"There is no reason for you to apologize. Did you take my book launch hostage? Nope. Did you insinuate that my life is a den of lies? Nope. Did you invite my father? Nope. So no apology necessary." Damn. She is a force of nature. If she knew that I was aware of his presence in the vicinity and I didn't tell her, I don't think that she would be so forgiving.

Addie

Okay, so the circus came to town. And just so you know, I have never been a fan of the circus. Caged animals doing tricks seems cruel and inhumane. And then, to add to my misery, I passed out in Jameson's arms. Can I just say that I am annoyed that I wasn't conscious for that? I imagine I would have enjoyed it. My lady bits agree. Anyway, heading back to the hotel, I notice that Jameson is softer. Not his body, but his attitude. No, his body is super hard and sculpted. Jesus, I'm so easily distracted.

After we arrive at the hotel, Jameson walks me to my room, and to my surprise, he comes in. What? Yes, you heard me. He picks up the phone to order room service and directs me to change and get comfortable. He is bossy. I like it this time. So I do what I'm told because, well, these Spanx are killing me, and I miss my yoga pants. Yep, I managed to sneak some into my luggage beneath George's watchful eye.

Our food arrives quickly. Sweet. Baby. Jesus. It's heaven on a plate. A double cheeseburger with fries that I quickly cover in ketchup. What? Condiments are my friend. My mouth salivates as I close my eyes to take my first bite. When I open them, I see Jameson staring at me. Like intensive, eye-exploration. Do I have ketchup on my face?

"What are you looking at?" I inquire. My mouth is still kind of full. I am so ladylike.

"Nothing." He clears his throat and continues to look for a movie.

He finds a movie. It's mindless, allowing me to simply escape the turmoil going on in my head. I didn't think he would even enjoy a romantic comedy, but considering the crappy evening that I just had, I figure he's just being nice. Weird. Between being ravaged emotionally, watching a movie, and enjoying my burger, I fall asleep.

I wake up feeling like I am in a cocoon. Safe. Cherished. Secure. I'm disoriented, but then the events of the previous night come rushing back, and I realize that I am in my hotel room. More critically, I am not alone. There is a man in my bed, holding me. Christ. On. A. Cracker. A man with a hard body. Did I pick up some random guy after the ordeal with my father? Wait, did I do the deed and forget about it? Crap, that's going to suck since I haven't had any action since …well, that's not important, but I would like to be an active participant if given the opportunity. And then I remember. Room service. Movie. Nice Jameson, who transformed into my caretaker. I move slightly so that I can get a look at my resident cuddle buddy. He is yummy.

"Enjoying the view?"

Crap. Busted.

"Um. I'm just trying to put the pieces of the evening together. Which begs the question, why are you still here?"

He releases me, and my lady parts sob. They are so emotional and a little clingy. Anyway, he moves off the bed and turns toward me.

"Well, at some point, you fell asleep, and I did too, so that's why."

I eye him suspiciously. "Okay, then. What time are we meeting, Nina?" I try to hide my disappointment that he has moved away from me. My feelings of abandonment are never far away. This is Jameson.

I remind myself he's only my publicist, not my friend. Just someone being paid to basically run my life for a while.

"Around nine for breakfast downstairs. I'm going to head back to my room, so I'll see you then."

"Thank you for everything you did last night. You know, I looked for my father for a long time but never found him. And now, he just pops up out of the blue." No reaction from him. Which kind of seemed like a reaction all its own. "Doesn't it surprise you that he was there last night?" I inquire.

I watch him. He looks almost vulnerable, but then a dark cast floods his eyes.

He blows out an exaggerated breath, runs his hands through his hair, and looks into my eyes. A couple of the buttons on his shirt are undone, and it's hard not to look.

"I knew where he was. My intel told me he was in L.A., but I had no idea that he was going to crash the party. It's my fault. I normally don't fail in these situations." So Mr. Handsome isn't perfect. Good to know.

"You mean to tell me that you've known where my father was and didn't tell me? And you didn't tell me he was *right here* in L.A.? What the fuck, Jameson? I deserved to have that information. Being blindsided was not my idea of a good time." My tone is scathing, but the hurt and exhaustion also come through. Fatigue blankets my body.

He rubs his handsome face. What? I might be mad, but I can certainly still appreciate this exemplar of the male species. Oh, wait, I need to remember that I'm mad and not allow my lady bits to control my mood. Thank God that men don't know how often that happens.

"I am so sorry. The story has legs. I released a statement that there is no comment at this time, but that can't hold them at bay for long. You are going to have to make a real statement. We have to control the narrative, which means that you will have to tell your side of the story."

First, I must be in an alternate reality; "stone face" doesn't usually apologize.

"Am I dead?" I deadpan.

"What?" He looks confused.

"You apologized, so I figured that I must be dead. Also, the thought of telling the world about my childhood traumas makes me extremely uncomfortable. I don't even know how to react to all of this."

He gives me a small, sad smile. Another phenomenon with this man. He cuddles, apologizes, and laughs. I think I need a stiff drink or a bar of chocolate. Possibly both.

"Alright, Jameson. I'm too tired to be mad at you. Just tell me the plan, and I will comply."

"Okay. Did you hit your head? Because a head injury would explain your complete willingness to go along with my yet-to-be-revealed plan."

"I suppose that we're both full of surprises. No, I didn't hit my head. I need to do this for Owen. Everything is about Owen for me—it always has been. I need to protect him. He's all I have." I close my eyes and exhale.

Jameson nods and says, "Then let's get started."

Jameson

I had no idea that I would learn something about myself last night. I do have emotions, no matter how much I'd like to deny them. I have spent so much time shutting them off that I forgot what it felt like to feel. I don't allow myself to be vulnerable. But holding her last night felt...right.

Shaking off my discomfort, I pick up the phone to talk to one of my buddies, who happens to be a private investigator and security expert. Grady served with me and is one of two people who I trust with my life. I need to be a step ahead of Addie's father, and he's the guy who can help with that.

"Jameson, what the hell did I do to deserve this honor? I haven't heard from you since...I can't even remember."

I am sure you've figured this out by now, but I'm not great with relationships—even relationships with those to whom I'm close.

"Grady, man, sorry, I know it's been a while. I need your help."

I fill him in on the situation and what the information that I need. The great thing about Grady is that he, too, has connections, but his run a whole lot deeper than mine.

"Sounds like this Addie person means something to you."

"Sure, I mean, she's a client. This is part of the job." This is something I keep telling myself because that's the only way I can feel in control. And I *need* to stay in control.

Grady chuckles. I roll my eyes. Same as with Harrison.

"Okay, I'll be in touch. Are you going to involve the police?" he asks.

"Not yet. I don't have a lot to warrant their involvement at this point." I also want to keep this on the downlow and control what the media knows.

We end the call, and I exhale. Would I do this for any client? Yes. It is my job to ensure that my clients are protected in any way necessary. And yet, this feels different. But I can't afford the distraction. Addie Snyder just became more than a client, which might be more dangerous than whatever scheme her father is running.

Addie

I met Nina in the coffee shop of the hotel, grateful to arrive before Jameson. She looks like a runway model, while I greatly resemble a homeless person. No offense to those who are homeless. Jesus, now I have probably offended people. Let me clarify— I have an "image" to maintain now with my new author "status." Whatever. Anyway, George would be so disappointed in me. But at this moment, I need comfortable clothes, chocolate, and coffee. Fortunately, I had chocolate at the bottom of my purse, and Nina already ordered coffee, plus I see a chocolate croissant calling my name. Poor Nina. She'll probably order her usual hideous fruit bowl and oatmeal. Cue the shudder.

"How are you?" She's worried. Her eyes scan my face.

"Well, I'm in shock, I'm terrified, and Jameson cuddled with me last night," I blurt. Seriously not my intent. I need to have a filter installed in my mouth.

"Well, I was referring to the reappearance of your father, but let's revisit that later. Tell me everything about Jameson and 'cuddling'." She uses air quotes when she says cuddling.

"No, thanks. By the way, cuddling is not code for sex." I try to look offended, but the thoughts in my head are chanting *sex, sex, sex*. Jesus.

Her eyebrows raise, and a smile tugs on her lips. "So, you aren't opposed to sex?"

"Stop! He isn't into me. I am a forty-something single woman whose life is a circus. Besides, every woman in the room eye-fucks him, and he could have anyone he wants." My voice hits a slightly higher pitch, and Nina narrows her eyes.

"You seriously don't see the way he looks at you when you aren't paying attention. He's totally into you. God, you should have seen him last night. He was so commanding and alpha. It was hot!"

I openly stare at her in disbelief. "Well, I'm sure he was concerned because I am his client, after all. Right now, I'm worried about keeping my delusional excuse for a father away from Owen. By the way, thank you for checking in on him. Is he okay?"

"No problem, sweetie. I love you both. I'm just worried about you. Of course, he is fine. I couldn't be more excited to hear from me since I am his girlfriend. By the way, I ordered you a chocolate croissant." She grabs my hand and gives it a squeeze.

I smile. My eyes fill with tears. I don't trust easily. My tribe is small. Nina is my person. She accepts me, warts and all. She evens orders me chocolate treats because she totally gets me. Is Jameson in my tribe? I think he might be. I feel like he's slowly taking down my walls.

"I will be fine once my father is out of the picture. There was a time when he had at least some goodness inside him, but now, he isn't a good man. He's bitter. I just want to protect Owen from the shitshow that is raining down on us."

"We will, Addie. Now, I hate to go back into business mode, but we still have the tour agenda to discuss. Our next stop is Boston. Do you want me to fly Owen out to meet you and Jameson? We can have one of the security guys fly with him."

"Security? What are you talking about, Nina?"

Jameson takes this opportunity to approach the table. His tight-fitting jeans that hug his delicious ass along with his form-fitting collared shirt make me a little light-headed. I almost forget about the discussion of security and my chocolate croissant. Almost.

"Ladies, good morning! Did you start without me?" His eyes volley between the two of us. Nina looks a little panicked, and I am pissed.

"Thanks for joining us, Jameson. I'm just filling Addie in on the idea of security. Something that I thought had already been discussed with her." Her frosty tone is pissed off.

"Yes, please, Jameson. Share the need for security with the rest of the class." I try to curtail my overwhelming annoyance.

"Well, I think that until we get a handle on the situation, we need to have security in place. Particularly for Owen. Look, I'm sorry I didn't tell you this earlier, but you have to admit, I am juggling a lot of balls trying to manage this situation."

Great. Now I'm thinking about his balls.

"I feel like we are experiencing the apocalypse—you have apologized twice in a span of two hours. So because I'm feeling particularly generous, and I'm exhausted from the shitshow that is currently my life, I will give you a pass. Well, another pass. I already gave you one yesterday. But anyway, please don't keep me in the dark. I'm not a delicate flower. I can handle it. I always have. and I always will."

"You have my word, Addie. I will keep you in the loop. Now, what do you think about having Owen come to Boston with us?"

"I think that would be great. I know I would be more relaxed having him with me." I smile at Jameson.

"Okay, I have some phone calls to return then, so I'll see you later." He turns and walks away. I admire his ass. What? You would be engaged in the view, too.

A smile tugs at my face. I turn my head. Nina is staring at me.

"What? He has a nice ass." I shrug and begin to enjoy my delectable chocolate croissant that the waitress just delivered.

"Yes, he does. Maybe once we have this situation resolved, you can explore a more personal relationship. A little tango action for your hoo-ha could alleviate your stress, too. I have a conference call to get on, so I am going back up to my room. We will chat later." She winks and leaves the table. I sigh. My hoo-ha agrees with her assessment.

Addie

As I walk back to my hotel room, I'm met by the familiar eyes of my father. I don't remember him being so manipulative. Cold. Calculating. Honestly, I just remember him being mostly emotionless. Distant. As if being in our lives was somehow a burden.

"Good morning, Addie. Where's your handler? I thought he would be glued to your side." He laughs. It's forced and a little creepy.

"What do you want?" My voice is hard.

"We have already established what I want, Addie—a little bonding with my children. I bet Owen would love that. He would probably like to get to know me." He smiles, but it doesn't reach his eyes.

My skin sizzles. Without even turning around, I know that Jameson is behind me. His protectiveness is palpable. He's like a ninja, which is both comforting and freaky. Ultimately, I'm glad we're staying in the same hotel.

"Mr. Snyder, I think you need to leave." His stare is cold.

My father holds up his hands in mock surrender. "Of course! We'll have plenty of time to hash out the details. I'm not going anywhere. I'll find you again at a better time."

He turns on his heel and retreats. I exhale while looking through my purse for a piece of chocolate. Jameson hands me a piece. I look up and realize that he has his own stash for me. Oh. My. God. That is possibly the sweetest thing, no pun intended, that anyone has ever done. And while I contemplate this very kind gesture, something shifts. I turn and meet Jameson's eyes. Before I can say anything, he pulls me against his hard, muscular chest, his hands firmly on my hips, and kisses me. Did you hear me? He is kissing me! As in panty-melting, lost-in-an-alternate-reality kind of kiss. My lady bits are singing the "Hallelujah" chorus in fucking harmony, people. They even master the high notes, which are a bitch. That is how mind-blowing this kiss is, and then before I can fully enjoy the moment, he pulls away. He fucking pulls away, and I instantly miss his touch. And his tongue. Shit.

"I shouldn't have done that. That was completely unprofessional." He rubs his hand over his ridiculously handsome face. We stare at each other.

At this point, I should be saying something. But my tongue, lips, and lady parts are still celebrating. Before I can formulate something coherent, he walks away. What the fuck is the deal with every man in my life simply walking away before I can say anything?

Addie

As I'm still recovering from the lip assault that Jameson inflicted on me, my phone rings. Of course, it's Dorothy. Like a moth to a flame, she thrives on anything chaotic or dramatic. I am sure that she's calling in regard to my sperm donor. I might as well answer, or she will continue to call.

"Hey, Dorothy. What's up?" I try to sound perky, but I'm a writer, not an actress. In the end, I sound flat. Again.

"Oh, Addie! I am calling to check on you! I just read about the reemergence of your father. How are you doing?" She sounds empathetic, which scares the shit out of me.

"I am okay. I appreciate you checking on me, but there's no reason to worry. Jameson and Nina are taking care of managing the press. I'm just still processing it all."

"Oh, I can only imagine how surprising that was to see him after all of these years. But that isn't the only reason I called. I want to apologize for Matthew and how awful he was to you when he came to your apartment."

I swear the universe is drunk. What is happening?

"Dorothy, that isn't necessary. It isn't the first time that he has been upset with me. I'm sure it won't be the last."

Is hell freezing over? When has Dorothy EVER apologized? It makes me extremely uncomfortable, but maybe she is sincere. Who am I kidding? This is just another farce.

"Addie, did you hear me?" She jolts me out of my state of confusion.

"Sorry, Dorothy. I have a lot on my mind this morning. What did you say?"

"I just said that we wouldn't be bothering you for money anymore. We are so grateful for your help all of these years, but it's time that we stand on our own feet."

"Wow, Dorothy, that is great and extremely unexpected."

"I know you don't have any reason to believe me, but we're trying. My psychic business is finally taking off, and I'm confident that it will continue to grow. If you ever want a reading, I'll do yours for free."

"That is so generous but completely unnecessary. I appreciate the offer, though." I feel like Ashton Kutcher will jump out any moment and tell me I've been punked. Plus, while I believe in people being intuitive, Dorothy is not that person. She's just a con artist. Unfortunately, there will be people who pay for her bullshit, sucked into her conniving ways. She is a master manipulator, so maybe that is her skill.

"Well, the offer is always there. I could probably give you some insight into this situation with your father." She sounds a bit giddy.

"Oh, Dorothy, I have to go. Someone is at my door. Thank you for calling and good luck with your business."

"Of course, Addie. We are here for you. Call me if you need anything."

We disconnect, and I have no idea how to process that call. And don't get me started on that kiss. I can still feel Jameson's lips. Does Amazon sell straitjackets? I feel like I'm going to need one.

Jameson

That was not my best moment. Let me clarify. Not to boast, but I am an excellent kisser. And the kiss was amazing. It felt right. However, I should not be tongue tangoing with my client. It is the old mantra, "don't eat where you shit." Jesus. One minute I'm seething at her father's presence, and the next, my tongue is down her throat. I liked it. A lot. She was so soft, eager, willing—and then like the asshole that I am, I walk away.

I sit at the bar swirling amber liquor in my glass. Yes, it might be a touch early for liquor, but desperate times call for desperate measures. Lost in my thoughts, I almost miss the sound of my ringing phone.

"Grady, have anything useful for me?" I ask.

"Well, I do know that the illustrious Mr. Snyder has been in contact with Addie's cousin's wife, Dorothy."

"Interesting. Do you know why?"

"My sources have photos of them meeting on several occasions. I'll keep my guys on them, and hopefully, we can uncover the answers. With Dorothy's financial issues, I would guess it's for monetary gain, but I can't find a money trail yet. I also noticed that he, too, is at the height of his own financial crisis, so I'm looking into a possible third party. I'll be in touch." We end the call.

Well, now that delightful amber liquor tastes like bile. It looks like Dorothy might be the ringmaster of the circus that has come to town.

Addie

I'm not going to lie. Jameson's kiss became the inspiration for my solo pleasuring-myself performance. Don't pretend you haven't done it, too. My vagina is so underused that it should have a sign that reads "closed indefinitely." It isn't as though I haven't had encounters. God, that sounds so…uninspired, a word that describes my sex life to a T. Okay, let's focus. I'm packing for our next stop, where I will finally get to see Owen. Just having him with me will ease the anxiety. I open the door and wrestle my suitcase into cooperation. I may have lost a wheel in the process. Poor Hello Kitty. I guess I'll have to purchase a new set. I grin.

As I make my way to the lobby, my stomach turns at the thought of seeing Jameson. My tongue is still recovering. But in true form, he greets me with his same stoic stare, glances at my suitcase with three wheels, picks it up, and motions for me to get in the car.

I settle into the cool leather seat and rummage through my purse for my chocolate. Finding the lost artifact nestled in the corner of the purse, I unwrap its heavenly goodness, plop it in my mouth, and moan.

"I want to apologize."

I open my eyes. Am I hearing an apology? It doesn't make sense because he simply doesn't apologize. And this would make three in twenty-four hours. Interesting.

"For what?" I love to feign ignorance. He is about to say he regrets the best kiss of my life, and I am trying to prolong the inevitable. Plus, messing with him gives me a bit of joy since it's his life's mission to annoy the crap out of me.

"For my inappropriate actions."

I stare at him.

"To what action would you be referring? I mean, there are so many." Okay, I do love seeing him flustered, and right now, he looks extremely uncomfortable and annoyed.

"Oh, for fuck's sake! The kiss. It was unprofessional," he growls.

"Oh, that. No harm. I mean, it wasn't that memorable, which is why I needed clarification." Liar. My lady parts are planning a walkout. They are currently making picket signs.

His eyebrows furrow, his eyes glaze over, and he glares. It's hot. I mean, if I was into the dark, brooding type, which I am not. It's a wonder that my nose isn't growing. He clears his throat.

"On another note, once we get to Boston, Owen's security detail will bring him to the hotel. They boarded the plane with no problem, and Owen has made friends with the entire crew."

I smile at the image because it is true that Owen touches everyone he meets. has probably asked out all the flight attendants, wrangled extra snacks, and managed to sit in the cockpit. I wish I were with him since this is his first time flying.

We continue to the airport with silence as our mutual companion.

Jameson

What does she mean when she says that the kiss wasn't memorable? Seriously. It continues to haunt me—how she tasted like chocolate and coffee. The way her eyes sparkled when I pulled away. And how confused she looked as I left her standing in the middle of the lobby. I get it. I'm an asshole. But this asshole needs to focus on keeping his client's career on track. I can't deny that I'm drawn to her. It just doesn't need to be my focus.

I watch her as we arrive at the Boston hotel. Her excitement about seeing Owen radiates from her body. My intel tells me that her father has indeed followed us here. I haven't shared that with Addie, or that Dorothy is somehow playing a part in the drama. I don't know what her endgame is, and until I find that out, I will simply have to keep her in the dark. I know what I promised, but as I try to stay ahead of the situation and keep the media at bay, I am reminded that while I might not be divulging all I know, I am trying to salvage this tour and prevent anyone from damaging her reputation. No one will steal the bliss that she should experience with her success. Not again.

Addie spots Owen. Both break out into big grins, and Addie runs to him. They hug and then jump up and down while Owen chatters on about the flight.

"They let me see the cockpit and everything!" His enthusiasm is contagious.

"Wow, it sounds like you had a great time!" I can see her relaxing. Her eyes glisten with joy-filled tears. Her smile is infectious.

"Yep. And the flight attendants were hot!" He giggles as Addie groans.

"Owen, remember what I said about using the word 'hot' to describe women?" She tries to use her stern voice, which is adorable.

He laughs, "Well, they were hot." I laugh. She sighs.

We check, in and proceed to our suite. I reserved the Presidential Suite with three bedrooms because it is necessary to be close to them. At least, that's how I'm justifying my actions. But I know that the lines are starting to blur. My emotional attachment is starting to overshadow my job, and while I rationalize my choice, it is obvious that these two people are becoming important to me.

Security is placed outside of the room, and they will accompany us everywhere we go. Of course, I haven't shared those details with Addie. Will she be pissed? Yeah but I'm doing this for her own good.

Addie

Seeing Owen eases my anxiety. His presence brings me tremendous peace. Calms me. Makes me whole. Watching Jameson with him expands my heart. Hearing Owen calling women "hot" annoys the crap out of me, and he knows it, which is probably the reason he continually does it. Typical *us* moment.

We are led into a luxurious suite that makes my apartment look like a shoebox. It's the Presidential Suite at the Four Seasons. It sounds pretentious and, well, let's be honest, it is, but I'm not complaining. Seriously, I want to live here forever. Owen screams at the top of his lungs with excitement—something about a media room. The living room features an expansive sectional paired with a modern wingback chair. I can imagine Owen chilling out watching his favorite movie, *Grease*. There's even a gorgeous kitchen that basks in the natural light from the window overlooking the city.

As I walk into my bedroom, I am speechless. It's exquisite. Elegant. The mattress is made by NASA. I mean, seriously, NASA, people. It's like lying on a cloud. Oh, and the bathroom has a tub so huge, I could potentially do laps if I even remotely liked to exercise. Which I don't...

So I won't be doing laps, but it's an option for someone. I'll probably just soak in it. You know, like a normal person.

I walk back out into the living room where Jameson sits perusing his emails. While the elephant in the room is still hanging out with us, I suppose it's up to me to lighten the tension. I can do this. You know, pretend that his kiss wasn't mind-blowing. Pretend that my lips aren't still tingling, and my tongue isn't still humming. Pretend that he hasn't made his way under my skin.

"Thanks for taking care of everything. What time is dinner?" I say, hoping my voice doesn't sound weird.

"I made reservations at a cool bistro at six o'clock. I think Owen will like it. We can go over tomorrow's schedule then. Oh, and I got Owen tickets to see the Red Sox play while you do your book signing." He says all of this without making eye contact.

"Sounds great. Well, we'll meet you in the lobby around 5:45." I'm hoping that this is a subtle suggestion for him to leave and go to his room. I need for his stupidly handsome face to go bye-bye.

He smirks and makes eye contact. I quiver.

"What?" Confusion blankets my face.

"We can meet right here. My room is next to yours." Christ. On. A. Cracker. Why does the universe hate me? Why does this stunning man have to be mere feet from me at night, when I have very dirty thoughts running through my head like a marquee in Times Square?

"Why are you staying here? I mean, in our suite." I am nervous. Fidgeting. Not making eye contact. I might be sweating. And for the record, those women who say that they simply glisten are liars. Those bitches sweat just like the rest of us.

"I want to make sure that your father doesn't make any surprise appearances. Speaking of that, you need to have a conversation with Owen. He needs to know, in case your dad approaches him."

"Is he here? Did he follow us?" I can't lie. I am a little fearful of his presence. Afraid of the unexpected, especially after my book launch party.

"Yes, he is here. This is why I have extra security, plus the media is already sniffing around, so I'm being cautious. You and Owen will have security with you both. I don't want any arguments. This is just a precaution until we uncover what Richard has in store."

"Alright, I'll talk to Owen at dinner. This is going to be so confusing for him. And why would you think I would argue with you? I am very easy going and adaptable." I smirk.

"Whatever gets you through the night, Addie. I just want you to understand that the actions I'm taking are in your best interest. Tell me, what does he know about his father?" His tone is soft, and I find myself staring at his lips. Sweet. Baby. Jesus. I need to get a grip.

"He was a baby when our father left. As time went on, Owen asked questions about why he didn't have a father like the other kids at school. I told him that our father had to go away. At the time, that satisfied him, but now, I don't know. He'll probably want to meet him." I sigh.

He hands me a chocolate out of his pocket. What the actual fuck. I take it, unwrap it, and pop it in my mouth.

Welcome to my life. A modern version of *The Twilight Zone*, and I hope that I survive.

Jameson

We head to the trendy restaurant that Nina alerted me to. She thought Owen would love it because of its sports-themed décor, and it might allow Addie to decompress from the shitshow that continues to follow her. The ambiance is casual, and the décor is funky. Cork-lined walls host black and white photographs of sports figures, while leather booths create an air of intimacy. The hostess leads us to our table. Owen peruses the menu, and with Addie's help, he settles on the steak with a side of fries. Addie takes a sip of her wine and exhales. I want to take her hand, but I don't. Instead, I nod, letting her know she has my support.

"Owen, I want to talk to you about something."

"Addie, I know all about sex. Remember, you told me that when I was a boy. Now I am a man. You don't need to tell me again." He's seriously the funniest person I've ever met. I want to laugh, but the timing would be totally inappropriate.

"This isn't about sex. This about our father," she whispers.

"He had to go away. I remember." He looks at Addie with the innocence of a child.

"Yes, and now he's back." She closes her eyes as the words slip through her lips.

"Oh. Can I see him? Maybe he will come back if he meets me." He smiles, and tears glisten in Addie's eyes. It takes everything in me not to offer her some sort of comfort.

"Buddy, you know how great you are, right?" she implores.

"You tell me all the time, Addie." He rolls his eyes and grins at her. It's the kind of smile that goes straight to the heart.

"Well, whether he stays or not, nothing will change how amazing you are."

"Okay. I hope he likes me. Maybe if he does, he won't go away again. When can I meet him?" She closes her eyes again and takes a deep breath.

"I'll see what I can do." She sighs as she takes an extra-large drink of her wine.

With a grin on his face, Owen digs into his newly arrived steak and declares, "I love my life."

Addie

It doesn't take much to locate my father. Since he has resurfaced, he seems to be everywhere, so it doesn't surprise me that he's taken up residence in the lobby as we arrive from dinner. I should have had another glass of wine. My eyes meet Jameson's, and he nods. That man has excellent nonverbal communication skills. I stop and turn to Owen.

"Buddy, do you want to meet your dad now?" I know the answer. I can no longer avoid the inevitable.

Eyes wide, he looks at me with so much innocence. Unconditional love and forgiveness pour out from his soul. While his enthusiasm is normally contagious, my stomach can't help but clench.

"Yes! I want to see my dad. Show him that I'm all grown up." He grins, and I cup his face.

"Okay, then. He's right over there." His face lights up like a Christmas tree. and we walk over to him—to the man that simply abandoned us. But in Owen's world, he is just his dad.

"Hi, Owen." My father looks uncomfortable yet smug. Like he has all of the power.

"Hi, Dad! I missed you. You left, but I knew you would come back for me." And with that, he hugs the man who abandoned him because of his disability. Richard looks uncomfortable as he pats Owen on the back. I try to hold my shit together. I can barely breathe. I just wish he would never have come back. The disappointment of his presence, coupled with Owen's inevitable broken heart, already hurts. But I can't break. Owen needs me. I am the only constant in his life.

Suddenly a piece of chocolate is thrust into my hand. I look up into Jameson's eyes. I mouth, "thank you," and he gives me a soft smile. I watch my father squirm while Owen chatters on and on. I can't hear anything he's saying; it's just all too difficult.

After a while, I say, "Hey, Owen. I think it's time to go to the room. It's getting late."

"Okay. Hey, Dad, will you still be here tomorrow? You aren't leaving, right?" My heart constricts. Owen's eyes beg for acceptance. He shouldn't have to beg—it should be given freely. And yet Owen's heart is still completely open to Richard.

"I plan on staying. I want to get to know you." His words lack conviction. They seem hollow. Empty. Owen hugs him again, and my father gives me a smirk. The feeling of dread escalates, and not even chocolate can ease the fear.

Owen is elated about the chance meeting with his dad, a.k.a, the sperm donor. I am trying to engage and be happy for him, but all I feel is impending doom. Maybe it's my gut talking, but I get the distinct sense that this is a game for him, like chess, where each move is strategic. I'm at a distinct disadvantage since I don't think that way about people. His motives are forced, and the timing is beyond coincidental. I didn't remember Richard as being calculating. My memories of him aren't unhappy, but they didn't match what my friends had. He wasn't a warm presence, but he did engage with me…most of the time. He did try to be a paternal figure to fill the void my mother left when she would disappear for days. Something shifted with him after Owen was born. I always thought that it was because of his disability, but now I am not so sure.

Jameson

Owen chatters on and on about his dad while Addie's face remains emotionless as we take the elevator to our suite. The impromptu introductory meeting left us both feeling on edge. She has her arm around him. I know she's struggling. I know that she wants to be excited for her brother, yet she knows there won't be a happy ending. I know it too.

As we enter the suite, I pull Addie aside.

"I know that this is a stupid question, but are you okay?"

"Nope. Not even a little bit, but what is my choice in the matter? Dick has me cornered. I just need to focus on the book tour and Owen. I have to trust that everything will work out, right? I mean, you do have a plan in place. Maybe it's time I learn to rely on other people."

I wasn't expecting that. The plan? Well, I don't need to tell her that it's still in the early stages. But for tomorrow, I know that we will be okay. Security is in place, and they know not to let Dick in the venue while Owen is at the Red Sox game. Bases covered. Pun intended.

While this situation is still volatile, I don't believe it will affect the hype surrounding Addie. Okay, that might be a bit of a lie. Sometimes it can ruin a person's reputation. I just have to bring my A-game and spin it to her benefit. Sleep will not come easy for me tonight.

Jameson

The bookstore is bustling as we make our way to the table where Addie will greet readers. Located in the heart of Beantown, The Book Nook is overflowing with anxious fans. She's visibly nervous, popping chocolate, nibbling on her fingers, and pacing so much I fear she will wear a hole through the floor. I walk over to her and calmly tell her they're ready to begin. Natalie, the store manager, is helpful and overly enthusiastic to the point where I wonder if she has an off button.

"Addie, are you ready? We are so excited to have you!" Natalie's nasal voice is accentuated by what I would describe as a singsong delivery. This is going to be a long day.

"Already? What if they don't like me?" She eyes Natalie with uncertainty.

"Well, they've been lined up for two hours, so I'm pretty sure you don't need to worry about that." This chick beams. Her larger-than-life teeth glow, and I hope she won't be hanging out with us the entire time.

For the next four hours, Addie patiently takes the time to chat with each person. She settles in beautifully, and in typical fashion, she owns the moment. When the last customer leaves, every single book is gone.

"Can a person lose a limb from overuse? Seriously, my hand might never be the same," she deadpans. Then she looks at me expectantly, but I'm distracted. For the last four hours, I have been getting news alerts. Someone filmed Owen meeting his father. Fuck. Not moving to somewhere private was a rookie mistake for me. This is what I get for letting my feelings get in the way. Now I need to figure out how to spin this to our benefit. What we don't want is for the public to believe that Addie is intentionally keeping Owen from his father. The outlets are reporting that Richard has been contacting Addie via email in an effort to reconnect, but she has rebuffed him. There are photos of emails that provide proof.

"I've never heard of that, but I suppose anything is possible." She was probably joking, but I can't handle jokes right now. I need to stay focused. "Let's head back to the hotel. We'll have room service. You have to be on *Good Morning Boston* for their nine a.m. segment tomorrow, so we need to arrive at eight for hair and makeup." I'm doing my best to act as if everything were perfectly normal. Unfortunately, she isn't fooled. I prepare myself for the Addie inquisition.

"You know, there was a time when I could dress myself along with doing my own makeup and hair." There is a sparkle of humor dancing in her eyes.

"You call your yoga pants and food-stained shirts dressing yourself?" I laugh. She glares. It's our thing. Then she flips me off. I love it. Jesus, I am so undone by this woman. She glances at me like she's reading my thoughts.

"Spill." Her eyebrows rise, and she folds her arms across her chest. Crap.

"What?" I ask, hoping we can skirt around the issue.

"You're acting weird. Like there's something you don't want to tell me. So spill it."

I run my fingers through my hair. "Alright. There's footage of Owen meeting Richard, along with photos of a trail of emails between the two of you." I look at her, hoping that she can tell me that those emails are fake.

"Are you fucking with me right now? Seriously? I have never exchanged anything with him. How would I? He fell off the planet when he left us. I don't even know where he lives, let alone have an email address. Trust me, I tried." She narrows her eyes at me. "You believe me, don't you? You don't think that I kept this from you, do you? Why would I do that?" Hurt shadows her face.

"I believe you, Addie. Whoever is doing this is savvy. I will get Grady on it to investigate the emails' origin. The coincidence of this happening right now seems very well orchestrated. We need to control the narrative. Tell the story in your words." I instantly regret saying "coincidence" since I am not ready to share Dorothy's involvement yet.

She waits, clearly pondering carefully. Then it seems like something clicks in her mind, and she looks at me with fire in her eyes. "What do you mean coincidence? Do you think someone else is involved?"

Well, crap. My job is to spin things, so I need to figure out how to do what I get paid for without making her suspicious.

I hesitate. "Not at all. Coincidence wasn't the right word to use. There are a lot of red flags with this whole situation. I just want to make sure that we cover all of our bases." I hope that was believable. Basically, I just spun some bullshit.

She stares at me like maybe she doesn't buy it, squints her eyes at me, and says, "Alright, let's do it. I can't allow all of this crazy to undo all of the good happening right now."

"Okay. Let me make some calls."

She nods in agreement.

We head back to the hotel. No "sperm donor" sightings, as Addie would say. Owen is safely in the room, awaiting our return. According to Owen's Instagram, he had a great time at the baseball game. Yep, he has quite a fan base with over two hundred thousand followers now. Seriously, he is having the time of his life. I even set up a meet and greet so that he could hang with some of the players. We enter the hotel suite, and Owen hurls himself at us, chattering about his adventures while Addie kicks off her shoes and face-plants on the couch.

"Gmmm smmm fmmm." The pillows muffle her voice.

"What was that?" I ask.

She raises her head and says loudly, "Get. Me. Some. Food."

I chuckle at her hangry request.

I order a large spread, and once it arrives, we eat in silence until Owen breaks the quiet.

"When can I see my dad again? We have so much to do together since he came back to me. Can we have dinner with him tomorrow night?" There is a hitch in Addie's breath.

"Let me see what I can arrange." She smiles at Owen, who instantly changes the subject to how many hot girls were at the game, along with how much junk food he ate. Owen and I carry the conversation while Addie retreats inward. She quietly gets up, kisses Owen on the head, and goes to her bedroom, closing the door behind her.

Addie

I didn't realize how exhausting and exhilarating a book launch could be. People were so kind and excited about my book. It affirmed me in a way that I have never felt. But by the end, I was done. Like, put a fork in me done.

When I got my first writing gig, my mother refused even to celebrate that milestone. I had been waiting for that moment where she would tell me that I was valued. That I was enough.

"Addie, I am so glad that you figured out it's better that you don't interact with the public. Since you don't care about your appearance, being behind a computer would serve you best. I suppose you want to celebrate. We could go to that diner that you love so much. Just watch your carb intake."

That diner was two counties over, and the reason it was my "favorite" was that it was the only place she would take me. Why? Well, then she wouldn't run into any of her country club friends. I heard you gasp. Do you know how many times I have been to the club? Once. That was only because we were celebrating my parents' anniversary, and we needed to "appear" as the perfect family unit. I was there a total of fifteen minutes before my babysitter took me home. After Owen was born, the club was never mentioned as a place where we would gather as a "family" again.

I shiver at the notion. With all of the success and the validation that I am enough, my mother's words still reside within me. Maybe they keep me humble. Or perhaps they are simply reminders of what one can do when they don't allow others to dictate their direction. I rose from the ashes after being beaten down from years of emotional abuse. And now, my past is threatening to invade my present.

After dinner with Jameson and Owen, I excused myself to retire to my room. I need a breather. I need to give some thought to how to navigate this situation with Owen and my father. How do I protect Owen's heart, knowing there will be no happy ending? I need an impartial person, so I call George.

Ever since our first meeting, George has become one of my people. His perspective on life is refreshing, and the fact that he doesn't give a crap what people think is exactly what I need at this moment. He picks up on the first ring.

"Addie! Oh, my God! I heard about your deadbeat daddy showing up at your big party. Guuurrl, your life is more dramatic than the drag show I went to last night. Those bitches got into it on stage and let me say, Spanx and testicles are things you simply don't need to see together. EVER! I need to bleach my eyes because I can't unsee it."

I giggle, which results in me snorting. His humor is the best medicine.

"I would have preferred that to the chaos that unfolded at the party by a longshot. Ugh! He is everywhere. What am I going to do? How do I protect Owen?"

"Oh, sweetie! I know you want to protect your brother, and let me say, he is so lucky to have you, but I think you are powerless in this situation. Is your hot publicist with the tight ass, a.k.a. Jameson, on high alert? I bet he is extra sexy when he's stressed out and in protection mode." I can practically see him swooning. He isn't the only one.

George is not wrong on that account. Jameson's sex appeal skyrockets when he's in protection mode.

"Yes...maybe...well, he's sex on a stick, but that isn't the point right now. Even if he is an excellent kisser." The words exit my mouth before I can stop them. I proceed to fill my friend in on the saliva exchange and the cuddling experience.

"Addie, it sounds like the brooding, hot publicist has a little attraction going on with you."

"Yeah, well, it isn't going anywhere. He switched back to business mode within seconds. I just need to keep my focus on this tour and protecting Owen."

"Well, you keep telling yourself that, but I bet that it won't be the last time his tongue finds its way in your mouth." He laughs.

"Whatever. I guess I should go and try to get some sleep."

"Take care, girlfriend. You are a warrior. Don't forget that."

We disconnect, and I absorb his words. Yes, I am a warrior. I just hope that I can win this war.

Addie

The ass crack of dawn arrives. I feel like I'm being watched, and sure enough, I peel open my eyes to see a sexy, brooding mirage. Oh wait, maybe I'm just having one of those hot dreams. I swear I get more action asleep, but I realize it isn't a mirage. There is an actual sexy, brooding man standing over my bed bearing coffee. The coffee is extremely attractive. Okay, so is the man.

"Rise and shine, sleepyhead." He reminds me of that annoyingly happy chick from the bookstore. She practically drowned in her drool as she eye-fucked him.

"Jesus, what time is it?" My eyes close as I inhale the aroma of the dark roast beverage he hands to me.

"It's seven. Walter is hanging out with Owen while we head to the station, and after your interview, you have the whole afternoon free."

"Free? Gee, Dad, what will I do?" Sarcasm drips like sugar from my lips. He licks his lips, and for a moment, I think he's going to take mine hostage. I turn my attention to my coffee.

I get out of bed, forgetting that I have no pants on. Underwear, yes. Short shirt, check. Underwear up the butt crack, another check. How does one remove said underwear from its current place of residence without drawing attention? I don't know about you, but I prefer to pretend that it isn't lodged in a dark hole and proceed to walk to the bathroom with my legs all funny. I also don't make eye contact as I shuffle along, moving my legs in a way that might allow my underwear to dislodge itself on its own -no such luck.

Once safely in the bathroom, I throw on my lucky yoga pants and semi-clean T-shirt. It's my "lucky" attire because I wore them the entire time I wrote the book. Also because I can't seem to locate anything else, so that makes them extra lucky. Jameson is waiting at the door with my purse and jacket. We head out, comfortable in our silence. He holds open the door to the car that awaits us.

"What are you going to do about Owen's request?" His tone is soft. It calms my anxiety and makes me feel like I'm not alone. I am, though. Alone in my brokenness.

"I guess I'll have to arrange it. Owen wants to get to know him, and I can't deny him, even if I can't forgive." I can't look at Jameson because I might cry.

"I can arrange it if you want me to." He takes my hand. For a moment, I breathe him in and relish the secure feeling that I have when I'm with him. As though he is mine. But he can never really be mine. I'm his client. And I'm too broken for him, too damaged by my circumstances. Besides, I know the type of woman that would attract him. They're sophisticated, elegant, confident, and sexy. They don't require chocolate for their anxiety, and they certainly don't have unexpected distractions that threaten their sanity.

I turn and look at him. "That would be great. Will you come with us?" It surprises me that I've even asked. I hate being vulnerable.

"I was already planning on it." He grins at me. I roll my eyes to hinder the tears that threaten to fall. This man, he threatens my heart, and I can't allow it because I won't survive it.

"I let the producers know that they could ask you about the Richard situation. This is our way of controlling the narrative. Share the story from your point of view. You can say as much or as little as you want, but we need to stay in front of this as much as we can." He looks at me for a reaction. I simply nod in agreement. As much as I would like to avoid the topic, I can't allow this situation to take away from all the good that's happening in my life.

He continues to hold my hand until we arrive at the studio. I don't try to analyze it. Alright, you know I am analyzing it. What does this mean? Does he make a habit of holding his clients' hands? I pop a chocolate in my mouth and close my eyes. Okay, so it's before breakfast. Don't judge me.

We walk into the green room, where I hear a familiar voice.

"There's my girl!"

I squeal and hurl myself at George. "What are you doing here? We just talked last night." I giggle as we hug.

"Well, a tall, dark, handsome man called me and invited me to hang with you for the rest of your time here. He felt like you needed a little cheering up. I was actually at the airport when you called. I got in late last night." Searching my face, he says, "I'm worried about you. And now that I see what you're wearing, I see this is truly an emergency." He "tsks" me under his breath.

I playfully hit him and laugh.

"Let's get you glamified." He claps and then does a little dance complete with jazz hands. Even his ridicule doesn't bother me because George has a way of helping me escape the dread and uncertainty that fills my gut.

I smile—it's a genuine, happy smile because, for once in my life, I realize that I am not alone. This quirky, unconventional group of people have crept their way into my heart. But I am still reserved. People leave. People can't be trusted. And I have a knack for being a very bad picker. Still, who knows how many appointments George canceled just to be here for me. That is truly an amazing act of friendship.

George and I chat nonstop while he swirls brushes around my face with an elegance that a ballerina might envy. Finally, he says, "Alright, beautiful. Ready to go wow your fans."

I look at myself in the mirror and smile at George. He is a magician.

"Yep. I am ready to go." I look over at Jameson. He is staring at me. Smiling. It is such a rare sight. His grin is so beautiful that I find myself staring back. Until the producer screams, "Five minutes!" and I am jarred back into reality. This dark, emotionless man brought George here to comfort me. He keeps chocolate in stock for me. He is kind to Owen.

I am so screwed.

Addie

C andance Williams is the darling of morning television—or at least that's what she'll tell you. Tall, blonde, and built like a supermodel, I am wondering if she eats. Her bright green dress accentuates her very perky boobs—the kind of boobs that wave and say hello. She looks at me like an afterthought as she rubs up against Jameson. You know how cats rub against you as a sign of affection (or to mark you as their own)? Well, this is the human equivalent. He's smiling at her, and I want to hurl. Ugh. The director ushers us to our chairs, calls, "One minute to air!" For the first time, Candance acknowledges my presence. The director points, and we are live.

"Addie, we're so excited to have you here!" She smiles at me like we're besties.

"Happy to be here, Candance." I smile. Not my real smile. I save that for people I like.

"Addie, your book has been such a phenomenon, but I know that some things have developed in your personal life that you want to talk about today. Tell us about the reappearance of your father." She furrows her brow and puts her hand on my mine. Is this for real?

"Yes, my father left us shortly after my brother was born. There has been no contact until recently when he showed up at my book launch in Los Angeles." Short and sweet. Is this over yet?

"That must have been difficult for you and your brother. Now, your brother Owen is disabled, correct?" She asks me like it's some sort of death sentence.

"Owen has Down syndrome, but he doesn't allow that to define him. He is a vibrant contributor to the community. He holds a job at a local grocery store near our apartment and is involved with the Special Olympics, where he plays basketball and softball," I say with pride.

"Oh, that is lovely and so very sweet. Do you think that your father left because of your brother?"

The question makes me cringe.

"I don't know the exact reason, but I do think there might be a correlation."

"It's so nice that you're still caring for Owen. The burden must be difficult." Her brows are knitted, and her eyes glisten with fake tears. I really want to punch her.

"We're a team, Owen and I. It has always been the two of us, and it's my honor to be his sister. Caring for him has never been a burden. He is one of my greatest teachers." I try not to sound like a bitch or incredibly preachy, but I have never been able to control my tone or facial expressions. Oh well.

"Addie, you are such a courageous woman. I am in awe of how you have taken on the challenge of such responsibility! Thank you for sharing this with us. Now let's talk about this amazing book you wrote." I want to revisit her insinuation that caring for Owen is somehow burdensome. that I am courageous for doing so. But instead, I simply focus on her next barrage of questions.

Jameson

Let me state for the record that Candance is a bit handsy. I mean, she is an attractive woman, but nothing about her is appealing. I see the glare from Addie. Honestly, it makes me happy that she might be jealous, even if nothing can become of us. Because, well, there is no us.

While Addie is busy with the interview, I take some time to read the email Grady sent. He included some grainy photos of the woman in question, who is Dorothy. He's trying to help me put the pieces of this puzzle together.

My mind wanders. I still feel Addie's hand in mine. Her warmth. Her vulnerability. I have never been drawn to a woman like I am to her. But it's a moot point. I can't blur the lines. Okay… I know—I've kind of already done that. It simply can't happen again.

I call Richard to arrange dinner. The conversation with her father is short. He agrees to the time, and I provide the address to the restaurant. As I end the call, I see Addie walking off the set and popping a chocolate. I should buy stock in Hershey. Her phone rings, and I know from the look on her face that it isn't somebody she wants to talk to.

Addie

As I walk off of the set, popping a celebratory piece of chocolate, my phone rings. Well, shit—it's Dorothy. I bite the bullet because if I don't, she'll stick around like a bad rash that simply won't go away.

"Dorothy." My tone is flat and heavy with annoyance.

"Addie! Oh my God, we just saw your interview. This whole situation is crazy, but you're handling it so well. You know, I had a premonition that someone from your past would come back into your life." *Slow your roll, soothsayer.*

"That's interesting. Anyway, it's fine. We're just taking it one day at a time." I say this hoping that I might believe it. Plus, I don't want to lay my cards on the table with her. I don't trust her. Her agenda isn't pure, and it has never been. She's out for herself.

"Addie, I'm family. You can be honest with me. I can only imagine how difficult this is for you to navigate. I'm happy to come, and support you. Just say the word, and I'll be there for you."

What. Is. Happening? Seriously, I feel like I'm living in a very warped nightmare. You know, the ones you have where you feel like you're actively trying to wake up to escape the horror? Yep. That's me.

Right now. And how the hell would she fly here if she doesn't have any funds? Oh right. I would be paying for it.

"Dorothy, I appreciate you calling. Really, I do. I just have a lot of things happening right now. When I get back to New York, we can do dinner. My treat, of course." I know the thought of a free meal will distract her.

"Oh, Addie! I would love that. Can I pick the restaurant? I want to try that new upscale French place in Manhattan. I bet you can get us in since you have celebrity status now. I can't wait to see you. Seriously, call me if you need to talk. I'm here for you." Cue the exaggerated slow clap for her Academy Award winning performance. What a tool.

"Will do, Dorothy. Take care." I go to end the call, but apparently, I don't take action quickly enough.

"Addie, wait a second. Do you know how Richard found you? I mean, all of these years of silence, and then *poof*, he's at your launch party? Just wondering if you know how that happened." My gut clenches, wondering why she's suddenly on a fishing expedition. The hairs on my neck bristle.

"I have no idea how he magically appeared after all these years. I imagine it's the publicity from my book because the timing is oddly coincidental." I'm not sure why I'm sharing this with her, but honestly, it isn't anything the rest of the universe doesn't already know.

"Oh, okay. Just wondering if there's anyone else involved." Her line of questioning borders on weird, but I shake it off since it all leads to some sort of conspiracy theory, which makes me feel like I'm in James Bond movie.

"Dorothy, I've got to run. Talk soon." I hit the end button. Chills run down my spine. I shudder, and when I look up, my eyes meet Jameson's.

"I fucking hate my family—except Owen. When they were handing out relatives, I must have gotten the leftovers." I turn away and pop another chocolate.

Fuck my life. If it isn't my father trying to mess with me, it is my cousin's wife. I liked it better when I was ignored—when my name didn't register with people, and I lived in a perfect state of anonymity. I feel like I'm in the middle of the perfect storm. Dorothy's call was a little unnerving. She doesn't need to know the details about what's happening. Plus, I don't trust her. I'm surprised she hasn't sold my embarrassing photos from their wedding. You know, the one where I tripped and fell into their cake. The face-plant in the chocolate deliciousness, where I may or may not have settled in for a few bites. I figured if my mouth was already there, why not indulge? Damn, that cake was good. Anyway, Dorothy's photographer got plenty of photos. Deeply rooted in my gut is the feeling that she's up to something. I should tell Jameson, but I'm probably being paranoid. I'll just be more guarded with her.

"What did she say? You seem upset," Jameson inquires. Concern crosses his face.

"Oh, the usual. She wants to support me. She even offered to fly here, which means I would be footing the bill, of course. Oh, and she asked if I knew how Richard found me, which I thought was odd. And she acted as if she had a premonition of his reappearance. Did I tell you that she believes she's psychic?" I'm rambling, but I still notice Jameson's face transition from a state of concern to an unreadable slate.

"Hmm, that *is* an odd line of questioning, but as you've always said, she is a little bit crazy." His demeanor is off, too. I want to question him, but I get distracted by the chocolate goodness he presents me as he talks.

Dorothy

She hung up on me. That bitch. I'm only trying to gauge how much she knows. But so far, it seems like I'm in the clear. Everything is falling into place—as long as Richard continues to play his part. He is a little unpredictable, and I'm praying he doesn't develop a conscience.

I rehash the conversation he and I had yesterday at a nearby bar.

"Dorothy, I'm not sure about this. Addie is going to find out one way or another. It'd be cleaner to bribe her directly." He's fidgety. Probably withdrawal from the pills he's been popping.

"Richard, don't worry. I have this all planned out, and it will benefit us both. Trust me, you won't have to worry about supporting your habits once this is all said and done. All the gambling you want, all the drugs you can handle—don't worry. Now, here's some cash. Call it an advance. You could use a fix, couldn't you?" He eyes the money and quickly takes it from me.

"I'm meeting them for dinner tomorrow night." He seems eager to proceed with my plan once he realizes that he can feed his addictions.

"Excellent. Make sure that you play the doting father, Richard. I've noticed that you aren't overly affectionate with your son. You need to remedy that, or this will never work."

Matthew's voice transports me back to the present moment, but I didn't catch what he said.

"Sorry, what was that?"

"I asked why you're so lost in thought. You seem far away." His eyes narrow. He knows me well. I won't share every part of my plan with him; he is a weak link. I can't allow anyone to get in my way—even my spouse.

Addie

We go back to the hotel. I'm doing my best to mentally prepare for this "family" dinner. Honestly, I would prefer to skip it, but this is about Owen, not me. George is coming over to help me dress, but as support for the three-ring circus that is currently my life. I can dress myself. Okay, maybe my fashion choices don't match his, so yeah... he'll probably end up dressing me anyway. But whatever. He's bringing wine. I need a little liquid courage to get through this evening.

As I wait for him, I scroll social media. I know, I know—Nina wouldn't be happy. But Nina isn't here right now. There are a crap ton of tweets about me. Seriously. *Me*. One Twitter twit, @goddess, keeps referring to the reappearance of my father, how my book is nothing but nonsense and keeps posting photos of Owen meeting Richard. Jameson has been able to control the press, but this "twit" is adding more shit to the current shitshow.

> @goddess: *Addie Snyder shuns her dad. #diva #nofamilyties #heartless*
> @goddess: *What is up with Addie thinking she's better than us?*
> *#herbooksucks #daddyissues #her15secondsareup*
> @goddess: *Addie is a chocoholic. #fatty #chubby #thescalehatesher*

Well, at least that isn't a lie. I do like my chocolate. But seriously, this person is mean. Teenage girl mean—and she has over a million followers. What the actual fuck.

I stalk out into the living room of the suite where Jameson is perusing his emails. His head jerks as I shove my phone in his face.

"Who the hell is this person?" My face hurts from all of my scowling. He looks at the feed but doesn't react.

"I have no idea. The bottom line, Addie, this is par for the course. There are trolls out there, and they will say hateful things. This is all a part of being in the limelight, and you are going to have to develop a thick skin." His tone is gentle. "And didn't Nina warn you to stay away from social media? Didn't she tell you that avoidance, in this situation, is your friend?"

"This limelight sucks. This twit sucks. This whole situation with my father sucks." I throw myself on the sofa like an unhappy toddler.

"For a writer, you might want to expand your vocabulary." He laughs. I glare and flip him off, stalking back to my room. As I slam my door, I hear him bellowing that I need to be ready by seven. Whatever.

Jameson

Something about the @goddess issue has me sure it's someone who knows Addie. I would love to pin it on her father or perhaps Dorothy, but all I can do is pass this on to Grady.

As usual, Addie is late. Since George arrived to help her get ready, all I've heard have been giggles and squeals. It's good to hear her laugh.

"Addie, let's go," I call. She hustles out of her room dressed in form-fitting skinny jeans that hug her just right and a white blouse that provides a peek of skin. Her cheeks are pink from laughing, and her smile is bright. She's heavily buzzed. I'm sure George doesn't think I know he smuggled wine into her room.

"Chill out! Where's Owen?" She struts toward me with a little swagger in her step. George is laughing, and I'm trying not to smile. So I smirk instead.

"I sent Owen down with Walter. They're waiting for us in the car." I watch her as she gathers her jacket and purse.

"Well, come on. This dinner is going to suck." She stalks toward the elevator, and I follow suit. My eyes linger on her ass. I'm not sure there's enough alcohol to get me through this night.

Addie

The hostess, who, by the way, can barely speak as she surveys Jameson's body, seats us in a cozy corner. It's probably ideal to keep us tucked away from the general public. I search for the nearest exit, you know, just in case I need to escape. If I were in a different frame of mind, I would have appreciated the restaurant's aesthetic. The mahogany bar is surrounded by leather stools, industrial lighting adding to the ambiance. It has a subtle retro vibe with its walls lined in vintage photos from the 80s. Owen loves the 80s, and he's obsessed with music from that era, so this is the perfect place for him.

It's just as well we are hidden away since we don't need to draw attention to what may happen tonight. It seems like a delightful place. Too bad I can't enjoy it as I zone in on the one person who is messing with my life.

My father is already seated, nursing his amber drink. Owen bounds over and settles in next to the sperm donor while I take the seat at the farthest end of the table. Where is the fucking waiter? I need a cocktail pronto—my buzz is dissipating. Owen is babbling on about all of the places he's seen since he arrived. I keep glancing at my watch, which indicates each time that only thirty seconds have passed since I last checked. Jameson keeps looking at me. Occasionally, he prompts Owen about various topics to keep the conversation flowing. I use the word "conversation" loosely because my father isn't engaging. He fidgets and doesn't make eye contact—such an asshole. I am jolted into the present moment by a voice calling my name.

"Addie? Is that you?" I look up and find myself greeted by a familiar face: Grayson Malone. The hottest guy in high school. He was popular, smart—the whole package. Every girl in school wanted to be on his arm. But since I wasn't in his social circle, I hardly thought he noticed me. Ladies, let me tell you that he looks even better now. His fitted designer suit hugs his muscular build, while his jet-black hair begs to be tussled. He smiles at me. Jameson clears his throat.

"Umm, yeah, it's me." I giggle like a high school girl and am instantly reminded why it's no wonder guys aren't banging down my door. Real smooth. My liquid courage is dwindling.

"You probably don't remember me. It's Grayson Malone—from high school." He smiles. It's genuine and kind. I pause. Holy shit! He *is* talking to me, looking at me. Me, people! I. Can't. Even. Okay, so I gather my wits and try to tackle the situation at hand. I need to get my shit together—fast.

"Of course, I remember you." I get up from my seat and embrace him. He's yummy. His arms feel strong as he draws me close to his body. "Do you live here in Boston?"

"No, I'm here on business. I live in New York." His eyes roam my face as he releases me, and I feel a little giddy with the attention.

"Oh, me too! I mean, I'm here on business, and I live in New York, too." I'm trying to be cool, but my nerves mixed with alcohol are a recipe for one hot mess.

"I heard about your book," he says sheepishly. It's adorable. "I read it. It was amazing. My sister will be so jealous when I tell her that I saw you. She loved your book, too. I think she's planning to go to one of your signings in New York." He pauses, then says, "I would love to get together. Can I have your number?" He looks at me with a boyish shyness that just makes him even more delicious.

Flustered, I'm stunned into silence. When I realize that he's waiting for an answer, I quickly hand him my phone, and he enters his information. Our fingers touch when he returns it. I send him a text, and he grins at me. My face hurts from smiling. He hugs me goodbye. And yes, I sniff him. Sue me. He smells woodsy and spicy. Once he releases me, he gives me one last grin and walks back to his table. I continue to stand there like an idiot until Jameson's irked voice brings me back to the current reality show going down at our table.

Let me pause this scene for a moment and explain the shitshow that has been my dating history. I told you earlier that I would, and I think this is the best place to keep my promise. My first date was in college. Seriously. Nobody was interested in a quirky girl who always had her nose in a book or writing in journals or who was the main caregiver for her brother with special needs. Carl asked me out during my freshman year of college. He was nice, predictable, and very boring. I lost my virginity to him because I felt like it was the right thing to do. It was something I felt the need to get done. Like it was an errand on my to-do list. Let me be clear if I could leave a Yelp review for that sexual encounter, my lady parts would have given him a one-star rating. We dated for a few months, and then he broke up with me. His reason? *I* was boring. Yep, his words. Mind you, this guy organized his pens by color and would lose his shit if they were out of place. I guess we just have different ideas about what constitutes a boring personality. Whatever.

There were others, but most were assholes who were put off by Owen. One called him "retarded," which is grounds for murder in my book. *Never* use that word. It's unacceptable. Owen and I come as a package deal. There is no room for anyone who isn't willing to open their hearts to both of us.

Then there was the Tinder period, insistently prompted by Nina. The whole thing was a disaster, and I decided to take Dora the Explorer's advice when she admonishes, "Swiper, no swiping." So, I've been living the life of a nun. A stern voice interrupts my trip down memory lane.

"You know, you didn't even introduce us to your friend." Jameson's voice is strained with irritation. I roll my eyes. He emphasizes the word "friend" like it's something sordid.

"I'm sorry. It was all so random. I simply got caught up in seeing him again." I smile. My lady parts are jazzed, but I noticed they were more subdued than they are when Jameson hugs me or kisses me. Instead of the "Hallelujah" chorus, they were chanting more of a "We will, we will rock you!" It's like lady parts karaoke. I shrug those thoughts away.

Jameson is glaring at me. Ignoring him, I look over at Owen, who is very invested in his meal, and my father, who looks as if he's having his last meal before his execution. You know, the typical family gathering served with a whopping side of dysfunction.

I sit back down and sigh. I realize that Jameson is staring at me.

"What?" I ask, my tone slightly clipped.

"Did you date him?"

"Umm, no. He's just a guy from high school," I tell him.

"Will you go out with him if he calls?" he inquires.

"Jesus, are you writing a book? What's with the inquisition?" I pause. "Wait a minute. Are you jelly?" I smirk at him.

"What's with the teeny-bopper 'jelly'? The word is jealous, and no, don't be ridiculous. I just need to know. Once you're in the public eye, everything changes. Your life is no longer private. You have an image that I need to preserve."

"Well, he probably won't even call." I shrug. "Even if he does, it won't be your business." I focus on my food. I can't shake the feeling that the more good things keep happening to me, the harder the other shoe will drop. It leaves me feeling unsettled.

Jameson

What. The. Actual. Fuck. We are seated at the table. Owen is chattering away at his emotionless father while I try to stay composed and keep myself from punching the asshole. Meanwhile, this pretty boy comes strolling along. I see his gaze roaming over Addie's body. I don't hear much of their conversation, but I know that Addie is giggly and nervous. He keeps touching her. It's hard to concentrate with my fists clenched and my jaw tight. I refocus my attention on Owen, who keeps trying to draw his father into the conversation. I notice that Owen looks uncharacteristically disappointed. Seemingly frustrated that he isn't getting any response from his father, he gives up and focuses more on the meal in front of him. How anyone could fail to be enamored by him is beyond me. This sweet human being is just happy being here. Everything brings him joy.

Since seeing Owen unhappy makes me uncomfortable, I decide to engage him on topics I know he likes to talk about, like his favorite shows, girls, and sports. They happen to be my favorite topics, as well. He chatters on, and I watch as Richard gazes at his phone. Thinking that I'm not watching, he texts a few times, and I notice his face goes pale. If I could get a hold of his phone, maybe I could find out who's making him squirm.

Between Addie hugging that douchebag, Owen being ignored by his father, and Dick getting distracted by his phone, I think that I might explode. This dinner has been a disaster. I am definitely getting a background check done on this Grayson character. What?! It's part of my job to make sure that my client is surrounded by honest individuals who won't take advantage of her, including potential "boyfriends." You don't believe me? That's fine. I'm just doing what I'm paid to do. What? You think I'm lying to myself? Well, denial is my best friend at this point.

Addie

Jameson is seething, and I am loving every moment. Every. Single. Moment. I turn my attention to my father and Owen. After barely uttering a word, even with Owen jabbering on and on about everything under the sun, my father does something I prayed he wouldn't do. He asks for time alone with Owen. Owen's face lights up, and my heart is breaking. This is just a chess game to my father, and my sweet brother is simply a pawn.

"Jameson, can you take Owen to the car? I need a moment with my father."

"Sure. No problem. Come on, Owen. Let's plan what we're doing on the last day of our Boston adventure."

"Okay, boss!" He laughs. He has been calling Jameson "boss" ever since he heard me say it. Of course, mine is laced with sarcasm. He turns to my father and hugs him. Owen gives the best hugs. Love simply radiates through him. My father stiffens and lightly pats him on the back. Like he's some sort of pet. His discomfort is palpable. Jameson and Owen head to the car, and I turn back to my father after assuring myself that Owen is out of earshot.

"Why would you want to spend time alone with him? You barely talked to him tonight. When he hugged you, you treated him like he had some sort of disease. I'm not going to stand by and watch him get hurt if you aren't all in."

"You can sit and judge me all day, Addie, but the reality is that I am his father. We can do this the easy way or the hard way. You let me get to know him, or I take you to court. The media circus will just bring more unwanted attention to Owen. Your choice." His eyes darken.

"Well, here is your choice. You can spend time with him, but these outings are supervised. I'm only doing this because I feel that Owen does deserve to know you. But make no mistake, he picks up on bullshit."

He smirks at me and leans toward me. The strong smell of liquor makes me gag. "Or perhaps you want to make this easy and write me a check to keep me away from him. I'll be in touch. Have a good night, Addie." With that, he gets up, turns, and walks away, leaving me standing there, wishing I had never written this fucking book.

Jameson

I hated leaving Addie to contend with her father, but Owen didn't need to be a part of that. While we wait in the car, we plan our next outing.

"Can we go to Boston Harbor? I want to see where they dumped the tea." He beams at me. My heart constricts.

"You know there isn't actual tea in there anymore, right?"

"Duh! I have Down syndrome, but that makes me special, not stupid." He laughs at me.

"Sure, we can do that and anything else you want. Did you like spending time with your dad?" Again, I'm asking questions to which I would rather not know the answer. I'm a fast forgetter.

"He doesn't talk much. Sometimes I don't think he likes me, but he doesn't know me very well, so maybe he'll like me later." He's still smiling. He's hopeful, and it makes me hate his father even more.

"I'm sure he likes you, Owen. How could anyone not?" I grin at him. The door to the car opens, and Addie climbs in with a smile plastered on her face. It's forced and doesn't reach her eyes.

"Addie, what did he say? Am I doing something with him?" His eyes are hopeful.

"He is going to give me a call tomorrow to plan some time with you. We can all go together. Whatever you want to do. I hate to miss the last day with you and, well, I think it would be a fun f-family outing." Addie stumbles on the word "family."

"Okay. I want to go to Boston Harbor, and Jameson is going too. Do you think our dad likes history like me? I wonder if that's something we have in common."

"I don't know, but you can ask him tomorrow." She exhales like she's been holding her breath.

I do what feels natural. I reach for her hand and squeeze it. This time, she doesn't let go. She gazes out the window.

When we get to the suite, Owen gets ready to watch *Grease* for what seems like the millionth time, and Addie goes out onto the balcony. The inner war continues, but again, I do what feels natural, and I follow her. She's pensive and doesn't hear my approach. I sit next to her on the plush sectional overlooking the shimmering lights of the city.

"He wants to spend time with Owen alone. I told him that it would have to be supervised. My gut tells me something is off about this whole situation." She turns and looks at me. "He couldn't even have a conversation with Owen, yet he is threatening to take him away. Owen is the only person that I have left. He implied that money would make him go away. But for how long? I know that if I start paying him, it will be another endless cycle. I already got trapped in that with Matthew and Dorothy. I don't want to repeat my mistake. Sometimes I feel like people only want me for the money. Never just me." Tears pools in her eyes.

I sit there, thoughtfully listening but not sure what to say. This is new territory, and I'm navigating it like a drunken sailor.

"I can't tell you what to do, but just know that I'm looking into it from all angles. I agree with you about the timing, and I'll do everything in my power to make sure Owen stays with you, where he belongs.

"You know how he wants to go to Boston Harbor? Well, I reminded him that there's no longer any tea in it, and he basically called me a dumb-ass." She laughs, and I feel the constriction in my chest ease.

"Well, Owen isn't known for his filter. That sounds good. I need a little decompression, and an outing with him always helps me stay in the moment." She gives me a slight smile. "Thanks for being so supportive. I know I'm just a client, but I feel safe with you."

Before I can correct her, before I can tell her that I feel like there is more to this relationship, her phone buzzes. She peers at the screen, and her face lights up. I look down and see it's Grayson. My jaw clenches. "Good night, Addie."

"Good night, Jameson." She doesn't look up at me. I go to my room, knowing that sleep will elude me.

Jameson

I spend the night tossing and turning. Unsettled, I put in a phone call to get the background check on Grayson going. I hope I find something. Of course, I'm the asshole who wants Grayson to be exposed as the bad guy so that I can look like the white knight. Then there's the part of me that just wants her to be happy, even though I can't be the right kind of guy for her. She needs someone good enough—the type of man who will commit to her. The kind of man who doesn't have his demons. I can't be hers.

I shower, then put on a pair of shorts and a T-shirt. I hope that I can get a little work done today before taking Owen to Boston Harbor. I venture into the living room, where I find Owen doing his best imitation of Danny Zuko while Addie assumes the role of Sandy. Both are giggling. They are truly in their element. I take a moment to watch them together. Their love for each other is consuming. Owen catches me watching them.

"Jameson, you can be Danny if you want to. He gets the hot chick!" He laughs and Addie scowls at him.

"Owen, remember we don't refer to women as hot. Try beautiful or pretty," she reminds him. It is a losing battle.

"No thanks. I just want to see some hot girls. Am I right?" He looks at me, wiggling his eyebrows. I can't help but laugh. Addie glares at the two of us and mutters, "Pigs," as she goes back into her room.

We head out to Boston Harbor, where we're meeting Addie's father, Dick. Addie reached out to him earlier since he never called. She only contacted him because she couldn't stand the thought that Owen would be disappointed. Owen was, of course, thrilled at the prospect of seeing his father again today. I purposely greet him as Dick, even though he has repeatedly told me he prefers to be called Richard. Yeah… that's not going to happen. Addie is quiet. She's cautiously observant of the exchanges between Owen and Dick. Dick keeps looking at his phone. He appears nervous and suddenly announces his departure.

"Something's come up," he announces. Fortunately, I have a tail on him, so maybe I can get more information about his angle. Well, hell—I know his angle; it's money, but I need to get the proof. He leaves without so much as a goodbye to Owen, who is visibly crestfallen, and I can feel Addie seething.

"What the actual fuck was that?" she whispers to me. "He threatens me, then does a 180 by agreeing to a supervised outing, and then leaves after less than ten minutes."

"I've got one of my guys following him, so hopefully we'll get more information soon. Let's enjoy our last day here. Owen deserves that."

She pops a chocolate in her mouth. "I wish I had a Xanax."

We stop for lunch at a nearby food truck and feast on lobster rolls. My phone rings, and I step away to take it. Thank God it's Grady.

"Did you get anything for me?" If I were one to pray, I would have sent a request to the big guy upstairs.

"Well, here's what's interesting. Once Richard left you, he headed to a nearby motel. Fifteen minutes later, he left with an envelope and guess who followed him out a few seconds after that? Dorothy. They ended up at a diner. I followed him to a casino, and he used the cash from the envelope to gamble. So, it's confirmed that she is giving him money."

"Well, I'm not surprised about a money exchange, except that Dorothy is broke, so we need to know who the source is in this scenario. Keep me posted." We disconnect. I head back over to the table, where Owen is laughing and Addie is rolling her eyes.

"Jameson, Addie is cramping my style as a chick magnet. Can we leave her and look for hot girls? You can be my wingman." He grins at me. Addie laughs, and I fist-bump Owen.

"Fine, you all troll for the ladies, and I'll head back to the hotel." Out of the corner of my eye, I see someone with a camera pointed at Addie and Owen. It's probably paparazzi now that Addie is in the public eye, but I can't be too safe. Wanting to protect them, I nonchalantly move to block the person's view and suggest we all go back together.

"You're a buzzkill, boss," Owen says, shaking his head in disappointment.

"I'll be your wingman another time." I hold up my fist to bump his, and he leaves me hanging.

"You guys are lame." Addie laughs at him. Her phone pings. I see that it's from Grayson, and my mood shifts from happiness to something darker.

Addie

The whole outing with my father is odd, but I do enjoy Jameson calling him Dick. I can feel my father's discomfort; he's annoyed with Jameson's presence. Owen doesn't let the heaviness of our father's attitude bother him. Instead, he dazzles us with historical facts, and afterward, he can't wait to get a lobster roll. But seriously, ten minutes into our outing and my father bails. Fucking bails? Part of me is relieved while the other part is completely outraged that he would not even put in the effort. And Owen, well, he is completely deflated. This amazing human who loves unconditionally is emotionally wounded, and that gives me murderous thoughts. I'm hoping Jameson finds out something we can use. The whole thing with my father is a ruse. If I thought I could get rid of him by paying him off, I would. But I know that he would just come back for more. He is a pathetic excuse for a father.

Owen is quiet after Dick leaves. He goes silent, probably processing what just happened. I quickly redirect him back to the history at hand, and within moments, he is throwing out historical facts and watching all of the tourists, but particularly the "hot chicks." I swear, if I hear "hubba-hubba" one more time, I might hurl. I notice that Jameson keeps his distance, surveying the area. While we're eating, he excuses himself to take a phone call. I watch him walk away. Okay, I'm watching his ass because it's a fine specimen. I wonder if he's packing. Not his "package," but a gun. Get your mind out of the gutter.

My phone pings and I look down. It's a text message from Grayson inviting me to meet him for drinks. It just so happens that he's staying at the same hotel, so we agree to meet in the bar at seven. Honestly, while I am excited that he's interested, I wish it were Jameson. I decide that I need some professional help in the what-to-wear department since left to my own devices, I would pick yoga pants and a T-shirt. Every. Single. Time. We head back to the hotel, and once I arrive in my room, I decide to call George and devise a game plan.

"Hey, girl! What are you up to?" His enthusiasm seeps through the phone. He makes me smile every time I talk to him.

"Just finished hanging with Owen and Jameson." I explain the whole ordeal with Dick and my text from Grayson.

"Guurrlll! You have more drama than that book you wrote! I am not a violent person, but this whole thing with your dad makes me want to go postal. What kind of person hurts a sweet human like Owen?"

"A selfish prick who's only interested in a payday."

"Well, he's certainly missing out. Owen is fabulous and he has great fashion sense... unlike someone we know." He laughs.

"Hey, I am getting better. Sort of. It is just so foreign to me that people care about what I'm wearing or how I look."

"Don't worry. You have me now, and you will look amazing tonight. We are going to glam you up, sista! I'll meet you in your room at about six. Grayson will be so hot for you that we'll need some firemen to put out the flames! Mainly we just need firemen for me." He laughs at his own joke.

"I knew I could count on you to make it about yourself." I giggle.

"Honey, I need to get laid. But since that isn't happening, getting you laid is the next best thing. Plus, you can make Jameson jealous with a capital J."

"I do need a little action, but I don't do one-night stands. Besides, Jameson won't be jealous. He hardly notices me." I say this as though I'm trying to convince myself. Jameson is not a commitment guy, and I'm merely his client. I know all of this, and yet I still need to make myself believe it.

"Oh, honey! The way that man looks at you makes me want to take a cold shower. His eyes smolder, Addie. He's hot for you. Lordy, I need to fan myself just thinking about it."

Sure, I would like to believe that he feels something more intimate than a professional relationship, but every time we get close, he takes ten steps backward.

"Let's just concentrate on the Grayson portion of our program, shall we?" I ask. "By the way, what have you been doing to entertain yourself?"

"What haven't I been doing? This city is full of willing and able men, but I'm a little picky. I've been enjoying meeting some very eligible men, but that's as far as I let it go."

"So, you are a romantic. No wonder we're friends. You want it to mean something, don't you?"

"I talk a big game, but honestly, I've been hurt in the past. As much as I'd like to be casual, I can't. So I'm just enjoying flirting and getting to know people while I'm here."

"I'm just glad you aren't bored. I've felt bad that we haven't been able to do more together outside of 'glamming' me. I love having you as a friend."

"Oh Addie, I love our friendship, too. Now stop getting all mushy. I'll be by later to make you even more fab than you already are. Don't forget to prune the promised land." He cackles.

I am stunned into silence. Before I can respond, he ends the call. Maybe George is right. Maybe I just need to get laid.

Jameson and Owen are deep in conversation about Owen needing a wingman to find some hot chicks when I return. The thought of another woman with Jameson makes me cringe. I have no claim. Sure, he kissed me until my panties almost melted off. and he seemingly knows when I need to be comforted, but he's my publicist. He would never go for a pleasantly plump forty-something woman who attracts drama like flies to shit. Nope, I need to redirect my attention to Grayson. Grayson's hot. He seems to think I am hot. I think my lady parts just rolled their eyes. Honestly, my lady parts aren't sure what to do. They have been doing the Rip Van Winkle for so long; maybe they're simply adjusting to the new hype.

"Sorry to interrupt, but I have plans tonight, so you all are on your own. George is meeting me at six to help me figure out what I'm going to wear." I don't make eye contact with Jameson, but I can feel the air thicken with tension.

"Where are you going? I thought we would go out to one of the more upscale restaurants since it's our last night in Boston. Owen is craving a steak." I know that he's eyeing me.

"Jameson, if Addie has plans, we can troll for chicks. She is a clock blocker anyway." Owen is overly excited by the thought of me leaving them to their own devices. Jameson laughs.

"It's cock-blocker, Owen, and we still haven't heard what Addie has planned. We're listening." He smirks. Both stare at me expectantly.

"Well, Grayson asked me for drinks in the hotel bar. It looks like he's staying in the same hotel. Not a big deal. Just two people having drinks. Reconnecting after many years." It sounds like I'm trying to convince myself. Why am I even giving an explanation? I'm a grown woman capable of making decisions for herself.

"Oh, well, then maybe we'll just stay in and have dinner in the hotel restaurant. You know, the one near the bar." He's enjoying this way too much.

"You don't need to babysit me. I'm fully capable of having a drink with a good-looking man all by myself." I'm pissed, and he's grinning. It makes him look even hotter, which makes me more annoyed.

"Jameson, I think *you* are a clock blocker." Owen laughs at his own joke, and Jameson shakes his head.

Jameson's phone rings, and he makes his way into his room to take it in private. Before he shuts the door, I try to make out the conversation. He is so secretive. I feel like he's keeping pertinent information from me. Thank God we're heading back to New York soon. Maybe I can get back to some sort of normalcy.

Who am I kidding? My life is probably never going to be normal again.

I head for my room. When George arrives, he is practically bouncing off the walls. I think he's more excited about this date than I am. I haven't been on one in years. My focus has been writing... and Owen.

George selects a blue silk wrap dress that molds to my body. I am not a size two. There is a two in my size, but it has one in front of it. Today's society labels me overweight. But looking at myself in the mirror, I smile. I feel good in my own skin. Finally. There is a lot rooted in my foundation that led me to believe I wasn't good enough. I could blame my mother for her lack of attention and her disappointment in my appearance. Or perhaps daddy dearest, who abandoned his family. There are a litany of factors, but at this moment, I feel hopeful that I am shedding a bit of the negative baggage I've been carrying.

"Girl, you look hot! I knew that dress would rock on your body. So, are you excited? Did you prep all the important areas?" He wiggles his eyebrows.

"We aren't going to have sex, George. Just drinks. And yes, I did prep those areas, but for me, not a man." I'm lying, and George seems to know it; he snickers. If I could get away with it, I would let all of those "areas" get overgrown like a field of weeds. It's such bullshit that women are expected to be "manicured" like a fucking lawn.

"I get it, but girl, you just never know. Maybe he'll be the perfect man! So I hope you dusted off the cobwebs. Nobody wants a dusty vajayjay." He laughs at his own joke while I roll my eyes. I swear, my eyeballs get more exercise than the rest of my body. I pop a chocolate in my mouth and strut out of my room. I strut because I want to show Jameson what he's missing. What? You know you would do it too.

I lock eyes with Jameson, and I notice as he scans my body. I shiver from his stare. Heading to the door, I purposely sway my hips, giving him an excellent view of my ass, and then I stumble. Fortunately, I'm close enough to the door that I recover by grabbing the handle. I turn and say, "Bye, guys. Don't wait up." Jameson's eyes grow dark, George grins, and Owen waves his hand to dismiss me.

Addie

I approach the bar and scan the seats, looking for Grayson. I spot him before he sees me, giving me a moment to appreciate the view. His white button-down is fitted, enhancing his muscular frame. His jet-black hair begs to be touched. It's thick, with a slight wave to it.

He turns toward me, and his face lights up. I walk toward the cozy table, which is illuminated by a flickering candle. He gets up to greet me with a warm embrace. I linger a bit, closing my eyes and inhaling his scent. He smells so good, but not like Jameson. That man has a scent all his own. Damn it. I need to stop making comparisons. I remind my lady parts that we are here to get to know Grayson. They sigh and reluctantly agree to have an open mind. Now that we're on the same page, I turn my attention to the man of the hour.

"I am so glad you were free tonight. I hope I'm not being too forward, but I couldn't stop thinking about you after I saw you last night." He smiles at me shyly. So. Freaking. Adorable. He seems nervous. The most popular guy in high school is nervous about a date with me! I'm seriously swooning.

"That's so sweet. I'm glad I was free, too. I'll be honest. I haven't done this in a long time." Why am I so unfiltered? Why do I always divulge too much information too soon? It makes me sound like a pathetic loser. *Ugh.*

"Well, I'm glad you decided to spend time with me." Our eyes meet. I smile at him. Oh my, I think he is going to kiss me. I'm torn between panic and excitement.

And just like that, we're interrupted by the waitress asking for our order. I ask for a glass of Chardonnay, while Grayson requests a scotch on the rocks. The moment is gone.

"Again, congratulations on your book. It's quite an accomplishment."

"Thank you. It's all so new—I'm still adjusting to all of the changes happening in my life. It's very surreal."

"You seem to be adjusting okay." It's cute that he thinks that.

"It has been quite a challenge." I fill him in on my father's reappearance and my struggles trying to navigate the media, and then I quickly redirect the conversation. No one wants to get too heavy on a first date. I certainly don't want him to run screaming. I ask about his work, hobbies, and the usual topics that typical people engage on a date. At least, I *think* those are normal topics. Either way, the conversation never lulls. It's comfortable.

"Ever been married?" he asks me. God, his dimples are precious.

"No. You?"

"Unfortunately, with work and everything, I haven't had the time. The women I meet seem so superficial, and I just want to find someone who wants to know me for *me*, not for my bank account." He inches closer to me.

"Understandable. Between writing and taking care of my brother, Owen, there hasn't been much time for me either." He touches my hand. It's warm and inviting. My eyes meet his, and I feel the hairs on the back of my neck tingle. Our waitress arrives with our drinks, and he releases my hand. I glance over to the bar, and my eyes meet Jameson's. He looks like he would like to explode, but instead, he nurses his drink while Owen sits beside him, trying to charm the waitress. Christ. On.

A. Cracker. I turn my attention back to Grayson and smile, but now my effort to not compare the two is ruined and quickly starts sucking all of the fun out of this date.

Grayson follows my line of sight and settles on my brother. "Hey, isn't that Owen? We can have him join us if you like. I would love to get to know him." Serious points for that invitation.

"No, it's fine. He's hanging out with my publicist, and they're on the prowl for chicks. Owen would be annoyed if we interrupted his evening." I laugh because it's true. He would be extremely snarky.

"Maybe some other time. Like when we get back to New York."

"That would be nice. We would love that." I grin at him.

We continue to chat. He asks me more about Owen, which endears him to me even more, and we reminisce about high school, although his experience was much different than mine. I was the quiet bookworm while he was the star of the school.

Time goes by quickly, and suddenly the bar is closing. I notice that Jameson and Owen are gone, and I'm aware of my disappointment. Grayson walks me to my suite, holding my hand. Butterflies flutter in my stomach. I lick my lips in the hope that he'll kiss me. He smiles. I smile. His lips are inches from mine. He leans in slowly, tantalizingly, until our lips finally meet. Our tongues tangle. He nips my lower lip. It's intense. Hot. For the love of Jesus, it is amazing, but instead of Grayson's face, my closed eyes picture Jameson. What. The. Actual. Fuck. He is ruining everything with his obsessive presence in my mind. Our lips disconnect, and we're both short of breath.

He smiles. "Thanks again for meeting me tonight. I'll call you when I get back to New York." His bourbon-colored eyes are hopeful.

"I look forward to it." I'm still trying to process kissing Grayson and picturing Jameson's annoyingly handsome face. Was the kiss hot because of Grayson or the thought of Jameson? Shit. Color me conflicted.

Jameson

I got the background check on Grayson. It was clean—*squeaky clean*. I mean, seriously, his list of volunteer stints is beyond impressive. He's perfect for her. That should make me feel good, but instead, it makes me angry. Never has a woman invaded me like Addie. When she walked out of the suite in that dress clinging to her delectable curves, I wanted to haul her towards me and convince her not to go. I keep reminding myself that she's just a client, but then I remember the kiss we shared. It was unforgettable.

"Earth to Jameson! Come on. Let's go pick up some hot chicks." Owen grins at me, dressed in a pair of khakis and a polo. The smell of AXE clings to the air.

"Buddy, how much AXE did you spray?" I cough, and Owen laughs.

"A lot. The ladies love it. Come on. Just follow my lead." He swaggers to the door. I wish I lived my life like Owen. He has adopted the mantra of total freedom. No limitations. Which is ironic, since society wants to cage him into a stereotype.

"Let's just go down to the lobby bar, and then we can get dinner at the hotel restaurant."

"Ugh. Are we stalking my sister? Are you going to be a clock blocker?" He narrows his eyes.

"It's cock-blocker, and no, I just thought it would be nice to have a drink first…to celebrate our last night here." It's not convincing.

"Uh-huh." Owen shakes his head. Even he knows the truth. Why can't I admit it to myself?

When we get to the bar, I see the douchebag, aka Grayson, practically sitting on Addie's lap. Seriously, he needs some lessons on honoring people's personal space. I order a scotch neat and try to peel my eyes away from them. Meanwhile, Owen is working his magic on the ladies. They surround him as he drinks his virgin daiquiri. I look over again to check out the "happy" couple. Yes, I am using air quotes because he isn't good enough for her…even though his background check suggests otherwise. I keep telling myself I'm doing this to make sure Addie is alright. Safe. That Grayson is being good to her. When our eyes meet, I know that I'm drowning in my own lies.

"Are you going to stare at them all night? It's creepy. I told you to follow my lead. Look at all the hot chicks hanging with us." He grins at me. "You need to loosen up. The ladies like someone relaxed. You always look mad. You don't need to frown all of the time." Owen has more game than Harrison, and that's saying a lot.

Relaxed is something I am not. I sip my scotch and hope that the amber liquor seeps into my body fast enough to give me some relief. Once we get back to New York tomorrow, I'm meeting with Grady to get the latest information on Addie's father. I am intrigued. He sent me a text before Addie left for her date and said that he needed to meet me in person. I nurse my drink, occasionally peering over at the cozy couple. She looks happy. Isn't that what I want for her? God, I am such an asshole. I finish my drink and settle our bill. Owen is less than thrilled about leaving, even just to move to the restaurant area a few feet away, but with the promise of a steak, he complies. Food is an excellent bribe with him.

We have a great time despite my mood. Owen's constant positive attitude keeps me from getting too down, and he keeps me smiling through the whole evening. He even gets a free dessert, just because the waitress likes him.

When we get back to the room, Owen heads straight to bed, and I decide to stay up and read. I know what you're thinking. You think I'm waiting for Addie. Well, I'm not. Okay, well, I just want to make sure she's okay. Plus, I like to read before bed. What am I reading? I have no idea. The words are blurred on the page. I hear voices outside the door. I try to make out what they're saying as I move closer. Then it's quiet. My heart stops. I just know that he's kissing her. The same lips that touched mine. Ugh. What is happening to me? I hear voices again and the turn of the knob. I race back to the sofa and resume my act of reading. My heart is beating wildly. I try to concentrate, but having read the same paragraph over and over, I already know that it's futile. As she sashays through the door, my eyes narrow at her. She flashes a megawatt smile before throwing a little sass my way. "Aww, you didn't have to wait up for me."

"Did you have fun, Addie?" I spit the words out like venom. It sounds harsher than I intend. I cringe, but I'm pretty sure my face maintains its cold, blank appearance.

"I did, indeed. We talked for hours. It was effortless. He is so interesting and accomplished. He volunteers at a variety of places. I mean, he is just so…impressive. You probably noticed how comfortable our conversation was since you stalked me." She cocks her head and smirks.

"Contrary to what you think, I was acting as Owen's wingman. However, I did see that Grayson was a little confused about personal space and that he was overly touchy. It seemed a little intimate for a first date." I really need to stop talking.

"Jealous?" I open my mouth to respond, but she immediately continues, "Well, it doesn't matter. You have made it abundantly clear that I'm your client. My dating life is not your business. And I *will* be seeing him again once we get back to New York. Goodnight, Jameson. Sleep well."

She heads to her room and quietly shuts the door. I saw the hurt in her eyes—the tears threatening to spill. The thought that I keep hurting her guts me. I know I won't be sleeping well again tonight.

Addie

As we head to the airport, and Jameson is back to acting distant. His usual banter with Owen is absent. His jaw is tight. The vein in his head protrudes. Honestly, the stick up his ass is much bigger than normal. This should be a relaxing flight home. *Not.* Meanwhile, Owen has charmed the flight attendants in first class. He has toured the cockpit and is currently being served a snack before we even leave the ground.

"What?" Owen catches me looking at him.

"Can you at least wait for everyone to board before you ask for a snack?"

He snickers at me. "I can't help it that I attract hot chicks who want to give me food. Did you see the selfie I posted on Instagram? All my friends are jealous." I roll my eyes.

Looking at his Instagram, I find that he has over a million followers now. For the love of Jesus. I laugh at some of the pictures from last night. The selfies of him with the waitresses are photobombed by the angry patron sitting nearby. Of course, that angry patron is Jameson. The vein in his neck is bulging. His eyes are narrowed. He looks pained, or perhaps a better term would be constipated. Why does that make me happy? I need to focus on Grayson. He sent me a sweet text this morning wishing me safe travels. I invited him to be my date for the New York book launch. I do like him. I am attracted to him, I think, but I keep comparing him to Jameson, which isn't fair. Okay, so I'm a little confused. Hopefully, I can get some perspective when we get home and I'm away from him. Spending more time with Grayson is probably the best way to get over my infatuation with my publicist. I need to keep reminding myself that he is a paid employee.

"You're in a pleasant mood today," I say to the man in question. "Did something happen to get your boxers extra twisty?" He turns to me, his face inches from mine -my breath hitches.

"Yes, as a matter of fact. My boxers are extra twisty because I have this client whose life is a circus rife with drunken clowns. So much drama, I can't even keep up with the cast of characters that continue to crawl out of the woodwork."

"Well, this client sounds lovely." I continue to smile, knowing that it's driving him insane. And yes, I know that he's talking about me. And yes, he is on point about my life being a circus. He puts his earbuds in and goes back to ignoring me.

We land at JFK, where Owen hugs every flight attendant before deplaning. He is totally in his element. A town car is waiting for us, and I realize that I can't wait to get back to my apartment. I miss the simplicity of my life before the success of my book—how uneventful it was. What I used to think was boring now looks rather appealing.

We pull up to our apartment building and unload our luggage. Jameson and Owen do some weird fist-bump routine before he gives me an abrupt wave with an indication that he will call later to go over our schedule for the week. There's a tug in my chest as the car drives away. Being with him for the last few weeks has given me an element of comfort. Safety. Something that I haven't felt in a while, if ever. I shrug it off, knowing that once I get into my routine, I'll feel better. And hopefully, my daddy drama will subside. My phone rings, and I see that it's Nina. I smile at the prospect of catching up with my friend.

"Hey!" I say.

"Welcome home! Thought maybe we could have a little girl time. Dinner on Friday?"

"Sounds good. I can't wait to see you." We chat a few minutes longer and end our call. I proceed to unpack all of the dirty clothes that Owen and I accumulated. At this point, it will take me weeks to finish doing laundry. My phone pings. I see it's Grayson. I'll be honest, I was hoping it was Jameson. I shake my head.

Grayson: *Hope you had a good trip home. Would love to see you. Dinner on Friday?*

Me: *The trip was good. Just trying to get back into my routine. I have plans Friday. Can you do Saturday?*

Grayson: *Saturday works. 7 okay? I can pick you up.*

I ponder that. Do I want him to pick me up, or should I just meet him? I'm waffling. Does he expect me to give up the goods? Do I even want to give up the goods? I am overthinking the question. My phone pings again.

Grayson: *I don't have to pick you up though. Hope I didn't scare you off.*

Me: *Sorry. Owen needed something. You didn't scare me off, but let's just meet there. It will be easier for me.* (Yes, I lied. Don't judge).

Grayson: *Okay. I will text you the address once I make the reservation. Looking forward to it, Addie.*

Me: *Me too. See you then.*

I put down my phone and smile. Maybe dating Grayson will shift my thoughts away from Jameson. Maybe spending more time with him will give me clarity.

Jameson

I drop my bags on the sofa in my apartment. It has been eight months since I moved in, and I just realize how sterile it is. Sure, there are the basics, but nothing personal. It's just another area of my life where I can't commit. Then I think of Addie's place, where every corner is jam-packed with books, photos, and warmth. Her place is a home. Her place is also a firetrap.

I was such an asshole to Addie today, but honestly, that's the only way I can keep my distance. The silence is deafening here. I miss Owen. I miss Addie. I miss their banter and Addie antagonizing me. I need to get out of my head. Fortunately, I'm meeting with a new client on Friday night. Chelsea Morrow is an up-and-coming artist. Her paintings are becoming a hot commodity internationally, and her agent contacted me to help navigate the publicity. I'm looking forward to diving into something new—a distraction from Addie.

As I unpack, my phone rings. It's Grady. Hopefully, he has some news about Addie's father.

"What's the word, Grady?"

"Well, it's interesting. My guy followed Dorothy into a seedy bar last night, where she met Richard and another man. The meeting was tense. Does the name Wendell Brooks ring a bell?"

"Isn't he a senator?" My mind is spinning, trying to figure out how any of this could be related to Addie.

"Yeah, and so now the trick is finding out what the three of them are up to and how Senator Brooks fits into the equation."

What. The. Fuck. Is. Happening? I can't even wrap my head around the insanity that is unfolding. What is Dorothy's end game?

"Just keep a tail on her for now. I'm not going to tell Addie anything yet until we know the whole story."

"Sounds good. I'll be in touch." We disconnect, and I'm left with a sinking feeling.

Addie

Friday night arrives, and I head out to meet Nina. We decided on a quaint Italian restaurant in the East Village. I would have been fine with a greasy diner, but I am trying to be open-minded since I don't like to step out of my comfort zone. I am greeted by a perky blond in a tight dress. I wonder if she can move. I wonder if she enjoys cheeseburgers or simply feasts on a buffet of kale.

"Can I help you?" Her tone is threaded with annoyance.

"Yes, I'm meeting Nina Bryant." I smile. She nods and proceeds to walk away after she looks me up and down with disgust. I suppose I'm meant to follow her, so I do. A greasy diner would never have been this rude.

Nina is wearing skinny jeans with an off-the-shoulder blouse. She looks gorgeous as usual. I'm grateful that George gave my closet an overhaul, although I did salvage some of my yoga pants and T-shirts by hiding them. Please don't tell him. Anyway, I picked a blue maxi dress that is both comfortable and functional—very important characteristics, especially since I am planning to carbo-load. Nina practically throws herself at me, and I laugh.

"God, I am so glad to see you. I feel like it's been years since we've seen each other. So, how is everything? I feel like so much has happened, and we haven't had time to chat, so spill." She sips her chilled martini.

"Can I get a cocktail before I spill my guts to you?"

Nina waves the waiter over, and while he's walking toward us, I see a face at the bar. Jameson. With him is a very attractive brunette who's caressing his arm. She is laughing. He is smiling. My insides twist. For fuck's sake, now *I* am jealous with a capital J. I order a double vodka and soda and turn my attention back to Nina. Nina raises her eyebrow and then follows my eyes to the bar. She says to the waiter, "Keep them coming."

"Alright, what the hell is happening with you and silver fox?" Nina inquires, using the nickname I used to refer to Jameson when I first met him.

"We kissed. It was amazing. He grew more distant, and now I'm going out with Grayson tomorrow night. End of story." Not quite the fun spiel I had planned, but now my mood has changed. I thank the waiter as he brings my cocktail. I would have hugged him, but I didn't want to scare him. I chug my drink. Sure, it isn't ladylike, but I don't give a crap at this point. "Doesn't matter anyway, as it appears that he's already involved with someone. And, as he keeps telling me, I'm just a client."

She laughs. "You have nothing to worry about there. That's Chelsea Morrow. She's an artist and his newest client. Look at his body language. He isn't comfortable with all the touching. You can tell. Jealous?"

"No. Yes. I don't fucking know. I'm so confused. Every time I'm with Grayson, I compare him to Jameson, which isn't fair. Grayson is the whole package. He's a good kisser, and he's kind, funny, compassionate, and good-looking. He doesn't get annoyed with my quirks. Wait, how do you know that is his new client?" My curiosity is piqued.

"Who are you trying to convince? Me or you? How do you feel when he kisses you?" she inquires as she gives me a smile.

"Well, that's the thing. When Grayson kissed me, I got all tingly, but I think it was because I was picturing Jameson." I cringe at the admission.

Nina raises her eyebrows and mutters, "Interesting." She taps her fingers on her chin.

"Anyway, I'm going out with Grayson tomorrow night, so maybe it will be different. I need a little distance from my publicist." I focus on my almost empty drink.

"Look, Jameson is different with you. Just remember, if you aren't feeling it with Grayson, then maybe you shouldn't be going out with him."

"I hear you, Nina. You never answered me. How do you know that she's his new client? Also, I would prefer to discuss *your* love life," I deflect. The whole issue with Jameson is so frustrating. I haven't heard from him in several days, unless you count the schedule that his assistant emailed me—which, by the way, I don't.

"Stop looking over there. Let's order dinner. The way you're drinking, you're gonna need some sustenance to soak up the alcohol. Drunk Addie isn't to be trusted." She laughs. "To answer your question, Harrison told me when I spoke with him today." Now *her* eyes are glued to the bottom of her empty martini glass. Interesting.

"Does he fit into your love life? I watch you two, you know. The sexual tension radiates off you both. It's a weird dance. Why aren't you hitting that?"

"Oh, my God! Did you just grow a penis? I am not hitting anything, least of all, Harrison. That man is infuriating. I mean, if we're talking about physically hitting, then I'm on board. Otherwise, I will pass." Her face flushes. "Let's not talk about men anymore."

"Agreed. I'm going to hit the head. I'll be right back."

Nina laughs, "No more alcohol for you." I smirk and make my way to the restroom. After checking myself in the mirror and giving myself a much-needed pep talk, I open the door and run into a brick wall, a.k.a. Jameson.

"Hey, Addie. Enjoying your dinner with Nina?"

I sway a little, and he puts his strong hands on my shoulders to steady me.

"Yes, I am. What about you? Enjoying your time with your 'client'?" I use air quotes when I say, client.

"Yes. Chelsea is a new client. An artist on the rise. She's getting ready to do an international show." He says this as if he's trying to explain himself.

"How wonderful! Is she a sculptor?" I grit my teeth as I ask.

He smirks. "No, she's a painter. Why do you ask?" Our faces are inches from each other.

"Well, she's awfully handsy. I just thought maybe she was going to sculpt you."

He laughs. Like a full-on loud belly laugh. "Jealous, Addie?" He holds my eyes with a penetrating gaze.

"Nope. I have a date with Grayson tomorrow night, so I'm focused on that." He grimaces. I smirk. Boom! Drop the mic, bitches! I walk away, swaying a little to the right and then to the left. It was my best impression of a pinball machine. Miraculously, I make it back to the table without falling. Instead of feeling smug, I feel empty.

Jameson

I see her as she enters the restaurant. My stomach drops, thinking she might be here to meet Grayson, but I'm relieved to see Nina embrace her. I am waiting for my new client, Chelsea Morrow, who happens to come in while my eyes are still lingering on Addie. As Chelsea walks toward me, I notice how beautiful she is. She's tall and willowy with long, wavy brown hair. Her short mini dress shows off her toned legs. Totally my type, and yet she does nothing for me.

"Jameson, it is such an extreme pleasure meeting you. Thanks so much for taking me as a client. You came highly recommended." She exaggerates the word "extreme" while she touches my arm and begins to rub it. A little touchy-feely, which is something I dislike in people I've just met. I move my arm, hoping it'll send a subtle message. I'm wrong. She simply moves her hand in tandem.

"Nice to meet you, Chelsea. I got all of the information I need from your agent, so now we can just go over the schedule and how things will work on my end."

Her smile falters. "Well, we can get to that later. Let's get to know each other a little better." She purrs while continuing to rub my arm. I laugh. Not the laugh where you think something is funny, but the kind that says, "Um, no," and I remove her hand from my arm. I happen to look over and notice Addie watching me. Part of me wants to explain that this is only a client, but then there's the other part that reminds me that Addie is only supposed to be a client too. I nurse my scotch, periodically peeking at Addie over the rim of my glass. She looks beautiful in her dress. I notice that she's animated in whatever she's sharing with Nina. I also notice that she's taking some rather generous sips of her drink.

"Chelsea, I don't mix business with pleasure. If that's what you're looking for, then we have nothing further to discuss."

Her smile drops while she regroups.

"Of course, Jameson. I apologize. I didn't mean to overstep any boundaries. Let's get down to business."

I start explaining to Chelsea how we'll move forward with her publicity this week, but I can't stop myself from continually looking over at Addie. When she gets up to go to the restroom, I excuse myself. As we share our usual snarky banter, there are two reasons why I continue to engage. One, she is under my skin, and two, I'm crazy. I must've lost my mind. I just can't seem to help myself. It's like an addiction. However, talking to her was a mistake—the realization that she is moving on with that douche left me feeling angry. Yes, I'm aware of my jealousy. It's irrational and confusing. She deserves someone who will make her happy. That person is not me.

I go back to my seat at the bar, and Chelsea is staring at me like she is trying to figure me out.

"You're in love with her. That's a huge relief. I was beginning to think I lost my touch." She laughs.

"I'm not in love with her. She's a client. I was just confirming some interviews for next week," I state emphatically. Lies. All lies.

"You look at her like she's the only person in the room. Like she's your oxygen."

I stare at her. Hearing someone say it out loud somehow makes it real. It heightens my discomfort. It makes me realize that I am on a runaway train, and there's no way to stop it. I need to jump off. I need to disengage. Pushing her away is the only way for both of us to move on. She needs a man who doesn't carry the emotional baggage that I have. She needs someone like Grayson.

Addie

un fact. I am a lunatic.

This emotional rollercoaster ride is making me nauseous. Or quite possibly, it's the alcohol. Either way, I'm lying in bed, dreading my date with Grayson. Maybe I should make a spreadsheet of the pros and cons. I am kind of a visual person. The interaction with Jameson confused me even more. He's always either super cold or scorching hot. And when I say hot, I'm not even talking about his looks. Even though I was pissed last night, I still wanted to kiss his stupid face. Ugh! My tongue currently feels like a cotton field.

I slowly leave the comfort of my bed. The tiny hammers in my head make my eyes hurt, along with the ringing in my ears. Oh, wait, that's my phone. God, who the hell is calling me? I don't even look over to see the name.

"Hello?" I grimace at the echo I feel in my head.

"Addie? Why do you sound so weird?" It's Nina's voice. Jesus, why is she talking so loudly?

"Well, someone drank the equivalent of a truckload of alcohol. So now that someone is dying. I think I need to cancel my life. Can you take care of that for me?" I say it quietly. It hurts to talk.

"That would be Jameson's job. You all need to talk. This tango you're doing is ridiculous. He wants you. You want him. Just do the deed for the love of God." She sounds annoyed.

"No, thank you. I'm good. Going out with Grayson tonight." I say it with conviction as I try to convince myself that this date is a good idea.

"Yeah, well, do you think you can give Grayson your full attention when you're still stuck on Jameson? I mean, won't your hoo-ha be confused?"

"First of all, please stop referring to my hoo-ha. Sure, we're experiencing a hiatus, but everyone has adapted. I am not having sex with anyone. It's a date and nothing more."

"Hiatus? Honey, your hoo-ha has checked into a nursing home. They're getting ready to call hospice. The situation is dire." She's laughing and, well, she might have a point.

"Stop. You're making me laugh, and that makes those little hammers in my head beat faster. I need water and aspirin along with a very greasy meal."

"Okay. Call me after your date. Hopefully, your hoo-ha will get a little action before they take her off life support." She laughs.

We end our call, and I head toward the bathroom, where the promise of relief resides in the medicine cabinet. I swallow the aspirin and a full glass of water. My door buzzer rings. What now? I shuffle to the door. My feet have also rejected the premise of moving quickly.

"Yes?"

"Addie, it's your father." He sounds different.

"Owen isn't here." I hope that will be enough for him to simply leave.

"I'm not here to see Owen. I need to talk to you." Reluctantly, I buzz him up. This is not helping my hangover. Why is the universe conspiring against me?

When I open the door, I'm not prepared for the look of regret that he seems to be wearing. Maybe it's my imagination. I move to the side as he walks into my apartment. He smiles a little as he looks around, taking in my small abode, and then focusing on my shelves of books. He runs his hands over them.

"You always loved books. Sometimes you would disappear for hours. When I would find you, you looked so happy." His expression is sad. Regretful. I notice that his hands are shaking, and his eyes are sunken.

"Books make me happy. They're my escape." Escape from the dysfunction. Escape from the reality of a loveless family. Escape from self-doubt. And right now, I would love to escape.

"Addie, I'm so sorry. I'm sorry for leaving. I'm sorry for the way this whole situation has unfolded. It wasn't my intention." His eyes are watery.

"What is your intention? You abandoned us and left me to pick up the pieces. I was ten. Mom couldn't cope with Owen after you left, so it all fell on me. Me!" I realize that I'm yelling. I take a breath.

"I know. I regret everything. There are things you don't know. All I can say is that once you're aware of the facts, you might be able to understand why I did what I did." He walks to the door and turns to me. "I'm proud of you, Addie." And then he leaves, and I'm even more confused than ever. My life seems to be a series of unfortunate events with a cast of characters I wish would leave me the hell alone.

Jameson

The day after my exchange with Addie, I feel like shit. I know what I need to do. I need to relinquish my duties as her publicist. Maybe I'll talk to Harrison and see if he can take over for me. It isn't good for us to work together with so much tension. A little distance will be for the best. I am excellent at justifying and rationalizing my actions.

Then I think about her date with Grayson, and my fists clench, my jaw ticks, and my heart constricts. I don't know when it happened, but at some point, Addie wormed her way into my life. She needs a man who isn't plagued by the darkness of his past and who doesn't break out into a sweat just thinking about commitment. But even if I turn my duties over to Harrison, I still want to get to the bottom of the drama surrounding her father, Dorothy, and how the senator fits into all of this.

I head into the office, convinced that this is the right move—that taking a step back is the best choice for everyone involved. I knock on Harrison's door.

"Come in." I step into his ultra-modern space with its floor to ceiling windows. Enlarged photos of the company's clientele decorate the walls. Clean lines and no clutter. Harrison has a bit of OCD, and his idea of design is that less is better. If he were a client, I'd have to publicize him as minimalist. Whatever.

"Well, well, well. What do we have here? I don't believe we've met. You've been avoiding me." His eyes twinkle with mischief.

"It isn't avoidance. It's called being busy. Addie's schedule has been insane, never mind my other clients. Oh, by the way, I met with Chelsea last night. She's all set to get started making the rounds. She has her schedule."

"Will you be paying her the same close attention as you do, Addie?" He smiles and wiggles his eyebrows.

"About Addie, I need you to take over her account. I think it would be best for everyone. Our interactions are becoming uncomfortable, and I feel like a little distance would be helpful." I can't even look him in the eye.

"Does this have anything to do with the little exchange you had with her last night?"

"Fucking Nina! Jesus, does she tell you everything? Is she the town crier?" I notice some defensiveness cross his face. There's something between him and Nina. Hmm…interesting.

"No, not everything, but she did seem to think that you two need to just go for it. However, I'll take over her account—for now. How about we table this discussion and have drinks tonight? You can tell me all about how you don't want to date Addie." He laughs, and I shake my head. "Even with the distance, I don't think it's going to help shake her presence." He speaks the truth, but at this point, I have no choice. I need to keep this professional.

"I'm meeting with Grady tomorrow." I'll fill him in on the latest information I have. "Hopefully, I'll find out what the hell is going on with Addie's father, the senator, and her cousin-in-law, Dorothy. It's the least I can do."

"So, you don't want to represent her, but you want to get to the bottom of her family drama. It sounds like someone has a heart," he says. I cross my arms over my chest.

"I just want to make sure that Addie and Owen are safe." I avoid eye contact with him because the truth is that they are both important to me. Imagining a life without them makes the emptiness I feel even darker.

"Come on. I'm done here, and I think you could use that drink. Have you told Addie about not being her publicist anymore?"

"No, I haven't. Her New York book launch party is tomorrow night. Can you handle that?"

"Of course. She deserves to hear about the change in representation from you, though. I hope you know what you're doing." There's a look of concern in his eyes.

I stay silent because truth be told, I have no fucking idea what I'm doing.

Addie

As I prepare for my date with Grayson, my stomach churns. He's a nice guy, but my truth lies in the reality that he doesn't stir me. My lady bits whisper "meh" when I'm around him, except when he kisses me, and I picture Jameson. Jameson sends them into a ticker-tape parade complete with those large balloons that take a whole group of people to wrangle. I love those balloons. Do you understand the chaos in my mind? Damn Jameson. He ruins everything.

I shift my mind to picking out an outfit. Fortunately, George has arranged my closet so that the selection process is easy. I decide on some fitted jeans that form to my curves with a frilly fuchsia blouse. One of the biggest blessings to come from this journey has been George. Not only did I gain a friend, but he has helped me obliterate how I view my body. I feel sexy and confident.

I meet Grayson at Gino's Restaurant & Pizzeria. A quick cab ride and I arrive. The hostess leads me to a cozy table in the back, where Grayson is sipping wine. He grins at me as he rises from his seat to pull out my chair. Always the gentleman. We make small talk, and the waitress brings me a glass of the house wine. I need a little liquid courage to tell him that as nice as he is, this isn't ever going to be anything but a friendship. Have you ever been with someone and you aren't present? Well, I'm having that experience now. I'm physically here, but emotionally, I'm absent.

"Alright, Addie. Spill." Grayson leans back in his chair as he observes me carefully.

"Spill what?" I scan the room, avoiding his eyes.

"I like you, and I want to spend time with you, but I feel like we aren't on the same page."

I meet his eyes. And this, my friends, is when I give the "it's not you, it's me" speech. The irony is that my whole life, in every relationship I've ever had, whether it was boyfriends or family, this was the speech that I always received—always feeling like I was never enough. Now, in a twist of fate, I'm saying those words to someone else.

"Oh, Grayson. I'm so sorry." I close my eyes and exhale.

"It's your publicist, isn't it? He's the one who's taking up all that space in your mind. Do you think I didn't notice how often you looked at him while we were at the hotel bar in L.A.? I was just hoping that the more time we spent together, the less you would think about him." Jesus, is he a mind reader?

I sigh.

"Yes. It isn't like anything will ever happen between us, but I can't help how I feel, and that isn't fair to you. You deserve someone who is a hundred percent invested, and that isn't me." As the words spill out, there's a sense of relief about being completely honest with someone instead of stuffing my feelings deep inside and allowing them to fester. I put on my big girl panties, and it feels pretty good.

He frowns at me. "Addie, I just don't get it. Why would you even waste time on a guy who isn't going to take things to the next level? I mean, seriously, I could have any girl I want. Right now, I could walk over to the bar and pick up that blond. She would be totally into me. But I'm sitting here with you, ready to move forward with you regardless. Jesus, I thought you would be different."

"Ummm…different? Why is that? Is it because of my looks? Because I'm not a size two like the cheerleaders from high school?" My insecurities are bubbling up and spewing out all over this conversation.

"Well, yes and no. No, because you were always such a bright light. I remember in high school how kind you were to everyone even if they were assholes to you. And yes, because I thought there wouldn't be any competition for your attention. Plus, I kind of have a thing for chubby chicks. Kind of a win-win." He winks.

"Wow, okay. I don't even know how to respond to that. I think I'm just going to go. I don't want to stop you from snagging someone more your speed." I chug my drink because I'm classy like that, stand up, flip him off, and strut out of the restaurant."

As my feet hit the sidewalk, I exhale. Tears prick my eyes. I flag down a cab and head home. My mother's tapes play in my head.

"Mom, I got invited to prom. Can we go shopping for a dress?"

Her eyes narrow. "Who in the world would ask you to prom?" Her tone drips with disgust.

"Milton Simpson. He's in my chemistry class." My enthusiasm has already dwindled. I don't know what I expected. My unrealistic expectations always get me hurt.

"I suppose we can go shopping, but it will have to be a plus-size store, and we'll go to the boutique in the next county. I don't want my friends to see me."

"Oh, well, that's okay. I can just go myself," I whisper.

"Take my card, and don't forget to buy a girdle or something that will hide all that fat." She hands me the card and walks out of the room. I stand there with tears streaming down my face.

Dismissed. My life has been a series of dismissals. But now I have the opportunity to create something with all of this discomfort. I have choices. I can take on the role as a victim, or I can take my place as a victor. My book was the first step. I wipe my tears, take a breath, and resolve that I will never allow anyone else's words to define me again.

Jameson

I'm meeting Grady at a nearby coffee shop, and I'm a little nervous about what's he going to tell me. I locate him settled in the corner. He waves me over, and I sit down across from him. He slides a thick manila envelope toward me. I hesitate.

"It's all there. There are photos of the various meetings between Dorothy and the senator, as well as Addie's father. Dorothy is the puppet master. There are also bank transactions that indicate Dorothy is making a hefty profit. You'll also see that she's giving a percentage to Addie's father. The only thing I don't know is why. I still have a tail on all three of them. Richard paid Addie a visit yesterday."

My skin prickles. My jaw tightens. "How long was he there?"

"Not long. Maybe fifteen minutes. Also, I still have a security detail on Addie. She took a cab and met Grayson. They went to a nearby Italian restaurant. She wasn't there long—didn't even make it to half an hour before she ran outside and grabbed a cab. Alone. And she was crying." He smirks at me.

I'm not going to lie. The fact that she didn't leave with him gives me a little thrill. Not even half an hour? What happened that she would leave so soon after getting there? What did he do to her that made her cry? My fists clench.

"Keep me posted."

He nods and leaves. I open the envelope and scan the photos. The desperation in both men's eyes is palpable. There is a secret tying these two men together, and Dorothy knows it.

I head back to my apartment. Several times my fingers hover above my phone, ready to call Addie, but each time, I shove my phone in my pocket. Tonight is the book launch. Dorothy is on the guest list, along with Addie's father. They were invited to avoid them crashing the party. Should be an interesting gathering. My phone pings. I look down and laugh. It's Owen.

Owen: Wingman tonight? Hot chicks!

His excitement radiates through the phone. God, I love this guy.

Me: Wingman it is.

I press send and close my eyes. I know I said I wasn't going, but I can't say no to Owen. And while Addie might not belong to me, I can protect her and Owen from whatever circus Dorothy brought to town.

Addie

George is coming over to "fluff" me. His words, not mine. And no, he isn't referring to the porn term, "fluffer." Get your mind out of the gutter. Anyway, I am a writer, not a pillow, but apparently, there's an appearance I must uphold, especially at this book launch. Cocktail attire. God, what I would give to just stay home with a good book and a jug of wine, some chocolate, and a hot threesome with Ben & Jerry. Maybe after things calm down, I can go back to my comfy life, and people won't be so interested in what I'm wearing.

The buzzer rings and Owen practically knocks me over to get to it. The chances are that he's eager to see if the girls coming with George to do my makeup and hair are "hot." Whatever. He's already decked out in a charcoal suit, crisp white button-down, and a blue tie. He looks sharp since George helped him out as well. George told me that Owen was a dream client.

Owen opens the door, and George walks in along with the hair and makeup girls. "How you doin'," Owen asks, wiggling his eyebrows and doing his best Joey Tribbiani imitation. They grin at him. He offers his arms to escort them to the bedroom so they can get set up where I will be "fluffed."

"Excited?" George scans my ratty robe, and a small "tsk" escapes his lips.

I roll my eyes. "No, not really."

"He hasn't called, has he?" George knows that Jameson has ghosted me. Poor guy has been my sounding board for man troubles all week between Jameson's behavior and the disaster date with Grayson. My picker is clearly off, and my abandonment issues are glaringly obvious. Thanks, Mom and Dad!

"Nope. Not a peep. Harrison sent me the itinerary. I suppose I will see Jameson tonight. I mean, he wouldn't skip this, would he? I need chocolate. The limo is picking us up at seven."

"Oh, honey, of course, he will be there. Let's get to work. You are going to knock him out with the dress I brought." He's practically giddy. I pop a chocolate, hoping I can relax.

An hour later, I emerge. My short hair is styled with soft wisps framing my face while the fitted fire-engine-red dress makes a dramatic statement with its exposed back. It makes me feel sexy, and that, my friends, is a huge accomplishment. George stands back, giving himself a standing ovation.

"Damn, girl! I am a genius." I worry about his lack of confidence.

"Don't hurt yourself patting yourself on the back," I smirk.

"Ha! I'll find myself a good man to do that for me…along with some other things." He laughs and winks at me.

"Please, no sex talk. I'm nervous enough about seeing Jameson. Sex just makes it worse." I head toward the living room, where Owen is waiting for me.

"'Bout time. Geez, girls take forever to get ready." At least some things never change.

"Alright, Romeo. Let's go. By the way, you look handsome." I grin at him.

"You look pretty, too. Now let's go. I'm hungry, and Jameson said he would be my wingman." He laughs. George nudges me in a silent I-told-you-so.

"When did you talk to him?" I try to act unaffected.

"Today. I texted him." Color me confused.

"And he responded?" I inquire.

"Yeah. Why wouldn't he? He's my friend." He looks at me like I'm a complete dumb-ass.

"Oh, well, okay. The limo is here, so let's get going." At least Owen isn't getting ghosted, and for that I am grateful. Owen has had way too much disappointment recently.

I hug George and thank the girls for their magical powers, then head to the limo. The driver opens the door for us. I try to remember to breathe, but the man in the limo is not Jameson. It's Harrison. Disappointment sends my heart plummeting. Harrison is great, but I have become dependent on his counterpart; he grounds me. I turn to Harrison and smile.

"You look beautiful," he says almost apologetically. He's trying to make me feel better. I get it, but my stomach is in knots, and I want to vomit.

"Thank you. I'm glad Owen is my date. So, um, where is Jameson? I thought he would be riding with us." I glance at my brother, who's busy appreciating his reflection in the window. Typical. A lack of self-confidence has never *been his* problem. Harrison looks at me with a great deal of compassion.

"He's meeting us there. There was another client that he needed to attend to."

"Oh, okay. Good to know," I whisper.

I turn my head to look out the window. I can cry when I get home. Tonight is about me. I just need to remember to breathe.

Addie

My book launch is being held at the Waldorf Astoria. I know, swanky for a girl who would rather eat chocolate and wear yoga pants. Sometimes I can't believe this is my life. Writing this book was a personal journey for me. It was a way to finally do something that wasn't centered around anyone else. I look over at Owen. He's grinning from ear to ear. He is my world, and I won't allow my father or anyone else to destroy that.

We pull up to the hotel. "Are you ready for this?" He smiles at me, and I nod. "Stay calm and mingle. You know how it works; you're used to this by now." Harrison's confidence is misplaced; I'm just as uncomfortable and uncertain as I was at the L.A. launch party. Jameson would have known that.

"Hurry up, Addie! Hot chicks are waiting for me." Owen bounces in his seat.

We get out of the car, and I take Owen's arm on our walk up the stairs. As we enter the ballroom, Owen quickly disengages. "No cramping my style tonight, Addie." Owen narrows his eyes at me.

I put up my hands in surrender. "I won't do anything to cramp your style, but please stay with Walter." Yes, we still have security, although Walter has become more of a friend, making Owen extremely happy.

"I'm not a baby. I'm a man." Cue my exaggerated sigh. This is our dialogue. Every. Single. Day.

"Yes, you are, but I need support tonight, so just stay close by, okay?" I ask, trying to stay patient despite my increasing stress.

"You're the star. You don't need me, Addie." He smiles, and with that statement—honest from his perspective, but untrue from mine— he strolls with Harrison and Walter to the bar. I suppose the pretty little bartender attracted him.

I see Nina approach. Thank God! Every guy in the room is fixated on her. Her beauty is effortless. She is dressed in a long, silk, golden dress in a mermaid cut, her back is completely exposed; her jet-black hair is gathered in a loose bun at the nape of her neck. Harrison looks like he might have a stroke. Interesting. I still don't know what the deal is with those two, but I am fascinated by their dance. She holds two cocktails, and she hands one to me.

"You are the best person on the planet." I close my eyes as I take a long drink.

"Only because I brought you a cocktail… but I do have an ulterior motive." She smirks.

"What's happening now? Can I just have one event that isn't marred by the shitshow that is currently my life?" At this point, I'm simply begging for a reprieve.

"Addie, your life is amazing. You're just surrounded by interesting individuals that may or may not need psychiatric help. Anyway, it isn't anything bad. The publisher wants to meet with you regarding another book." She takes a sip of her martini, waiting for my reaction. Another book? Ugh. Okay, I know this is supposed to be wonderful news, but I have so many moving pieces in my life, I can't even begin to think about another project. But maybe what I need is a distraction.

"Can I have a few weeks before I start? My life resembles the inside of a mental ward. I need some time to decompress." I would give anything to have some creative mojo. An escape sounds lovely. My laptop called and asked if it still has a job. Seriously, I haven't written in what feels like an eternity, but I don't even know if I can focus with this much stress pressing down on me.

"Absolutely. By the way, you look stunning. How was the limo ride?"

"If you're referring to the limo ride where Harrison was standing in for Jameson, it was uneventful." I feel my eyes starting to fill with tears, but I refuse to give them any attention. Instead, I take a large drink from my wine, hoping that the alcohol will relax me.

"Harrison's here?" Her eyes dart around the room. She finally finds Harrison, and a slight smile tugs on my face. His eyes bore into hers. This is fascinating. Jesus, is it hot in here?

"What exactly is the deal with you and him? Inquiring minds want to know." I am so grateful that the subject has moved on to something else.

"Nothing to tell. We were together once a very long time ago. That ship has sailed." Sadness shadows her face.

"I don't know. When he saw you, he looked like he was about to have a stroke." I smile at her, and she glares back.

"Okay, since neither one of us wants to talk about two particular men, let's simply enjoy the evening celebrating the amazing you." We turn and walk to the bar to refresh our drinks—and I see him. Jameson is here, and his eyes are focused on me.

Jameson

I spend all day reading through the information Grady gave me again and again. My eyes sting. My backaches. I had asked Harrison to take my place tonight. It has been seven days since I've seen or contacted Addie. Yes, I'm an asshole. Yes, I might be considered a coward, too. But finding out the answer to this mystery surrounding Addie's father may help me make some sort of amends for my actions.

Just when I think it's a lost cause, the pieces start coming together. It was hard to see before because it appears as though there's a fourth party involved—Addie's deceased mother. And holy shit, this information is going to blow Addie's mind. I need to get to her before the other players in this game do. I shut down my computer, throw on my tux, and text my driver.

I arrive in record time, which is amazing since it's New York, and the traffic usually sucks. Maybe the universe is smiling on me. I enter the ballroom and notice Addie immediately. She looks stunning and relaxed as she chats with Nina. I don't move. I simply watch her, knowing that she has infiltrated my emotional barriers. With her quirky, sarcastic, sassy presence, she is the someone that made me feel again.

Just as I am about to move toward her, our eyes meet. But as I approach, her father appears, and from the look on his face, he might be about to spill what I have just uncovered. Shit is about to hit the fan.

Dorothy

I survey the room. It's elegant and full of important and influential people. Everyone is in place, and it's almost showtime. Honestly, I am so pleased with how everything has fallen into place. It was almost effortless. Hopefully, Richard will keep his mouth shut. He's been extra twitchy. Maybe it's the drugs. I have noticed that he almost seems remorseful, which isn't the ingredient needed for tonight's big reveal.

Matthew comes back from the bar and hands me a drink. I sip as I watch the chess game that I orchestrated.

"You'd better have a way we can we afford this new tux and your designer dress. Addie isn't helping us anymore, and I have better things to do than apply for jobs."

"Oh, darling. Don't worry about it. I have everything covered. My psychic business is taking off, and, well, I have other endeavors. Watch and learn." I start to walk over to where Addie is standing with Nina. Matthew reluctantly trails behind. I have left him out of this little plan of mine because he is weak and pathetic. He might have run to Addie if he knew what I was doing, especially if he thought he could get a handout for it. I kept him in the dark for his own good; we'll get a lot more money this way. Intentionally hurting Addie isn't something

Matthew would want to do, but that's because he doesn't understand how these kinds of deals work.

The moment we reach her, Richard begins to spill his guts, and her publicist rushes in like some sort of white knight as Addie's life is about to implode. This was not how it was supposed to go.

Addie

Why does that man have to look so hot? Why can't he have an ugly day? Jesus. Then I remember that I'm mad, but the rest of my body hasn't gotten the memo, and there is a lot of celebrating with high fives. Traitors.

As he moves toward me, I hold my breath. Our eyes lock, and everyone else ceases to exist. And then my father appears. What the fuck have I done to the universe? Can I have one celebration where the circus shows up late?

"Addie, I need to talk to you," says the man who has helped fund my therapist's European vacations. He looks sad, scared, and almost regretful. Sweat glistens on his colorless face. His hands are shaking, and his breathing is labored.

"Can't this wait?" I'm hoping he at least agrees to give me until tomorrow, but I hadn't had any interaction with him yet when he didn't step over the boundaries that I tried to establish.

"No, it can't." His eyes dart around the room, and then I see Dorothy approaching. Well, this can't be good. I'm sure you're wondering why she was invited. Well, apparently, one of my two publicists seemed to think that inviting them would *prevent* the shitshow. Seems like that decision will probably bite me in the ass. Matthew is slinking behind Dorothy, looking as if he would rather be somewhere else. Nina presents me with another cocktail. I love Nina.

I can't help but marvel at Dorothy's appearance. It looks like she just walked out of a fashion magazine. Her perfectly coiffed hair, manicured nails, and Michael Kors evening gown make me shake my head in disbelief. How in the hell can she afford to look like that? I mean, I hate to be petty, but I think it might be difficult to shoplift a designer dress… maybe she has improved her stealth skills. Whatever. I need to focus on the current episode of "How Can We Fuck Up Addie's Life. In this episode, daddy dearest is either about to spill his guts or vomit.

"Addie! Oh my God, you look, well, so much better. It is so odd to see you in actual clothes that don't have food on them." She turns her attention to Richard. "Is this a family reunion? You must be Addie's father. I'm Dorothy. I'm married to your nephew, Matthew." She offers her hand while throwing him all kinds of looks that I don't understand, but my father doesn't respond. Instead, he stays focused on me, tears in his eyes.

"I'm sorry, Addie. If I'd done the right thing from the beginning, none of this would have happened." I feel a hand grab mine, and without even looking, I know it's Jameson.

"Richard, don't do this. You will ruin everything!" Dorothy spits. Her eyes narrow, and her face oozes rage. Matthew's eyes dart around the room. People's conversations screech to a halt as they unexpectedly find themselves with front-row seats to the show. I hope everyone has a drink. Shit seems to be getting real.

"Wait, you all know each other? Can someone tell me what the fuck is going on?" I realize that I'm yelling and drawing even more attention to myself, but at this point, I don't give a shit. Cameras are flashing. People are holding up their phones, recording the scene. It is the least of my worries at this point.

"Addie, I'm not your father, and I'm not Owen's either." He spits the words as if they were choking him. My mind spins like a roulette wheel as I try to comprehend them. A voice jolts me back into reality.

"Who is my dad?" The voice belongs to Owen. "I just got you back, and now…"

"I'm sorry, Owen. I'm not your father."

Before I can reach for him, Owen turns and runs out of the room. Jameson is hot on his heels. People are yelling. Dorothy looks like she's going to explode. Richard collapses right in front of me. I hear someone scream, "Call 911!" Chaos ensues, and I stand stunned for a moment, my brain unable to comprehend what just happened.

Coming to my senses, I race out of the room in a desperate attempt to find Owen, leaving Dorothy and Richard behind. The elevators are too slow, so I dash down the steps, almost falling on my ass in my insanely high heels. Making it to the entrance, I see Jameson try to grab Owen, but Owen is too fast. I hear tires screech and metal crunching as Owen darts into the intersection. A car rams into him, despite its brakes, squealing to stop, and his body flies back, landing in the street. He doesn't move.

Have you ever had an out of body experience? Apparently, I am having one. I feel like I'm watching a movie. Everything is moving slowly. People are gathering to help. Sirens are blaring. Jameson is doing CPR. Someone is holding me. Faces run together.

People talk about how, when you are about to die, there is a running reel of your life. While I'm not physically dying, I'm having that experience emotionally. Owen as a baby. Owen's first steps. Owen's snarky comebacks. His laughter. His love. I can't lose him. He's all I have. He's everything. Why does everyone leave me? Why am I not enough?

I am guided into a limo. Voices continue to echo. I'm not sure if they're talking to me. Am I in shock? I shake uncontrollably. A blanket is wrapped around me, but it doesn't take away the chill. I hear someone ask, "Is he alive?" I realize that the voice belongs to me.

Nina envelops me in a hug while Harrison holds my hand. She looks at me. Tears run down her face. "Yes, he's alive."

I nod, and then I crumble.

Addie

My body quakes. Loud sobs fill the car. Time passes without my knowledge, and suddenly I'm being guided into the hospital. The smell of antiseptic and death permeates the air. I hear a voice—I think it might be Harrison—barking at the nurse outside of the emergency room.

I'm not sure how much time passes. Someone offers me coffee. I don't answer. I'm lost in my own thoughts, thinking about my life without Owen. Thinking about how this book has changed the course of my own life, and not in a good way. Thinking about how this book has now changed Owen's life irrevocably. I hear someone saying my name over and over. I look up and meet the eyes of a man who I assume to be the doctor.

"Is he alive?" I ask, terrified to hear the answer.

"He is, but we are taking him to surgery. He has some internal injuries, as well as a broken leg. Someone will let you know once he's in recovery. I won't sugarcoat this, Ms. Snyder. He's in critical condition. I hate to add more bad news, but your father had a heart attack. He is currently in the ICU. There is a cardiologist assigned to his case who will be out to speak with you soon. If you want to see him, I can get one of the nurses to take you." He waits for me to answer. Nina speaks up, indicating that it won't be necessary. He turns to leave.

"Thank you." Always polite. I didn't feel the need to explain that Richard isn't my father. At this point, I have no idea what is going on, but I do know that I need to get my shit together if I'm going to be there to support Owen.

"Nina, can you go and get me a change of clothes and Owen's blanket? He's going to want that when he wakes up." She meets my eyes and squeezes my hand.

"Of course, Addie. Whatever you need. We're here for you." Out of the corner of my eye, I see a figure approaching. It's Jameson.

I go to him as if it's the most natural thing in the world, and he wraps me in his embrace, whispering, "I'm so sorry," while he strokes my back. I draw back from him to look at his face. His clothes are covered in dried blood. His eyes are wet with tears. He looks as lost as I do.

Reluctantly, he releases me and goes over to Harrison. They glance at me periodically as they exchange words. I only hear bits and pieces of the conversation, but it's enough for me to realize that Jameson is keeping something from me. But what could it be?

Addie

Hours pass. Shifts change. At some point, I fall asleep on a chair in the waiting room. Someone is shaking me by the shoulder, and I slowly open my eyes and adjust to the harsh lights. Nina is holding my hand.

"Ms. Snyder, Owen, is out of surgery. We removed his spleen. He had a small brain bleed that we fixed, and we had to put pins in his leg. The next twenty-four hours are critical. We have put him in a medically induced coma to help him heal. I will have a nurse come and get you once we get him settled in the ICU. He'll be in the room next to your father's. We thought it would make it easier for you to be with both of them." Gee, that's swell. I don't want to see the man who has been masquerading as my father. My questions about the man who I thought was our father would have to wait. Owen is my main concern.

"Thank you," I whisper. I hear a collective sigh of relief, as if we were all holding our breath.

"I need to get some air." I rise from my seat and walk toward the doors.

"Want some company?" Jameson's voice is cautious.

"Um, sure. That's fine." We walk to the doors. Cool air greets me, reminding me that fall is on the horizon. I find a bench a few feet from the entrance and sit down. Jameson settles next to me. Our thighs touch. My hand itches to link with his.

"Addie, I'm so sorry about this whole situation." He rubs his face and turns to look at me.

"Why? You didn't create this mess. Right now, my focus is Owen, and the rest of the answers to this episode of *The Maury Povich Show* regarding who my daddy is will have to wait."

A slight smile crosses his face. "I know I didn't create it, but I could have helped you avoid being blindsided. Addie, I found out about Richard right before your party. I have had my buddy, Grady, investigating him. I had an inkling that there was something amiss. When I received confirmation, I tried to get to you. I was on my way to tell you. He just beat me to it."

"Are you fucking kidding me? If you had an inkling, don't you think you could have given me a little clue? I feel like you've kept me in the dark this whole time, only giving me tidbits of information just to pacify me. You might have felt like you were protecting me, but you weren't. Jameson, you disappeared. No phone calls. No responses to text or emails. You fucking ghosted me. I felt abandoned, and honestly, all of this could have been avoided if you would have just clued me in on the information you had, even if you didn't have everything figured out. We could have worked on this together, but you shut me out. Oh, my God! Owen wouldn't be in the ICU if you'd just kept me in the loop."

I realize that I've been screaming and that people coming and going out of the hospital are gawking. He reaches out to touch my hand, but I flinch.

"Just go, Jameson. You aren't wanted here." I stand up and move toward the door.

"Addie, please. I know I screwed up. I know I should have told you what I knew, but honestly, I felt like I was doing the right thing for you and Owen. If I could go back, I would do things differently. Please let me help you and Owen. Please." I've never seen him so vulnerable, and if I wasn't so pissed, it might have meant something. But at this moment, I am numb. My brother could have been killed because of him and the secrets he promised he wouldn't keep.

"Goodbye, Jameson." I walk through the doors and don't look back.

Dorothy

I sit in a dark corner of the hospital waiting room. I am incognito, decked out in a trench coat, a hat, and my Kate Spade sunglasses, because there is no excuse for my fashion not to be on point, even while spying. I watch the scene unfold. The doctors are updating Addie on her brother and Richard. Her distraught state. Ugh. All of these people fawning over her as if she's important.

And just when I'm getting bored, Jameson and Addie walk outside. I follow at a respectable distance and head over to the smoking area that provides the ideal spot to overhear their conversation. Well, their voices are raised, so actually, anywhere would have been perfect. I can't help feeling almost giddy over the exchange. I have a front-row seat to their relationship dissolving. This couldn't work out any better. Addie deserves nothing but misery. She has stolen everything from me... especially the funds Matthew should have inherited. And it should be *me* who has the bestselling book. It should be *me* who is wildly successful. I dress for it; I have the personality for it—that special something that makes a star. Not her. Never her.

Jameson watches her walk back into the hospital, and after the door closes behind her, he flags a cab. I realize my opportunity has risen. He doesn't have the final piece of the puzzle. His little minion, that useless PI who's been attempting to follow me and gain information, has fallen short. Jameson needs me. And his need will give me my freedom. I can get the money that will buy me a new life away from all of this. Away from Matthew, who is no more than a weak link—I'm sick of his inadequacy. Away from Addie and her annoying fanbase. This is my moment, and I am going to seize it.

Jameson

I watch Addie retreat. The feeling of failure is palpable and just another reminder of how I let down the people I care about—my brothers-in-arms, my mother, and now Addie. I run my hands through my hair. She just needs time, I tell myself. The best thing I can do for her is to wrap up the loose ends surrounding Dorothy and Richard… or maybe I should just leave it. She has already endured so much pain. I am in a quandary.

I flag a taxi and head home. My mind wanders to the first time I met Owen. His snarky, cheeky attitude about not letting me in their apartment without the password. Watching him capture the hearts of everyone he meets. I had never met anyone with Down syndrome before, and I'll be honest, I had some preconceived notions, but he shattered my assumptions. He has quickly become my best friend. *"You'll always be my wingman, right?"* Tears prick my eyes.

As I sit in the backseat of the cab, the driver peeks at me in the rearview mirror. I realize that I am mumbling to myself. Reasoning out the chaos that has infiltrated my brain. I shake my head in an effort to clear it. He stops in front of my building as I toss him some bills, my phone rings. Hopeful that it's Addie, I whip my phone out of my pocket, but it's an unknown number.

"This is Jameson."

"Well, well, well. I understand that Addie has dismissed you. It seems that you might need some information that will get you back into her good graces."

Ugh. It must be Dorothy. I need to play along because I know she has the missing piece of the puzzle.

"Dorothy, what do you want?" I growl.

"I give you information, you give me money," she purrs.

"So, you are essentially bribing me."

"I would call it a mutually beneficial business transaction. You get back into Addie's good graces, and I get some financial gain in order to create a new life somewhere else."

"How much?"

"One million should do nicely. Cash, of course." Her smug tone seeps through the phone.

"It will take me a while to get that type of money."

"I will give you twenty-four hours—I'm not unreasonable. You're a smart guy, so don't do anything stupid. I am watching you. If you slip, I'll simply go to the media with my information. There are plenty of those gossip rags willing to pay good money for what I know."

"There's no way I can get that kind of money in twenty-four hours. I need more time."

"You see, that isn't my problem. I'll be in touch." And with that, she disconnects. I grin to myself as I stop the voice recorder on my phone. Gotcha, Dorothy.

Jameson

True to form, Dorothy calls within twenty-four hours demanding a meeting at a seedy bar located in Harlem. I enlist the help of two FBI agents who served with me. Todd Thomas and Gil Thorpe took my recording along with the information that I had received from Grady to build an extortion case against Dorothy. They supplied me with a wire along with a canvas bag full of marked bills.

I enter the bar, my eyes adjusting from the sunlight to the dank, dark décor. Dorothy is tucked away in the corner. I make my way toward her while staying vigilant of my surroundings. I don't trust her not to throw a little surprise into our meeting.

"Hey, Jameson. Sit down. Let's have a drink." She gazes at me as she taps her fake fingernails on the table.

"No, thanks, Dorothy. Let's get this transaction over with so that we can all move on with our lives."

"You said *we*. So cute. What exactly do you see in Addie? I mean, she is so plain. She's chubby, and then there is that disabled brother." She shudders as if Owen is some sort of sickening illness.

"Addie and Owen are two of the most amazing people on the planet. You aren't good enough to utter their names," I say through gritted teeth. My fists are clenched. I don't believe in hitting women, but she challenges my restraint.

"I'm a writer, too. I mean, I was writing long before Addie. She copies everything I do. Always trying to one-up me. That book she wrote should have been mine. Her success and fame should be mine. She stole it from me. She's always stealing from me." Now she's ranting. Her eyes are bulging as she whisper-shouts.

I try to pacify her. "Oh, I had no idea you were a writer too. Well, now, with this money, you can make a new life and pursue your writing again."

"Yes, that is exactly what I am going to do. Just have some loose ends to tie up. Here is the information I told you I would provide in exchange for the money. You're going to be floored when you read it. It looks like Addie's mother was quite the conniving bitch. The apple doesn't fall far from the tree. Addie has always been in it for herself."

She slides the manila envelope toward me. Her words, "Just have some loose ends to tie up," concern me, but I have it all covered. She is easily falling into the trap that I've set for her.

"Anyway, it doesn't matter. Her life is destroyed. She has lost everything she has ever loved, and her career is ruined. My work is done." She giggles. Her delusion is disturbing.

I don't tell her that since the disaster at the hotel, Addie's book is holding at number one on every list known to man. She is a media darling. The public is rallying around her and Owen. She is loved, especially by me.

Holy shit.

I am in love with her. I love Addie Snyder—and the realization doesn't scare me.

"I guess you're anxious to get going. Here's the amount requested. Now don't contact Addie ever again." I hand her the bag containing a tracker I slipped into the side pocket. This meeting was never about arresting her now. No. The FBI wants to continue to observe her.

They don't think she will leave the country, but they're covering all the airports and bus terminals just in case. She is so obsessed with Addie that they believe her next move will be to contact her. Walter is still with her, and I have kept him abreast of what's happening. He has become a fixture anyway, as he and Owen really bonded. The FBI wants to bide their time as they continue to build a solid case.

"Aren't you adorable? So protective of your chubby buddy. Well, don't you worry. I'm going to start a new life, and I'll finally get everything I deserve. Fame. Money. Hot men. I'll get it all!" She has crazy eyes, and it is seriously disconcerting. It makes me want to pop a piece of chocolate to help me relax. Jesus, I miss Addie.

"Now, Jameson, we are going to walk out together. I have a car waiting. You won't try anything because I have several media outlets that would love to publish my story about Addie and her daddy issues. It doesn't paint her in a very good light. So we will simply part ways. Pleasure doing business with you. Give Addie my best. Tell her to lay off the chocolate."

We walk out, and she gets into the waiting car. As it pulls off, I give a thumbs up to the guys in the unmarked van. The driver is an FBI agent as well. She won't be going anywhere without their knowledge. Now we wait for her to make her next move.

Addie

It has been twenty-one days since I last saw Jameson. Not that I'm counting. My new home consists of the chair that resides next to Owen's bed. He hasn't woken up yet. He made it through the critical twenty-four hours, and his doctors remain hopeful. He is no longer in a medically induced coma, so now it's all up to him. He has always done the exact opposite of what I want, so it isn't a surprise that he's not awake yet. Richard, on the other hand, is at death's door. I haven't gone into his room, but the doctors have been keeping me apprised of his status. Oh, and would you like to hear the irony? I'm listed as his power-of-attorney, so I get to make the decision about whether to pull the plug or not. You can't make this shit up.

The door opens, and I look up. It's Nina.

"Hey, sweetie. How are things today?" She reaches for Owen's hand and sits down in the chair on the opposite side of his bed.

"No change. The doctor is still hopeful, though." I sigh.

"Well, that's good. He just needs time. Have you made a decision on Richard?" She knows my dilemma and has been amazingly supportive as I find my way through this situation.

"No. As soon as Owen wakes up, I will make that decision. I just can't right now." I close my eyes.

"Of course. I get that. How about I stay here with Owen, and you go home for a bit? Get a shower. Take a nap. There's a car waiting for you."

George breezes in looking like he just came off the runway just as I say, "Are you trying to tell me that I smell?" I raise an eyebrow.

"Well, yes. Honey, you haven't left in days, and the hospital smells better than you do." A small smile plays on her lips.

"Oh, dear." He tsks, shaking his head as he looks me up and down. Seriously? Doesn't having a family emergency give me an excuse to be less fashionable?

"You don't approve?" I tease. It's the first time I've felt the heaviness lifting, even if it is just for a moment.

"I. Can't. Even. Nina is right, and I'm going with you. You need a little George time and so does your wardrobe." He smirks. I roll my eyes but secretly need his sense of humor and friendship more than ever.

"Okay. I'll go, and I guess you can come, George. However, I'm only showering. I'm coming right back."

"Correction. You're showering, but I am styling your hair, and you will be wearing a cute pair of jeans with ones of those tops I will pick out for you. Trust me, you'll feel so much better with a little self-care. I *will* allow you to go without makeup, though. That is my only concession. I'm not totally unreasonable."

I sigh. He laughs.

"I know you don't want to hear this," Nina blurts, "but Jameson calls me every day to check on you and Owen. At some point, you need to sit down with him. He has the full story on Richard."

"I know, but not now. I need Owen to wake up first. Then I'll deal with the rest."

"Fair enough. Go, and I'll be here when you get back. Oh, and Walter is going with you two. You know, just in case crazy lady jumps out at you."

"Do you think Dorothy is going to emerge? It's been quiet for three weeks. That's the longest I've gone without hearing her annoying voice."

"I don't know, but it would make me feel better if Walter was with you."

"Did Jameson put you up to this?" My eyes narrow.

"He just wants you to be safe." She reaches for my hand. It's warm and comforting. "Go and take some time for yourself. Let George take care of you. Then come back. Owen would probably appreciate you more if you didn't look like you slept in a dumpster." George laughs as Nina squeezes my hand. I am too tired to argue.

"Okay, Nina. You win this round. Just call me if there are any changes."

"Of course, I will."

I rise from my chair, kiss Owen's forehead, and head to the door. I glance at the room to the right. As if I was on autopilot, I walk right in for the first time and observe the man in the bed. I have a hard time feeling compassion for him, yet there is a part of me that is overflowing with sadness. What kind of life can you live based on a lie? Oh wait, maybe I can relate to him since the whole foundation of what I believed about my life has crumbled. You're probably wondering why I'm not angry with my mother. Well, there's currently a "no vacancy" sign in the feelings department. I simply can't deal with any of it.

Of course, I'm curious about the mysterious man who impregnated my mother and what the backstory is. I also wonder if Owen and I have the same father. And then I think about my mother's last words: "I'm sorry." I had always dismissed them, as I thought it was simply a blanket statement. There are so many things that come to mind where an apology would be in order. The way she verbally assaulted me with her disapproval of everything I did—everything I was and wasn't. Her excessive drinking. Leaving me to raise Owen myself because of her lacking maternal instincts. Honestly, Owen wasn't a burden to me. He filled a void of love. He simply accepted me for me. He's the only person who allows me to believe I'm good enough, that I'm simply enough by being me. God, I love him so fiercely that it's physically painful.

George entertains me with stories about the twig-like models he has to deal with along with a potential love interest—or boy toy, as he refers to the guy in question. We enter my apartment. I strip off my clothes and get in the shower while George raids my closet for something appropriate to wear. I am going to the hospital, not a party, but whatever makes him happy. Feeling a little more human, I wrap myself in a towel and head into my bedroom.

"Feeling better, princess?" He smiles softly at me.

"Yes, I guess I needed that shower." I shrug.

He narrows his eyes. "Honey, I didn't even need to know the room number; I just followed my nose. Okay, here are some options. I think this floral top would cheer you up; otherwise, here is the pink one that you seem to not complain about when I suggest it." He snickers.

"Why can't I just wear my yoga pants and T-shirt? Those bring me comfort, and after all, I am going through a hard time." I pout. Giving my best "poor me" look.

"Look. Crisis doesn't mean compromising fashion. Did you see Jackie Kennedy looking like she just rolled out of bed following the death of her husband? The answer is no, and I am not letting you walk out of here looking any less than fabulous. It will lift your spirit. Trust me."

I let him fuss over me while trying not to admit that I do feel better in my colorful top and fashionable jeans.

"Thank you, George. You have no idea how much your friendship means to me."

He gives me a bright smile and says, "Baby girl, you are a light in my life. You and Owen have become part of my family, and I will do anything for you. Besides, I'm waiting for that broody hottie to claim you."

"Well, I don't think that's in the cards. I have a lot that I'm juggling."

I gather some things that Owen might want when he wakes up. I say *when,* because there is no other alternative.

As we head out to the waiting car, I'm accosted by the sight of Jameson as he heads toward me. As he approaches, I notice the dark circles under his eyes, his wrinkled clothes, and the sadness that hollows out his face. He looks as bad as I feel. Oh crap, who am I kidding? He still looks hot. Shit.

"Jameson, what are you doing here?' My tone is harsher than I expect it to be. He flinches.

"I know you don't want to see me, but we need to have a conversation. Nina told me you came home, so I thought I would try to catch you before you head back to the hospital." Jesus. Nina seems to be the town crier. Please, Addie. You need to know everything." His eyes plead with me. George nudges me forward. Even Walter smirks. Traitors.

"I'll meet you back at the hospital. Take your time. I'll troll the halls for hot doctors." George wiggles his eyebrows before getting into a cab. I shake my head, trying not to smile.

Walter nods at Jameson as if they have some silent language, and he gets into the car with George. It was like Walter just handed me off to Jameson. Whatever. At this point, I am too tired to argue.

I close my eyes and exhale. All the fight has left my body. Exhaustion has made me vulnerable, but he's right. I need to know. "Alright. Let's go to the diner around the corner. Let me call Nina. I want to check on Owen." Do I want to go to the diner? No. Well, yes, but only because I'm starving since food has not been at the front of my mind. Honestly, I don't want to know the sordid details that resemble something from a Spanish soap opera, but I also know that I need the details in order to move forward.

I step away to make my call. It rings, and she answers, "I know you're mad, but this shit needs to be dealt with, and avoiding it won't help you."

"You don't understand. I can only deal with one thing at a time. Right now, Owen is my priority."

"Stop using Owen as a distraction. He is healing in his own way. Deal with this before he wakes up. He will have questions, Addie. Wouldn't it be nice to have the answers?"

I close my eyes and sigh. Ever the voice of reason. I'm grateful I have her to guide me when my vision is so clouded.

"I hate it when you're reasonable. Call me if there are any changes."

"Of course, I will. Love you, Addie."

"Love you, too." I disconnect the call. I guess I have no choice but to face my new reality.

We head to the diner in uncomfortable silence. Awkward isn't even the right word to use for this situation. Jameson holds the door, and I'm assaulted by the sweet scent of vanilla and coffee. My stomach growls loudly. Jameson's eyebrows rise.

"You haven't been eating, have you?" he inquires, knowing the answer.

"No. My appetite is on vacation with the shitshow that is currently my life." I avoid his eyes.

We find a booth in the corner. The waitress brings us water and a carafe of coffee. I am grateful that I have a menu, so I don't have to look at Jameson. You know, his stupid-handsome face. Ugh. Once the waitress takes our order, I reluctantly release my menu, the only barrier between my eyes and his.

"Let me start by saying I am an asshole. I should never have ghosted you. I also should have kept you in the loop about Richard. I wanted to gather more information before I slammed you with this mess." The shadow of regret blankets his face.

"Did that hurt? I mean, you just admitted to making a mistake and being an asshole in one sentence." I give him my cheeky grin.

He shakes his head. "I handled everything wrong. I thought I was protecting you, but instead, I fucked everything up. I've been a mess not being able to be there for Owen. For you. And having this information is eating me alive."

I cock my head, trying not to read into his admission. That, quite possibly, he feels something for me beyond being a former client. "Well, let's relieve you of the burden. Share what you know. I might as well stop avoiding the inevitable."

"Okay, and then when the time is right, we'll discuss us." My breath hitches at the very thought that there might be an "us" to discuss.

I shake my head. "There is no *us*, Jameson. I can't do this." I point my finger at him and then back at me. "My whole life has been a series of people lying to me. Abandoning me. I can't deal with that shit anymore. So please just tell me what you know, and we can go on with our lives. Separately."

He swallows. A shadow of emotion clouds his face, but it disappears as he proceeds to deliver my life sentence. At least, that's the way I feel that the information he has will forever change my life. Owen's life.

Before he can spill what he knows, our waitress delivers our food. Normally, the golden pile of pancakes partnered with bacon would delight me. It would bring me comfort. But my appetite has evaporated and is replaced with a deep sense of dread sprinkled with nausea.

"Okay, proceed." I lift my eyes from my plate and stare at Jameson.

Surprised by my lack of food enthusiasm, he starts talking. "Alright. Richard has known since you and Owen were born that he wasn't your father. Your mother had been having an on-and-off affair with a very influential man. He was married and had no intention of leaving his wife. Your mother broke off the affair after she got pregnant with you. But after you were born, she resumed seeing him. He didn't know about you. Then when she got pregnant with Owen, she did the same thing. Meanwhile, she tried to convince Richard that he was indeed the father of you both. What your mother didn't know was that Richard was sterile. Of course, he didn't share that information with her. So she tried to pass off both of you as his, and he went along with it. He had always wanted kids, and he knew that your mother couldn't love you the way you deserved." He takes a breath, giving me a moment to process this information.

"At least Owen and I have the same father." Somehow that gives me a little comfort. At the same time, I realize that this must be the source of my father's random distancing from me—before Owen was even born, Richard was living a lie. That must have been hard on him.

"Richard left because he had found out who the father was and realized that he just couldn't continue the charade. Plus, he was overwhelmed at the thought of raising a child with special needs. He couldn't step up."

"Well, at least one thing is true. That he left because of Owen's Down syndrome." I close my eyes and inhale deeply. Jameson reaches across the table and takes my hand. I let him. I need the connection and the safety it provides.

"I think I know the answer, but why now? Why did all of this happen now?"

He takes a breath and continues. "The timing of your book's success and all of this coming to light is not a coincidence. You already know that Dorothy was involved after what happened at your New York book launch. She found Richard as well as your birth father, and she took advantage of them."

I didn't think of Dorothy as savvy. I have always thought that she was a few fries short of a McDonald's Happy Meal. (Shameless endorsement, as I love their fries!). Okay, my inner dialogue needs to end so I can find out the rest of the dirt.

"I can only assume it was for money. Shoplifting wasn't a career where she was hugely successful, and her psychic business probably wasn't very lucrative either." I smirk.

"Yeah, so once she found him, she provided him with all kinds of proof, and my PI was able to track wire transfers to an account that belongs to her. The monetary gain was the result of blackmailing your birth father while giving partial payments to Richard for his assistance in the charade. He was in bankruptcy, so this seemed like an easy way to make a buck, I suppose." He pauses and looks at me like he's waiting for me to break.

"So how did Dorothy know all of this, and I didn't?" I inquire.

"Well, that is an excellent question. I met with her the other day. She called me with a business proposition. She said if I gave her a million dollars, she would hand over the information on your birth father. Otherwise, she would go to the media. She has no idea that I recorded our conversation. It's all been turned over to one of my buddies who works for the FBI." He gives me a cocky grin.

"Well, thanks, but why would you do all of this without me? That bitch has been a thorn in my side for years. Her rainbow-unicorn, love-and-light crap was always a façade. She was always out for herself." Honestly, I am a little hurt that I seem to be the last to know everything. And, by the way, this is *my* life.

Jameson smiles at me and says, "You needed to focus on Owen's recovery. I just wanted to alleviate some of the heaviness that you must be feeling. My way of atoning for my actions. You have a lot on your plate." His expression is soft and caring.

"It's not a plate, Jameson. It's a fucking buffet, so what's one more serving? Are you going to tell me who our father is? Inquiring minds want to know." He squeezes my hand and slides a large envelope toward me.

"Everything in this envelope will give you the information you want. Paternity tests, letters from your mother to your biological father, and there is also a letter to you from your mother."

"Oh, a letter from my mother. That should be interesting. Can you just give me the CliffsNotes version? I'll look at all of this later, but right now, I just need a name," I beg.

"It's Senator Wendell Brooks." He watches me. I can only assume that he thinks I might implode or perhaps scream, but I surprise us both by simply nodding. I had wondered why the senator was at the book launch in Los Angeles. I remember the odd conversation we had and how familiar he seemed to me. Now it makes sense, but then, it felt like he was on a fishing expedition. The irony is that he is a very conservative politician whose sole purpose seems to be cutting services that benefit individuals like Owen. What a douche. And yes, ladies and gentlemen, he is my father. Just peachy.

My phone pings with a notification from Nina. I look up at Jameson, my eyes wide. "I need to get back to Owen." He throws some bills on the table and says, "I'm coming with you." I don't argue. We race to his waiting car and head to the hospital.

Dorothy

I watch them. It is sickening. What does that hot piece of man see in that chubby bitch? Sitting in the corner, I observe the interaction. The touching of hands. It's disgusting. Time is running out for me. After the money exchange and the ease with which I slipped out of the bar where I met Jameson, I have been lying low. I know that I should leave the country, but I want to see how this all plays out. I want to see Addie finally get what she deserves. Misery.

Matthew disappeared weeks ago, leaving a note saying that he couldn't be a part of this. I guess he found out what was going on—although how he found out, I still don't know. Well, he wasn't part of it, to begin with, but who cares? He was weak. Pathetic. He weighed me down. Good riddance.

I take a sip of my coffee and adjust my disguise. Today, I chose a platinum-blond wig that might rival Dolly Parton's hairstyle, designer sunglasses, and my very fashionable trench coat paired with a pink scarf. I needed a little color today. It is very James Bond. I decide that while they are over there canoodling or whatever, I'll head to the hospital and see if I can find out any information about the esteemed patients. Maybe they will both die. I don't care. They are just a means to an end. What happened to Owen wasn't part of the plan, but it is what it is.

As luck would have it, I arrive at the hospital to find Owen alone. That bitch, Nina, is always hanging around, acting like she's better than everyone else. And the big, bulky henchman they hired is nowhere to be found. Perfect. As I'm about to enter the room, I am stopped by a nurse.

"Excuse me, but only family is allowed in this unit. Are you related to the patient?" Her eyes narrow at me.

"Oh, why yes, I'm his cousin. I've been so terribly worried, and Addie has been so wonderful keeping me posted. I thought I would come and give her a break. That's what family does for each other." I smile at her, trying to appear like a doting family member. Acting is hard sometimes. I dislike Owen. He gives me the creeps with his slow speech that I sometimes can't even understand and his weird appearance. Retarded people are worthless. That's why Addie was made fun of in high school. She was always protecting her brother. Too bad the car didn't just take him out. The world wouldn't miss him.

"I had no idea! Addie never mentioned you. Go ahead and go in. I suppose you know that Owen just woke up asking for her. He has fallen back asleep, but we expect that since his body is still healing. Addie is on her way. Her friend Nina just stepped out to make some phone calls but will be back soon. We're so relieved! He is such a sweetheart." She turns to leave, and I grin. Seriously, people underestimate my ability to get what I want. Now is my time.

Addie

B y the grace of God, traffic is not an issue. It's like the parting of the Red Sea. Anyway, we arrive. Just FYI, Jameson is still holding my hand, and well, I'm not going to lie, I fucking love it! I know you're wondering if I've forgiven him. Well, the jury is still out, but I do know that he cares for Owen and for me. He fits with us in our little tribe of people. The family that I picked instead of the dysfunctional biological sort. He is human. And humans make mistakes. So yes, I forgive him, but I am still working on the trust part. And my fear of being abandoned. I have a lot to work on, but Owen comes first. The rest will fall into place. I need to tell him.

As we exit the car, we sprint like O. J. Simpson in that rental car commercial before he decided to break the law and go on a wild ride in his Ford Bronco. We reach Owen's room, and next to my brother's bed stands Dorothy. Her eyes linger on him as if she is contemplating her next move. Remember the love, light, unicorn, and rainbow shit that she spouts? Well, it has been replaced with venom, disgust, and anger. Will the real Dorothy Snyder please stand up? Fortunately, I have shed my tolerance for bitches. If Jameson weren't here and there weren't any witnesses, I would probably kill her. I have mad ninja skills when prompted. At least in my mind, I do.

"What the hell are you doing here?" My heart is racing. Rage is bubbling. At that moment, Jameson and Walter flank me. Walter doesn't speak a lot, but his presence is commanding, and he truly cares for Owen. Even in the middle of this madness, I feel safe.

"Oh, I was just visiting my sweet cousin. Is that a crime?" Her statement is devoid of any emotion.

"Dorothy, you don't even like Owen. But I do know that you're a conniving bitch. I know you received money in exchange for keeping the senator and Richard's secret. How did you even know?" I stare at her. She laughs.

"Oh, Addie. You were always so naïve and incredibly stupid. Always thinking that you're better than me. How did I know? That's easy. Your mother told me." She smirks.

"Why would my mother confide in you? You weren't even close."

She giggles. This is when I believe she's losing it. Like, several slices short of a full loaf of bread. Notice I always reference food. It's my thing. Okay, now back to the wicked bitch of the west wing.

"Your mother made a deathbed confession. She thought I was you, so naturally, I went along with it. It was like divine intervention that I was there to listen. I recorded it so your actual father could celebrate that he is a daddy and, of course, so I could have leverage with him financially. Richard was in the middle of bankruptcy, so it was easy to get him on board to help me for the right price. It was my security blanket in case you cut us off financially. When you did, well, I had no choice." She is grinning like a fucking Cheshire cat. Ugh. Well, that explains my mother's last words of "I'm sorry."

At that moment, two very attractive gentlemen approach us flashing their FBI badges. Don't judge. It's been a miserable three weeks, and eye candy is always welcome. Jameson nods at them and then looks at me like he has a story to tell me. Dorothy looks surprised.

She starts laughing hysterically, like a lunatic. I wonder if the agents have a straitjacket with them.

"Go ahead, boys. Take me in. You have nothing on me. Just like all the arrests before, they can never make anything stick." At least she is consistent in her penchant for denial.

Dorothy struggles against the cuffs that restrain her hands. She spits and kicks at her captors. The two agents are probably surprised at her strength, so the cutie with the blond hair uses his stun gun. Best. Moment. Ever. I should have bought one of those years ago. Maybe she would have left me alone. Her body jolts. She looks like a flailing fish. They take her away. Bye, Felicia!

"I'm so sorry, Addie," Nina says from behind me. I turn around to face my friend. "I stepped out to get some tea after I called you. I never thought she would show up here." Nina's remorseful eyes fill with tears.

"Oh, Nina! I could never blame you. She has always been narcissistic. Always looking out for number one. I'm not surprised that she showed up. If I weren't in the throes of living this nightmare, it would make for great fiction. Unfortunately, you simply can't make this shit up." I walk over and envelop her in my arms.

Walter touches my shoulder and says, "Addie, I walked down the hall to get a cup of coffee. I am so sorry. If anything had happened to Owen, I would—"

I don't let him finish, instead, I give him a hug. "Walter, I don't blame you either. We are so grateful for your friendship."

George struts in and gasps, "Oh my God. What did I miss, and who were those hotties escorting that poorly dressed woman with that hideous wig out of this room?"

I full-on laugh, complete with tears rolling down my face.

"George, that was Dorothy. You know, the bitch who's married to my cousin."

He scrunches his nose. "Well, Jesus, I can't unsee that fashion mistake she was wearing."

"What's going on?" I pause and turn to look at the source of the voice.

"Well, hello there, sleeping beauty." I grin at Owen and grab his hand. Tears stream down my face.

"What happened?" Owen asks. I can tell that he's frightened because he's gripping my hand like a lifeline.

"Do you remember anything?" I ask, trying to decide what I should and should not tell him.

"I remember what our dad said. You know, about not being ours." Sadness morphs his usually happy features. "Addie, why doesn't he want me?" He looks at me with such dejection that my heart breaks for him. For us. It guts me to see him feeling like he doesn't belong. But he does. To me.

"Owen, I want you. It's you and me against the world. Always." I just want to erase his hurt and anguish. "After you heard the news about Richard not being our father, you ran off, and Jameson followed you. A car hit you, Owen, when you ran into the street," I explain.

"I'm sorry that I didn't look both ways like you told me to. Are you mad?" He looks worried. This guy. He is my whole world. My landscape would be colorless without him.

"Oh, Owen. No, I'm not mad. I'm just so happy that you're okay. I love you, buddy. You are my heart. The world is a better place with you in it." I squeeze his hand.

"I love you too, Addie. I'm glad you're my sister."

I'm grinning like a fool when the nurse walks in to check his vitals.

"Hubba-hubba." He wiggles his eyebrows. And he's back. The nurse laughs.

At this moment, everything feels right. The most important people in my life are in one room.

Smiling, I look around, and standing in the doorway, I find none other than Senator Wendell Brooks. My smile disappears. Fuck. My. Life. Could I just have *one* moment free from this shitshow?

Addie

I was so focused on Owen that I wasn't aware of his presence. How long had he been standing there? The senator, our father, is standing in the doorway. Wendell Brooks is a formidable man. He is handsome and tall with salt-and-pepper hair. His Armani suit accentuates his fit physique. Normally, he looks powerful. But not today. The power that normally radiates from him has been twisted into vulnerability and uncertainty. I move toward him while George and Nina distract Owen. Jameson follows me, but I shake my head at him. He nods in agreement with my silent request. He stands nearby like a safety net. My guardian. My protector.

I straighten my back and guide Brooks into the hallway. Jameson's presence gives me strength.

"Can I help you, Senator?" My voice wobbles. I want to sound confident, but my emotions take center stage.

"Addie, I want to explain." His tone is cautious.

"Explain? What, that you were carrying on an affair with a married woman, fathered two children, and then paid money to a woman who was bribing you to protect your own image? I know how your politicians twist things. So please, enlighten me on how the fuck you are going to explain this mess." I'm on a roll. But deep down, I know that we're both victims. Both pawns in a chess game that Dorothy orchestrated. But at this moment, I need a release.

"There are no excuses. I didn't know that your mother was pregnant or that I had two children until I was confronted by Dorothy. And then, well, I panicked. I thought that if I responded to her demands and paid the amount she asked, it would buy me some time. I was wrong." His eyes meet mine. I notice our similarities. Our eyes. Our mouths. It's surreal after all these years of believing that Richard was my father.

He continues. "I want to get to know you both. I know that so much damage has been done, but I would like to try to make amends for my actions. For my absence."

"I don't know. Since I haven't had time to process this, I can't give you an answer. Please give us some space." Tears prick my eyes.

"Of course, Addie. It isn't my intent to inflict more pain. Here is my card. My cell number is on there. Please call me when you're ready." I take the card, and he gives me a caring smile before he turns and walks away. I exhale and turn toward Jameson. He opens his arms, and I don't hesitate as I walk into them. I feel safe. Secure. It feels right. It feels like home. I close my eyes. In this moment, everything disappears. It's just the two of us.

I step back from the embrace and walk back into Owen's room, instantly missing my connection with Jameson. I compose myself. Owen doesn't need to know the shitstorm that is swirling around us.

"Who was that?" Owen inquires.

"Just a reporter. No one important. How are you feeling?" He looks so small and vulnerable.

"I hurt, but the nurse gave me some medicine. Now I feel sleepy." He struggles to keep his eyes open.

"Sleep, buddy. I'll be here when you wake up." I give him his blanket. He snuggles with it, just like he used to when he was little.

"I love you, Addie." He takes my hand, tears pool in my eyes. Seriously, I have cried so much, I might be dehydrated.

"Owen, I love you too. So very much." As he closes his eyes, the tears flow. A combination of relief, happiness, and grief shower my face. My whole life has been centered around empowering and loving Owen. He is my biggest teacher. I have spent years guarded, hesitant about getting close to people. The fear that they will leave permeates new relationships, so I build a wall. Is there room in my heart for Jameson? When he held me, I felt my heart expand. I'm in love with him. I know it, and it scares the shit out of me. How do I allow myself the luxury of giving my heart to someone when I'm held hostage by abandonment and trust issues? There isn't enough wine or chocolate in the universe to get me through this. I have spent most of my life navigating it alone. Maybe it's my turn to be cared for, cherished—to finally feel safe with another person. Can I do that? Can I allow someone in and trust them with my heart? Those questions will have to wait. My next step is letting Richard go. It'll be time soon.

Jameson

I am so consumed by watching the emotional exchange between Owen and Addie that I miss the senator's approach. When I see him standing there, watching his two children, I observe a broken man. The anguish is palpable. I move toward him, ready to remove him from the room, but Addie shakes her head. Message received.

She straightens her back and walks over to him, guiding him into the hallway. I stand nearby as a backup, but I know Addie won't need me. The more time I spend around her, the more aware I become of her capacity for badassery when it comes to Owen.

I step back into the room as she confronts her real father. Both appear vulnerable, and I can only hope that some good comes from this. I turn and walk over to Owen. He is grinning at something George is telling him, his eyes sleepy, and all is right with the world. His eyes find me.

"Are you crying? Tough guys don't cry. Danny Zuko doesn't cry," he teases.

"Real men aren't afraid of emotion. Glad you woke up because I need my partner in crime back."

"Partner in crime? I don't want to go to jail." He looks concerned.

"It's a saying, Owen. I meant my wingman. I just missed my friend."

"Were you scared I would die?"

I pause. This is the question that I need to consider carefully.

"After the car hit you, your heart stopped. Do you know what CPR is?"

"Is that when someone helps make your heartbeat again?"

"That's right. I did CPR on you. Your heart started beating again, and then the ambulance brought you here."

"Jameson, you saved my life. You are my hero. You need a cape like a superhero." He grabs my hand, grinning.

This guy. He has no idea that he and his sister have brought me back to life.

"I love you, Owen. I can't imagine the world without you in it. Go to sleep, buddy."

"Okay, but you'll stay, right?"

"Of course, Owen. I will never leave you or your sister."

He falls asleep with a smile on his face.

Addie

The whole day was an emotional vacuum, and since Owen is on the mend, I feel comfortable going home, and confronting my demons. The manila envelope that Jameson gave me holds my life story. It's sitting in my purse, giving me the stink eye. I need chocolate.

"Headed home?" Jameson asks.

"Yeah. Owen is doing well, and being at home might ground me a bit."

"Do you want company? I mean, to go through the envelope, like a support system." His face softens. and he almost looks sheepish. Freaking adorable.

"Thank you for offering, but this is something I need to do by myself. I feel like this might be the catalyst to help me move forward and come to terms with Richard."

"Of course. Well, call me if you need me. I will see you tomorrow."

"Tomorrow?"

"Owen and I have a date with video games." His eyes dance with amusement.

"How are you all going to do that? He doesn't have one here."

"Yet, Addie. I am getting him the mega-daddy of all systems." He's grinning at me, and boy, do I love that smile.

"Jameson, don't spoil him," I scoff.

"Spoil him? He just survived a horrendous experience, and he deserves to have some fun. Plus, it's purely selfish. I get to hang with him and play video games. Win-win."

"Ugh, you are such a guy. Fine. You all do your video stuff. I will see you tomorrow then."

"I have a car waiting. Can I give you a ride home?" His eyes roam over my face and settle on my lips. Is it hot in here?

"Oh, okay. That would be great."

We head to the car in compatible silence that makes me wonder if there is hope for us after all.

Addie

After Jameson drops me off, I walk into my apartment and exhale. This day has been a series of unexpected events peppered with an almost unfathomable amount of information. It has been overwhelming. I change my clothes, putting on my coziest pajamas with chocolate kisses all over them. What did you expect? Broccoli? I pour myself a healthy serving of wine and settle on the couch with the taunting manila envelope.

Opening it, I unearth photographs of myself with Richard, bank transactions, paternity results, and a letter from my mother. How on earth did Dorothy get these? If she weren't such a crazy bitch, I might admire her ingenuity. Like ripping off a Band-Aid, I decide to read the letter first. I take a big drink of wine and begin.

Dear Addie,

If you are reading this, then obviously, I am no longer living. Let me start by saying that I should never have been a mother. I wasn't cut out to be unselfish. You were also this loving, giving child, and

I just didn't know how to respond to it. I was raised in a cold, sterile home. I didn't know any other way.

I made so many mistakes. My life has been a series of regrets. First, Richard is not your father. I had an ongoing affair with Wendell Brooks. I had met him at one of the many philanthropic causes that I was involved in, and we clicked. I didn't care that he was married, and when I think back on it, I don't know that I ever really loved Richard. Wendell was charismatic and influential. He loved me deeply. Then I got pregnant with you and panicked. I broke things off with him. He was devastated.

Richard and I were never overly intimate, but I made sure that the timing matched so I could pass him off as your father. I thought I was doing the right thing. After you were born, I was depressed. I missed Wendell so much, and there was such a void in my life without him. I would see him at functions with his wife. Jealousy pulsated through me. I wanted him for myself. I needed him. Life without him was so empty. So we resumed our affair, as he felt as strongly as I did. He brought out something in me that no one else could. He made me a better person. I know that you didn't get the best of me. Only Wendell did.

When I found myself pregnant again, I knew I needed to choose. The love of my life or another child. Wendell never wanted children. He thought they would hinder his political agenda. So I broke things off with him. Truthfully, I thought about having an abortion. I even went to a clinic, but in the end, I couldn't bring myself to go through with it. Surprised? Me too. Putting something ahead of my own needs was a foreign concept. When I told Richard, he laughed at me. He confessed that he was sterile. That he always had been, and that he knew you couldn't be his. He told me that he was willing to be a father to you, however, he would not be part of this charade with a second child. I suppose, in his way, he loved you. I begged him to stay for the sake of appearances. He agreed, but only after I signed over ownership of several properties that had been given to me by your grandfather.

When Owen was born, I couldn't even look at him after they told me he had Down syndrome. I allowed the nanny to take over and deal with you both. You stepped right up and became every bit his mother. As you remember, Richard left not long after your brother was born, along with cleaning out one of our bank accounts. He was always greedy.

Now you know my secrets, how imperfect I was, even though I tried so hard to pass myself off as the woman who had it all. Do you want to know another truth? I was jealous of you. That is why I always picked at you, criticizing your appearance and anything else that would bring you pain. I was envious of the way you lived your life, not caring what others thought, how you loved Owen despite his imperfections. It disgusted me, really. The only person that I really loved was Wendell, but even that wasn't enough. He eventually discarded me, saying that he needed to make it work with his wife and that a mistress was getting harder and harder to cover up, what with his political career. I knew he would never leave her, especially since I had children. Oh yes, he knew about you both. I blurted it out one night, as I couldn't keep it a secret any longer. He knew that Richard was the "father" and that Owen had a disability. But we never discussed you children beyond that.

I am not asking for forgiveness. I am merely letting you know about your father's identity. What you do with that information is totally up to you.

Mom

Woah. That was a lot. I mean, not much of the letter was a surprise, but being jealous of me was a total "holy shit" moment. I can't even wrap my head around that. You would think she could at least sign off with "love, Mom" instead of no emotion at all. Oh right, who am I kidding? She was the coldest person on the planet. I shiver at the notion.

I sort through the photos. There are so many with Richard. He appears as the doting father, looking lovingly at me. Did he ever really care about me? Was I simply a pawn in his game of greed and power? No wonder I'm so fucked up with abandonment and trust issues. The impulse to call Jameson is strong. Instead, I finish my wine, and with that comes the revelation that it's time to let Richard go. Tomorrow marks the beginning of Addie Snyder's new reality.

Jameson

Addie walks into Owen's room the next morning. Her expression seems to be frozen in perpetual surprise, her eyes radiating questions.

"I'm surprised to see you here," she whispers, not wanting to wake Owen. He had a great night according to the nurse, and he's set to be released in a few days.

"Why is that, Addie? I told you I'm here to stay. When things calm down, we're going to discuss our relationship. Until then, I am here to support you and Owen."

"Oh, well, um... okay. I am too emotionally exhausted to banter with you." She pauses. "I opened the envelope last night. There were lots of photographs of me with Richard and, well, there was a very detailed letter from my mother." Her eyes stray from me and focus on Owen, whose eyes are fluttering open.

"What are you all talking about?" Owen's sleepy voice asks.

Addie walks over to Owen's bedside and kisses his forehead. "Nothing, boo. Just excited that you'll be released soon."

"Ugh. Don't call me boo. I am not a baby. I am a man." He smirks.

"Okay. Hey. Look who's here!" She moves aside to reveal me.

"Duh, Addie. He's been here all night. That's what best friends do." He grins at me.

"You've been here all night?" Her eyes soften as she looks at me.

I nod.

"But why? I mean, he's doing well." She cocks her head to the left as she studies me.

I shrug and respond, "He's my best friend. That's what best friends do for each other as he said." I give Owen a high five.

"Buddy, I need to talk to Jameson for a minute, so we'll be outside, okay?"

"Are you all going to kiss? If you kiss my sister, that's cool, but don't do it in front of me because that's just gross." Addie blushes, and her eyes dart to the floor.

"Just talking, Owen, but I'll keep that in mind when I do kiss her."

"Oh, for God's sake, we are going to be in the hall. There is no kissing happening here or at all." She huffs, turns on her heels, and walks out into the hallway.

"She is mad at you, so I don't think you'll be kissing her." Owen states.

"Not yet, but soon." I laugh.

Addie

I am pacing in the hallway, waiting on Jameson. Kissing? Seriously, what the hell has he been saying to Owen? There will be no kissing. Okay, maybe, well, because he's so yummy, and his kisses make me breathless. Stop it, Addie! Your fake father is in the next room, and you are about to pull the plug. Get a grip! I compose myself as Mr. Hottie ventures out to meet me.

"Okay, so tell me about the letter your mom left." His eyes are laced with concern.

"It was a long, cold letter telling me everything I already know. Several things were new like she was jealous of me and some other random shit. She didn't even sign it 'love, Mom'." I shake my head.

"Addie, I'm so sorry. I can see why she was jealous of you, though. Your warmth and compassion, for a start, plus you are so damn funny." His smile is so hypnotizing.

"Wow, um, thank you. I think Owen has a lot to do with that. He just makes me better." I shrug off the compliment.

"No. It's you, Addie. Don't minimize the amazing human you are." His tone is laced with frustration. "I see you, Addie. I see kindness. I see *you*." His hand caresses my face as he looks deeply into my eyes. I gasp while tears threaten to fall. No one has ever said that to me. Letting people in has been hard. Trusting them has proven even more difficult. But if this turbulent journey has taught me anything, it is that I have a core group of people who have my best interest at heart. In a way, finding out the truth has enabled me to start healing.

"I think it's time to say goodbye to Richard. Can you go with me?" I blurt. I can feel that my eyes are pleading.

"Of course, Addie." He reaches for my hand, a brief smile tugs at my lips.

We walk into Richard's room. The machines beep, and the scent of death lingers. Jameson follows me to Richard's bedside.

"I don't know what to say to him. My whole life has been a lie." I gaze at Jameson as if he has the words that I long to say.

"The life you created with Owen isn't a lie. That's your foundation, Addie." Woah. That was profound. If I weren't drowning in my own emotional ocean, I would address his willingness to be so open another time.

"You're right, of course, but I'm still processing everything. I feel like at this moment, I need to state my truth to him. To somehow find a way to forgive him so that I can move on with my life."

"Go ahead, then. Speak your truth to him. I'll be right beside you."

I close my eyes and take a deep breath, and Jameson squeezes my hand.

"Richard," I whisper. "God, I don't even know where to start. I wish you could have just told me the truth. It would have saved all of us a lot of heartache. I keep thinking of those moments when you were present. Remember the dollhouse you built me? It was so detailed, even down to the tiny furniture. That dollhouse fueled my imagination. I made up stories about the family that lived there. A family much different than the one I experienced growing up. I think that's one of the reasons I've become a writer. You did that for me. Thank you for that. And while I'm hurt, confused, and angry as hell over this whole situation, there is a part of me that has tremendous compassion for you. I want you to leave this life knowing that I have forgiven you. I hope you find peace." I exhale and nod to the nurse.

Tears streak my face as I say goodbye to the man who gave as much as he took. Jameson holds me while we wait for him to take his last breath. The steady beep of the heart rate monitor is replaced with the dreaded solid tone that fills the room.

"Time of death, 8:56 a.m."

Addie

I t's been a week since Richard passed away. I find forgiveness and grief to be formidable companions. There is the little girl in me who is saddened by the loss of the man who was my only father figure. The necessity of embracing the grieving child will allow me to work through the mixture of feelings that could swallow me whole if I allow them to. I can't do that. I can't allow the people who I knew as my parents to have that much control from the grave. I gave them too much power while they were alive. It's time I take my life back.

The anger has dissipated, replaced by understanding. Don't get me wrong, I am not ready to get to know my actual father, but someday I might be. In the meantime, he has honored my request for space, and we have exchanged a few text messages and phone calls regarding Owen's progress. Baby steps.

Sometimes my life feels like somebody trying to stand on a hammock. I teeter. I fall. I get up and try again. I am embracing my humanness and allowing others to be human, too.

Today, Owen is being released from the hospital. One month of living in a hospital puts things into perspective. Thank God! Not just because I'm grateful that he survived, but he's also becoming a royal pain in the ass. I get it. He's bored. He wants to get back to his life. Which, by the way, is going to be difficult. We can't go back to our Brooklyn apartment without an elevator, so we have to stay at a hotel for the next three weeks until he gets his cast off. I figure room service will be an excellent consolation prize.

"Who's ready to kick this popsicle stand today?" I enter Owen's room with several boxes and bags. The room is overflowing with flowers and gifts. Seriously, I might need to hire a moving van. Christ. On. A. Cracker.

"Addie, this is a hospital, not a popsicle stand. When are we leaving? Where is Jameson?" He keeps looking over my shoulder. Cue the eye roll. Jameson is now his favorite person. He has been for a while, but his popularity expanded when he bought Owen a top-of-the-line gaming system with two controllers, so they can both play. They have spent endless hours killing zombies. And because Jameson and Owen are so charming, the nurses have turned a blind eye to their pastime, as long as they keep the volume down. These two could charm a tree. Sigh.

"Whoa! One question at a time. They're working on the paperwork now, and I have no idea if Jameson is coming here or not." Jameson and I have not addressed our mutual attraction. With everything going on, we have just partnered to get Owen better. That has been the focus. After doing this solo for so long, it's nice to have someone to balance me.

As if he knew we were talking about him, Jameson appears in the doorway looking hot. Jesus, does this man ever have an off day? Ugh. Today, I did put on deodorant and brushed my hair. That's probably the most I've done in a few days. George would lose his shit. However, he did give me a "fashion pass" since my life is beyond chaotic. Pretty nice of him. He said it with his eyes closed as if the sight of me was too hideous to handle. Oh, and he brushed my hair and applied makeup to ease his discomfort. I think he has given up.

"Good morning, Owen. Addie." His eyes linger on me, warm. It's moments like this when I feel like he sees me. Like he truly gets me. Goosebumps prickle my arms.

"Jameson, Addie thinks this is a popsicle stand. Tell her she's wrong." Owen looks annoyed. We have spent way too much time together during his hospital stay.

"It's a saying, Owen. So, are you ready? I have a car downstairs, ready to take you to the hotel." He starts packing up the boxes and bags while the nurse goes over Owen's discharge papers with me.

This man. God help my heart.

Jameson

I stand outside Owen's room, listening to their exchange. Watching them interact has become one of my favorite pastimes. I carefully observe Addie. Exhaustion clouds her face. She needs a break, and fortunately, I have arranged everything. It's all a part of my grand plan to prove that I am worth the risk. That *we* are worth the risk. I smile to myself. As if she feels my presence, she looks over at me. A small smile forms.

"Good morning, Owen. Addie." My eyes meet Addie's. I see her, really see her. The connection is undeniable.

"Jameson, Addie thinks this is a popsicle stand. Tell her she's wrong." Owen looks annoyed. I chuckle. You can't help but fall in love with Owen. And his sister. Shit, I haven't truly loved anyone since my mother. Yep, they shattered my barriers and completely embedded themselves in my heart.

"It's just a saying, Owen." I laugh. "So, are you ready? I have a car downstairs, ready to take you to the hotel." I start packing up the boxes and bags while the nurse goes over Owen's discharge papers with Addie.

I take my time while periodically looking at her, hoping that I can make her trust me. See me. Know that I will cherish her. Know that if we are together, I will keep her safe, loved, and treasured. It's going to take a lot of work, but I have enlisted the help of Nina, Harrison, and, of course, Owen. As a gesture of respect to him as the man of the family, we had a bro talk a few days ago, and I asked him if it would be okay if I dated his sister.

"Aren't you already doing that?" he asked me with a tone that could only question if I am a complete dumbass. Which, by the way, I am.

"No, we aren't, but I'm going to need your help convincing her to be my girlfriend," I told him.

His eyes widened, and he said, "Gross. I'm cool with you hanging out with her. Can you still be my wingman?" His face was full of mischief and humor.

"Dude, I don't think you need a wingman. You do a fine job on your own." I laughed.

"Fine. Be her boyfriend, but you still have to hang out with me." His face was serious.

"Owen, I will always have time for you. We're brothers from another mother." I grinned at him.

"Okay, I won't be a clock blocker." He laughed, and I rolled my eyes.

I'm quickly brought back to the present when I realize that Addie has been talking to me, and I haven't heard a word she's said. Note to self: work on listening skills.

"Sorry, what?" I turn my attention to her.

"I said, are you ready? The nurse is bringing a wheelchair, so we can finally leave this hell hole."

"Sure. I'll take this stuff down and meet you both at the car." She cocks her head at me as if she's trying to figure me out. I kiss on her on the cheek and walk out the door, grinning and whistling as I walk down the hall.

Addie

Okay, what just happened? He kissed me on the cheek, and he is whistling. Jameson doesn't whistle. I look at Owen, whose smile squeezes my heart.

"Do you know why Jameson is acting so weird?" I inquire, giving him my best "mom" glare. It never works on him, but an A for effort. I have it mastered.

"Addie, he's not acting weird—you are. Let's go and order room service. The food here sucks." In true Owen form, it always comes down to the food. When he was in first grade, he told me he never wanted to go to prison. I asked him why, and he informed me that a boy at school had a father in prison. His father told him that the food was awful. Whatever works.

The orderly comes with the wheelchair, and Owen settles in, asking him if he can do some "wheelies." I groan. Cue the eye roll once again. I swear, my eyeballs are in the best shape since they're the only part of my body that exercises.

Once we get to the hotel, I notice Nina waiting for us.

"Are you the welcoming committee?" I ask, wondering why she's here, since the last time I spoke to her, she told me she would be in meetings all day. Color me confused.

"I cleared my afternoon. I thought Owen and I could hang out. Maybe go get some lunch and then some ice cream. Give you a little breathing room. I know it has been a tough few months." Everyone needs a Nina in their lives.

"Oh, Nina. I don't know. I'm sure he's tired. Maybe—" I'm interrupted by a very annoyed Owen.

"I'm a man. I will make my own decisions. I want to hang out with Nina." The two of them grin at each other, looking at each other as if they have some sort of secret. What is happening? Everyone is acting so weird. I feel like I'm on an episode of *The Twilight Zone*. Maybe I'm just tired. I am going with that. A nice bath and a nap are at the top of my list now that Owen is going to hang with Nina.

"Okay, go. But if you get tired—" Again, I'm interrupted by Owen, who throws his hand up and puts it over my mouth. Nina stifles a giggle.

When he removes his hand, I put on my fakest smile and say, "Have fun, you two! Stay out as long as you want." My tone drips with sarcasm. Jameson laughs. I love this group of people. They are my tribe: even Jameson and his incredibly handsome face.

Nina wheels Owen toward her waiting car, and I turn to Jameson. "Well, thanks for your help. I can take it from here." I try to sound confident, but the reality is that once he leaves, I'm scared that I won't see him again. He ditched me as a client, and I think he's only supportive because he feels obligated. Guilt has a funny way of holding people hostage. You know, because he kept pertinent information to himself and because of the shitstorm that followed because of it. There is no way he would ever fall in love with someone like me. People leave me. That's what they do. The problem this time is that I don't know if I will recover if he leaves my life completely.

"Trying to get rid of me?" His eyebrows furrow.

"No, I just thought you probably have better things to do." I avoid making eye contact.

"Come on. Let's take this stuff up to your hotel room. Maybe we can have that talk about us." My eyebrow rises. I can only do the left one. It's one of my talents. I'm not bragging. Just pointing it out, so don't be jealous.

I have lost my capacity for words at this point. We get on the elevator and I press the button for floor five, but he presses twenty. He's smirking.

"Why did you press twenty? My room is on five." Radio silence. So when the doors open to the fifth floor, I start to get off, but Jameson grabs my hand and says, "Addie, trust me." Well, hell, what's a girl to do when this unbelievably hot man is begging me to stay on the elevator? I nod. I comply. For once, I don't argue. We ride the rest of the way in silence. I can't help but notice his mischievous grin.

We arrive on the twentieth floor, and he scans a card to access the floor. When the door opens, I find out that this is the penthouse. The room is opulent in its décor. Elegant sofas and wingback chairs are grouped in the living room. A sliding door reveals a terrace that overlooks the cityscape. It is breathtaking. As my eyes scan this incredible space, I notice that the dining room table hosts what appears to be my ideal feast: a bottle of champagne ready to be opened and bouquets of chocolates. I turn to Jameson, who has a shit-eating grin on his face. What. Is. Happening?

"Um, this is a mistake. I didn't reserve this." My voice wavers with emotion.

"I did. I took the opportunity to upgrade you, and I had this arranged for us." He moves toward me and takes my hand. "Addie, I'm crazy about you. Everything about you. Even when you're a complete neurotic basket case."

"Is this supposed to make me fall into your arms? Because I'm pretty sure that calling me a neurotic basket case doesn't make me want to do that." At this point, I'm trying to contain myself. I mean, I want to kiss his stupid face even after his semi-insult.

"I'm telling you that I love every part of you. I love that you pop chocolates when you're stressed. I love that you hate dressing up, and you prefer living in your yoga pants. I love that you are fiercely protective of Owen. I love that you write to write and not for the celebrity status. I love the capacity you have to draw people to you. But most of all, I love you." He moves closer. Our faces are inches apart. My breathing speeds up, and my heart races. This hot, brooding man loves me, and I am standing here mute. No words. I'm frozen in disbelief.

I close my eyes and whisper, "I love you too, Jameson. Somehow, you have broken down my walls. Be patient with me. I'm not used to being vulnerable. All I know is that people I love leave. It can be a lonely existence." Tears spill from my eyes.

His lips graze my forehead while his thumb wipes away my tears. "You're never going to be alone again. I'm here for you and Owen. Addie, it's your turn for someone to take care of you. I want to cherish you and I would be honored if you would allow me to be your person. Can I be your person?"

I open my eyes and nod. This man sees me, really sees me and loves me anyway.

He leans down and kisses me. Our tongues dance. My lady bits are fist-bumping. And I am lost in a simple kiss. A kiss that signifies something that feeds my soul.

Our lips pull apart. I give him a smile and ask, "Does this mean you're my boyfriend?" I giggle.

"Do you want me to be your boyfriend?" He smirks.

"Yes, I think I would very much like that. Now, were Nina and Owen in on this little ruse?"

"Of course, they were. I even got Owen's permission. By the way, I received on the condition that I would continue to be his wingman. I reminded him that he doesn't need one."

"You talked to Owen? Oh, Jameson, that is positively the sweetest thing I have ever heard." I am seriously overwhelmed. I am swooning at his love and respect for Owen.

Seriously, ladies, I think he might be a keeper. How cute is that? I walk over to the table where Jameson pops the cork off of the champagne and pours me a glass. I pop a chocolate from the bouquet. Not because I'm anxious, but because I can. He knows that chocolate rules and flowers drool in my book. He knows me.

He hands me a glass and pours one for himself. "To new beginnings." Our glasses clink, and I let the bubbles tickle my throat. I grin and think to myself, *It's finally my turn, and life has never looked so promising.*

EPILOGUE

Jameson

I take a moment to take in the view. While the vineyards surrounding our extravagant villa are gorgeous, my line of vision is drawn to the woman who captured my heart. I love the way her lips purse as she thinks. Her eyes close as she takes a sip of her coffee. Relaxed. Happy. I can't imagine a life without her and Owen. It makes me realize how empty and colorless my existence used to be.

Addie is open to developing a relationship with her biological father. Her pace is slow, but I think that with all of the abandonment and trust issues that she brings to the table, it's understandable. Do you know the most beautiful thing I'm privileged to watch? It's the budding bond between Owen and Wendell. It is natural. It is comfortable. Most wonderful of all, Addie stepped back from it, allowing the two of them to figure it out for themselves. After all the crazy that surrounded us for months, the circus has officially left town. We are going to be okay.

After a lot of consideration and subtle pressure from Nina, Addie decided to write a memoir about her life. With the false facts floating around the internet, she thought the best course of action was to control the narrative. I wonder where she got that excellent advice? Anyway, I think that the book has been a therapeutic release of sorts. I admire her willingness to be so vulnerable on a public level, which she fought in the beginning. I am so fucking proud of her.

Before we came to Italy, I went ring shopping. I'll admit that I'm terrified of asking her, but not because I'm afraid of committing—I'm scared that she won't say yes. I spent months trying to get them to move in with me. We have spent every moment together, but for some reason, she finds excuses. Irrational excuses. Like that I don't have enough bookshelves for her literary collection, or that my furniture won't blend with hers. Stupid reasons. At least to me. So, I bought a house complete with a library that would accommodate her book addiction- still a no. I will not be deterred. This step in asking for her hand happens to be one of the most frightening actions I have ever taken. Which is crazy, since I have jumped out of a plane in war-torn countries, taken out insurgents, and lived for weeks in trenches. Seriously. I'm terrified.

I asked Owen's permission, of course. He rolled his eyes and told me to, and I quote, "Shit or get off the pot," which I suppose was his way of giving me his blessing. Nice. God, he makes me laugh. He sees life in color.

The ring I selected is simple. Understated. Totally Addie. Custom made. It's a one-carat diamond surrounded by emeralds. It isn't flashy because Addie would hate that. I know she's skittish, so I have been patient, but I will say that it still feels like throwing a Hail Mary pass.

"Morning, Addie." I keep my voice low, hoping that it isn't wavering with emotion.

"Morning." She grins at me, her eyes closed. God, that smile lights up my world. I sit next to her and grab her hand. We sit in compatible silence while I try to formulate my delivery. I have been practicing, but at this moment, I know I just need to speak from my heart.

"Where's Owen?" I take a sip of my coffee.

"Oh, he's with Antonio. They went to a café so Owen can scope out the ladies." She giggles. Antonio is the caretaker of our villa. He and Owen have formed a tight bond.

"So, I've been replaced as his wingman?" I say it like I'm annoyed, but I'm not. Besides, Antonio is a good guy and apparently "hot as fuck," or at least that's what Addie says to Nina when she thinks I don't hear her as they chat on the phone. Whatever.

"I suppose so. Are you going to survive?" She smirks at me.

"Yes, I'll survive. I have my hands full with you." I laugh. "When are Nina and Harrison arriving?"

"Tonight. I hope they don't kill each other in the process." We're both still wondering what the hell is going on between them. Every time I ask Harrison, he changes the subject. Interesting. There is a dance with them. The sexual tension is thick.

"Oh, I'm sure they'll be fine. So, are you done with the revisions?" I know her focus has been a little scattered, but since Nina is coming, she's had to buckle down. The publisher is breathing down her neck, which means Nina has been on her ass.

"I have some work to do today, but it should be done by the time they get here." She closes her eyes and sighs. I take in her beauty. She looks happy. Content. Loved. Cherished. Everything I promised when I pledged my love to her. In all honesty, her presence in my life has eased my PTSD issues—along with the psychiatrist Addie urged me to see. It seems that I will do just about anything she asks. She is a powerful presence.

"Addie."

She opens her eyes and turns to me. I'm down on one knee, a chocolate rose in one hand, and a ring box in the other. She gasps. Probably more about the chocolate rose because, well, it's chocolate, and I can guarantee she's wondering where I was able to find such an amazing creation. I digress. Focus, Jameson. This is the moment.

Addie

I t certainly has been a whirlwind of activity. Dorothy got what she deserved. A prison sentence that should keep her far, far away for a very long time. The trial was a media circus, but that was tame compared to the months leading up to Dorothy's fall. We handled it. Together. Jameson has been my rock. A true partner in every sense of the word.

Matthew divorced Dorothy, and aside from the trial, I haven't seen or heard from him. I'm not expecting to since we now know that we aren't even related. I mean, even when I thought we were family, he did everything he could to destroy that bond. Good riddance. I do hope he finds his bliss. I am so evolved now that I feel a little like Oprah.

I'm sure you're wondering about the senator, a.k.a. my father. He opted not to run for another term. His approval rating took a hit. Surprised? Yeah, me neither. Anyway, we're taking it slow. Like, sloth slow. I'm sure you'll be shocked to know that I may have some trust and abandonment issues that I'm still working on. The memoir has been cathartic and has gotten me to a better place. Wendell has been very patient with the whole process. Together, he and I told Owen that he is our father, and they're working on their own bond. I will say that he's extremely patient and loving with him. And honestly, if nothing else happens with our relationship, I am grateful that Owen now has a real connection with our father. And, I am staying out of the way, allowing them to forge their own path. That was all Jameson. He urged me to let Owen figure this out for himself, which is not my usual way of approaching things where Owen is concerned. It is possible that I don't know what's best sometimes, but especially in this case.

Speaking of Jameson, I am jolted back into reality as I open my eyes. There he is, on one knee with a stunning ring. I see his lips moving, but my ears are roaring. I am sure he's saying some romantic things. I am frozen. Paralyzed by my own neurotic state of fear. I have held him off from living together. I have used excuse after excuse, but yet, here we are. He's proposing. And the only thing I tune into is, "Please be my wife." Wife. Something I never thought would happen to me. A partner. Someone to walk with me through life. Cue the ugly cry. Did you know there are women who cry without their skin getting blotchy or snot running out of their nose? That isn't me. But this man is wiping my tears and helping me blow my nose while I stutter my answer, which, of course, is yes. Yes, to a life full of everything I never thought I deserved. Yes, to trusting other people to have my back. Yes to it all. I finally have my happy ending. It just took me a while to catch up to it.

Nina

This man is infuriating. Sitting in first class, Harrison looks like he walked off the cover of *GQ*, sipping his bourbon and generally annoying me. Oh, he isn't doing anything to me, it's just his presence. His ability to get under my skin. *Ugh.* Great. I said "ugh" out loud.

"Problem, Nina?" He smirks.

"No problem. Could you possibly turn down the volume on your drinking?"

"What? That's ridiculous. You can't turn down the volume on drinking. I don't even know what that means." His brow is furrowed as he looks at me.

"The clinking of your ice in the glass and your sipping is too loud. Those are just two examples."

"Is my breathing too loud?"

He's teasing me. Even I know I'm being ridiculous, but I can't admit that to him. How am I ever going to survive this trip with him? Focus. This isn't about me. It is about celebrating my best friend's engagement. I mean, I kind of deserve credit since I did initially introduce them. I always knew they would be perfect together.

Harrison's voice jolts me out of my thoughts. "I asked you a question. Is my breathing too loud?"

"Well, your chattiness certainly isn't quiet," I scoff.

"I can't win with you. Look, we've got to agree on a truce. I know that you're angry with me, but I can't change what happened. This is about our friends. Let's try to get along."

I hate it when he's reasonable. Unfortunately, he is right. I guess I can fake it until I make it there. Thank God there will be copious amounts of wine.

"Are we in agreement?" he asks.

"Yes, we're in agreement," I whisper.

"Wait, did you just agree with me, because I couldn't hear you. I guess my drinking is a lot louder than I originally thought." He laughs at his own joke.

"You heard me. I am not repeating myself. I love Addie and Jameson, so I'll be nice. For now."

"Maybe, Nina, just maybe, we can reconcile our feelings while we're there." Before I can say anything, he puts his earbuds in and shakes his ice cubes in a rhythmic fashion.

Reconciling my feelings is exactly what frightens me.

Acknowledgments

To my family. I am so grateful for their support and encouragement, tolerating my moods, and being willing to let me escape into another world. You are my heart.

To my friend and taskmaster, Kristi Jedlicki. I appreciate your willingness to keep me focused. You read the garbage I sent and helped me fuel it with magic. I can never repay your commitment to helping me along this path.

To Christie Stratos of Proof Positive. Thank you for your guidance and honest feedback during the development of this book. Your experience was incredibly valuable to me during this journey.

I was taught to write what I know. My inspiration for the character of Owen resides in my oldest son, Bailey, who was born with Down syndrome. Both of my boys are my greatest teachers, but Bailey encourages me to simply accept life on life's terms. He isn't plagued by worry or stress. Instead, he basks in the beauty of life.

To my tribe of beautiful women that continue to support, inspire, empower, and accept my twisted brand of crazy, I love you all. You help me be the best version of myself.

For more information on Down syndrome,
go to www.ndss.org